D1021036

Ghostwriter

Ghost

A Novel

writer

TRAVIS THRASHER

New York Boston Nashville

This book is a work of fiction. Names, characters, places, and incidents are the product of the author's imagination or are used fictitiously. Any resemblance to actual events, locales, or persons, living or dead, is coincidental.

Copyright © 2009 by Travis Thrasher
All rights reserved. Except as permitted under the U.S. Copyright Act of 1976, no part of this publication may be reproduced, distributed, or transmitted in any form or by any means, or stored in a database or retrieval system, without the prior written permission of the publisher.

FaithWords
Hachette Book Group
237 Park Avenue
New York, NY 10017

Visit our Web site at www.faithwords.com.

Printed in the United States of America

First Edition: May 2009
10 9 8 7 6 5 4 3 2 1

FaithWords is a division of Hachette Book Group, Inc.
The FaithWords name and logo are trademarks of Hachette Book Group, Inc.

Library of Congress Cataloging-in-Publication Data

Thrasher, Travis, 1971–
    Ghostwriter / Travis Thrasher. — 1st ed.
        p. cm.
    ISBN 978-0-446-50558-1
    1. Authors—Fiction. 2. Writer's block—Fiction. 3. Fans (Persons)—Fiction. 4. Stalkers—Fiction. I. Title.
    PS3570.H6925G56 2009
    813'.54—dc22   2008044699

THIS BOOK IS DEDICATED TO MY UNCLE,
CHRISTOPHER BREAZEALE,

*who died at the age of thirty-six.
His spirit, and his stories, live on.*

Ghostwriter

Dennis Shore Bibliography

That California Trip (1997)*
The Glorious Trade (1999)*
Breathe (2000)
Echoes (2001)
Marooned (2002)
Sorrow (2003)
Run Like Hell (2004)
Fearless (2005)
Scarecrow (2006)
Us and Them (2007)
The Thin Ice (2008)
Empty Spaces (2009)

*Book out of print

Part One

The Lunatic Is on the Grass

On his knees, Dennis Shore cries out.

But it does no good, and it never will.

"Say something."

But nothing is said.

The wind beats at him, the field flat and endless, the ground lifeless. The dark heart of the sun fades, and with it, so does hope.

A curse tears out of his mouth.

He shakes and tightens his body and glares at the sky. The words bleed in his mouth, fiery and tingling.

He curses again, louder, as if his words are not heard.

And then he takes the lighter and flicks it. Once. Twice. Again and again until it finally ignites.

He watches the photograph burn, wrinkling and glowing until it slowly wisps away to nothingness.

Just like Lucy did.

And just like he will.

The Warning

(Ten Months Later)

1.

Terror should start in the dead of night, with rain trickling off the rooftops and thunder bellowing in the sky. But for Dennis Shore, it began with the simple ringing of his doorbell.

It was midmorning, already warm and looking to be clear and hot all day. Two weeks ago, he had gotten back from driving his daughter cross-country to college in California. Despite having the house all to himself now, the old routine remained the same: getting up, taking a walk along the river, coming home to the aroma of coffee, and heading up to his office on the second floor of the hundred-year-old Victorian mansion. Yet even though the routine was the same, nothing about it felt as it had in his former life. His life when Lucy was around, when she could take the walk with him and make the coffee for him and interrupt his writing when she needed to. When she was alive. The anniversary of her passing approached, and Dennis found that nothing was the same without her. Including his writing.

His morning commute consisted of climbing the stairs to the room two doors down from their bedroom, overlooking the lawn and the Fox River below. For many years now, he had spent his mornings in this room, facing the computer screen, clacking away at the keyboard, staring through the blinds at the trees and the river, letting his imagination roam free. That imagination had been very good to him. It had been very good to his family. But ever since learning about Lucy's cancer, it had virtually disappeared.

Now he found himself going through the motions, like a businessman shuffling papers all day long without ever really doing any work. Instead of arriving at his desk a little after eight each morning, Dennis found himself dropping into his expensive leather chair around nine or nine thirty. He might surf the Internet and check out the national news and see what movies were coming up and spend a thousand other minutes wandering in a thousand other spaces. He spent a lot of time on e-mail, something he had neglected when Lucy and Audrey were around. At least there was some pleasure in knowing how surprised his fans were to receive a personal e-mail from their favorite author.

On this particular morning, the Tuesday after Labor Day, he was watching yet another political satire on YouTube when the doorbell rang. The ring always sounded wrong to him, like it was ringing in an old church rather than a suburban home. Certain things about this house would always be old, even if he replaced them. Maybe it was the acoustics or just his imagination (the small bit that remained), but the doorbell seemed to echo a bit too long.

Dennis used to hate interruptions during his writing, especially when he was in midthought or midsentence. But now these interruptions were almost welcomed. Climbing down the creaking wooden stairs, Dennis opened the door.

And for the first few seconds as he stood at the entryway, he was sure his eyes were playing a trick on him. Or he was dreaming. That's right. He was dreaming, and he would wake up soon.

But he knew that wasn't right. He felt the sunlight on his bare arms and smelled autumn in the air, and he knew he wasn't dreaming because he hadn't dreamt since Lucy passed.

Dennis stood at the door, staring at a tall skinny girl who was white as a ghost. Her black eyes and raven hair were the two things that stood out: eyes that didn't blink, that didn't move, that looked dead; and long, stringy hair that fell all the way to her waist.

As he noticed the hair, he noticed something else.

Both of her hands shook. And on each of her arms, just below the sleeves of her short-sleeved shirt, brownish-purple bruises stood out like grotesque tattoos.

Before Dennis could say anything, she made a simple declaration: "The book cannot come out."

But even though he stood there startled and speechless, Dennis knew exactly what she was talking about.

He had wondered when this day might come.

2.

Dennis wanted to say something—what exactly, he wasn't sure—as he glanced out toward the lawn, freshly cut from yesterday. Nobody was around—no television crew or joking friends or anybody capable of explaining what was going on. Finally he reached out and touched the girl's shoulder.

She winced in pain, her pale ghostly face grimacing. He stared once again at the bruises evenly placed along her arms. He wondered how they got there.

"Are you okay?" he asked as his eyes watched her trembling body. "What're you doing here?"

"You're Dennis Shore, right?" Her voice sounded hoarse, as though from screaming.

He hesitated to answer the question, thinking back to the incident with the fan a few years ago. "What do you want?"

"Answer the question. Are you Dennis Shore?"

"Yes."

The eyes remained lifeless, unmoved.

"You're in a lot of trouble."

"What are you talking about?"

"I'm talking about someone who wants to hurt you the way he hurt me. And I don't think he'll be as gentle with you as he was with me."

Something in her voice was off. Her angry eyes and almost fearful trembling body contradicted each other.

"Who are you talking about?"

"I was hoping you'd tell me. I was hoping you could tell me who did this to me."

"Who did what?"

She dropped to her knees and began crying. Crying and cursing. Dennis knelt over and touched her back. She pulled away at his touch.

"Can I get someone—"

"Don't you call a soul. Don't call anybody. I swear on my life—don't call anybody."

"What's your name? Are you cold?"

"Of course I'm not cold," she said.

"You're shivering."

"I've come to warn you, Dennis."

"Warn me about what?"

"Are you going to let me in or make me stay on your doorstep so the neighbors can watch?"

Dennis couldn't help looking around again, knowing nobody else was there. Then he stepped away and let the gaunt girl walk past and into the house.

She didn't ask whether she could sit on the couch in his living room. She sat at the edge, her arms still trembling. Dennis noticed her bony ankles, so frail they looked like they could snap any second.

"Do you need help?"

"You're a writer, right?" she asked him.

"Yes."

"Don't worry, I'm not a deranged fan. I haven't read any of your books. But *he* has."

"Who?"

"The guy who did this. The guy who did this to me. The guy I can't get out of me."

She wrapped her arms around her legs as though trying to make herself into a ball, as though she was trying to hide.

"He just kept saying the same thing over and over."

"What's your name?" Dennis asked. "Please—are you okay?"

"If it starts it will be impossible to stop," she said, her voice throaty, grainy.

"If what starts?"

"That's what he kept saying to me over and over again. If it starts it will be impossible to stop."

His eyes found the purple bruises.

"That's nothing. You should've seen what else he did. You should see my back. And my stomach."

"*Who* did this to you?"

"I haven't even read anything by you. I just lied and told him I had. Not even to be cool, you know. Just to say I had. I think I saw a movie or two. I don't know."

"I'm sorry but I don't understand—"

"Yeah well, I don't understand either, Mr. Shore. I go to a bar the other night and meet this interesting guy who buys me all these drinks, and one thing leads to another and then the guy starts beating me. Not in the face. But in other places. And he does other things. And he's angry. This guy is the angriest guy I've ever met. But he's also just—I don't know. Crazy. And he keeps talking about you. About Dennis Shore this and that. All while he's hurting me."

"Look, we need to call the police."

"No."

"If you'll just settle down for a moment, I'll—"

"You settle down. You don't get it. *You* have to stop it now. The book can't be published."

"What book?"

"*Empty Spaces.*"

"It's not out yet."

"I know that. I'm trying to tell you it can't be published because if it is you'll suffer."

Her words made sense, but the way she was speaking them and this entire scene made none at all.

"Just listen—okay? Just tell me your name, and I'll make sure—"

Suddenly a scream tore from the girl, startling Dennis so that he stepped back and almost tripped over an armchair.

"I know why I am here, Dennis. Do you?"

A vein lined her forehead, her lips pouty and full.

"I live here. And it's okay, I'm going to get you some help—"

Once again she howled. "Do not mock me."

"I'm not mocking you."

"I know all about you."

He nodded.

"I know all about you, Dennis, and you need to stop that book from being published."

"Okay, sure. Why don't we just settle down and talk about this?"

"There is nothing to talk about. Not anymore. Not now. Not after what you've done."

"What's your name?" Dennis asked, inches away from her but not touching her.

"It's Samantha. And I know."

"Good. You know. That's good."

She shook her head, her eyes narrowing. "Don't patronize me, Dennis. I know things. This guy—this monster. He told me. He told me right before . . ."

"Right before what?"

"Right before he took from me. Right before he took something that didn't belong to him. Right before he hurt me."

Dennis looked into her dark, probing eyes.

"The same way you took from him."

He didn't breathe. He didn't move. He just stared at her, the white skin and the dark eyes and the twitching body.

Samantha rubbed her hands as though she were cold even though the room was warm. With a glance that didn't waver, eyes that didn't blink, she spoke clearly.

"You've done something, and I don't know if he wanted me to warn you or not. You need to understand—you've done something and you need to be careful."

"Careful about what?"

"This man wants to hurt you. And it's all because . . . Plain and simple, the book cannot come out. It can't be released. *Ever.*"

3.

Dennis wanted to back up and retrace the moments from waking up. Was it something in the coffee? Perhaps a full moon approaching? Was he still in bed having a long, drawn-out nightmare that he would from?

Nothing explained the girl sitting across from him.

Yet even though he had a hundred questions, Dennis didn't want to talk about his next book.

He wanted to change the subject.

Permanently.

"Where are you from?"

"Does it matter?" she asked.

"I just—if you have family—"

"My family's all from downstate. I've been living in Chicago since college. For the last few years."

Dennis couldn't help sighing, feeling uncomfortable and unsure what to do.

"I'm not mad."

"Excuse me?" Dennis asked.

"I'm not crazy. I know—I heard about it just like everybody else. The girl who broke into your house a few years ago. Said she was your biggest fan. Went all Kathy Bates on you? I know. I'm not that person. Like I said, I've never read anything by you."

"Okay."

"Plus, I even rang the doorbell."

"And you came here to warn me?"

She licked her dry, cracking lips. "How many times do I need to tell you?"

"But I don't understand."

"I hoped you could give me a little more information on the guy who raped me."

He stared at her as her eyes bored into his soul.

"That's right. I said it. And as much as I've tried, I can't get the stench of him off me."

"When did this happen?"

"A couple weeks ago."

"Did you report it?"

"Of course not. I don't even know who the guy is. What his name is. Nothing. I was hoping you could tell me."

"I don't know who you're talking about."

He felt something inside of him ache. He guessed her to be around the same age as his daughter. He wanted to put an arm around her, to call the authorities, to rush her to the hospital, to do something. But he doubted she would let him do a thing.

"You don't have any crazy relatives? Any crazed fans that have been terrorizing you lately? Nothing?"

Dennis shook his head.

"He acted like—when he was hurting me, he kept saying your name over and over again."

"Are you—do you need anything?"

"Oh sure. Maybe the last five years of my life back. Then

I wouldn't be at the wrong place with the wrong people, and I wouldn't happen to meet the wrong guy. I always meet the wrong guy but this—this was different. He was different."

"Samantha—look . . ."

"No no no," she said. "I didn't come here for sympathy. I came here to tell you. Some crazy guy has a thing for you. And he said the next book couldn't come out. So there, I told you. And that's it."

She stood to leave.

"Don't—hey, let me just call one of my friends. I have a buddy who's a cop."

"No thanks. I've dealt with them enough in my life."

"Can I get you anything?"

"Yeah. You can give me the name of the guy who did this to me."

"So you can report him?"

She laughed, a low, maniacal laugh that made Dennis's skin crawl.

"I don't want to report him," she said. "I want to kill him."

Dennis watched as she opened the front door and glanced back at him. A wave of prickles washed over his skin as he noticed her smile.

It was the kind people wore when they were dressed in their Sunday best, lying on their backs in a casket as mourners passed by.

4.

"I couldn't get her to stay."

"Did you want her to stay?" Ryan Cummings asked as he sipped from the cup of coffee Dennis gave him.

"Not exactly. But I didn't want her to go either."

"She drive here?"

"She walked down my driveway toward the road and disappeared. I didn't hear an engine start."

Ryan gave a wry smile. "Maybe she was a ghost."

"That's funny," Dennis told the deputy.

Ryan had been a friend since years ago when he professed to be a big fan. Ever since *Breathe* broke out and became a bestseller, Dennis discovered more and more self-professed fans everywhere, from the grocery store to his dentist's office. Ryan was a nice guy, the sort of cop who probably wouldn't write you a ticket if he pulled you over for speeding.

Dennis met the affable young man after the garage incident—the second since Dennis's launch into fame. The first and more harmless incident, the one the media found out about and reported, involved a high school girl who showed up at his house in the middle of the night to get an autograph. He had laughed it off, but it had shaken Lucy up pretty badly.

The garage incident happened months later, and the only people who knew about it were the local authorities. Dennis hadn't even told his wife or daughter.

"You don't think she's talking about Sonny, do you?"

"Sonny Jacobs? No way. That guy's still in a nuthouse over in Tinley Park. He was harmless. Sonny would never hurt a girl. And a girl would never talk to Sonny."

Sonny Jacobs was the bipolar, alcoholic fan Dennis found in his garage one afternoon, holding a loaded gun, talking about cowriting a book with Dennis. The gun turned out to be empty, but nevertheless it was a scary experience. Dennis had called the cops and a host of them had swarmed his house.

It had luckily been when Lucy and Audrey were spending a weekend in downtown Chicago.

"What do you think I should do?" Dennis asked.

Ryan wasn't dressed in his uniform since he was off today. It wasn't unusual for Dennis to see the deputy when he was off. Dennis used Ryan as a resource for his novels. The young guy with the crew-cut hair and boyish looks enjoyed assisting Dennis in his writing projects.

But there hadn't been a writing project in some time now.

"You wanna report it?"

"I'm not sure what I'd report."

Dennis had told Ryan everything. Well, almost everything. Everything except the girl's accusation that he had stolen something.

Dennis kept that comment to himself.

"She didn't take anything, did she? Did you threaten you?"

"No."

"Then there's nothing to do."

"What if she really was raped? What if the story is true?"

"Then she needs to report it. You said she lives in Chicago, right?"

"That's what she said."

They were in the same room that Dennis and the girl had been sitting in, a separate room right off the entry to the old mansion. The house had been built in 1895 and renovated several times since, the most recent right after Dennis and Lucy moved in seven years ago. The rooms had high ceilings and intricate woodwork, especially around the fireplace in the living room.

"She didn't look like she was lying," Dennis said.

"Think she's on anything?"

"I don't know. She didn't act like it. But I'm not a good judge of that."

"Want to file a report?"

Dennis shook his head. "No. The last thing I want is press. I got enough of that last time. I think it only breeds more intruders and craziness."

Dennis went to the kitchen to get a bottled water. Ryan followed him and took in the view of the backyard. The deputy stared out at the sunlight beaming off the river behind the house.

"You have quite a view."

"That's what sold us on the place. Lucy always wanted a house by the river."

Ryan looked back at him, a sad smile on his face. "Last time I saw you was at the funeral."

"Yeah. Saw a lot of people that day."

"Sorry."

"Me too."

"Where's Audrey?"

"Took her to college a few weeks ago. All the way in southern California."

"Where's she going?"

"Biola. She got a scholarship there."

"Never heard of Biola."

"It's a Christian college." Dennis rolled his eyes. "That's something she takes after her mom."

"How's that going?"

"Her being at college or me being here alone?"

"Both."

"Well, Audrey's loving it. And as for me, despite the visit from Little Miss Spooky, things are normal." Dennis shrugged. "Ask me in a month."

"Okay."

Dennis scanned the lawn and its crisscross pattern. He peered through a window that could use cleaning, looking out toward the river that never stopped and never died.

The deputy patted his back. "Don't look so worried, buddy. Maybe she'll get some help."

"Yeah, maybe."

But for some strange reason, Dennis didn't think so. And all he could hear were the words she had said in that frightening, unnatural tone: *"The book cannot come out. It can't be released. Ever."*

Dennis did his best to make small talk with Ryan about his books and writing and the fact that Ryan's aunt so-and-so just read all of his books and eagerly awaited the new one.

The new one that must not be published.

Dennis soon found himself telling the deputy good-bye, wondering if he had imagined the whole thing.

Things like that only happened in the pages of books and on the movie screen. This was real life, which consisted only of living, breathing human beings you could see and touch. That's all.

Just because he wrote bestselling novels about the supernatural didn't mean he believed in them.

5.

At four that afternoon, the doorbell rang again.

Dennis was half asleep, watching ESPN. He bolted off the couch toward the door, hesitating as he grasped the handle. He knew it was the girl again. It had to be her.

He wondered if he should call the cops.

Finally he opened the door, surprised to see a tall man in a brown uniform.

"Hello, sir," the UPS driver said, asking him to sign for a package.

He didn't need to open the box to know what was inside. For a long time he just stood there, staring at the package.

Eventually he opened it.

The new book had arrived.

2002

A week's worth of rain had kept the streets wet; the leaves stuck to the sidewalks. The afternoon was windy and overcast. The tall figure, twenty-one years old by ten days, walked down the deserted avenue toward the brick building on the corner. One of the only windows—small, circular, and painted black—had one crimson word scrawled on it: *Bookstore*. A nondescript door opened to a long, narrow interior that used to serve as the local watering hole. Remnants of the old place still remained, including the bar itself, which now served as a checkout counter.

Inside was the smell of incense, the colors of Halloween. Lamps were kept dim, draped with black linens or lit with dark bulbs. Exotic music played softly along with other background noises—chimes, running water, even birds. The smells and sounds were not those of a typical bookstore, but this store on the north side of Chicago was known for more than its books.

The man browsed for a few minutes but hadn't come here for that. He had called ahead. A woman—big all over, including her hair that looked like a bad wig, her meaty arms and hands, and her eyes that seemed to look everywhere without seeing anything—sat behind the counter smoking a cigarette.

She didn't appear interested in asking him whether or not he needed help.

"I called about the book on deaths. Last name is Reed."

The woman seemed bored as she looked him over. "Cecil or something like that?"

"Cillian Reed."

It took her a moment to get off the stool she sat on. She disappeared through partial drapes and returned holding a hardcover book with a Post-it note attached to it.

"*The Visual Guide to Death.* That the one you're looking for?"

He nodded. The woman didn't appear fazed in the least. She put the book on the counter, checking the front for a price. She found the tag on the inside, and for the first time her face took on some expression.

"They tell you it's fifty-seven dollars?"

He nodded and took three twenties out of his wallet. This obviously surprised the woman, though she didn't seem easily surprised.

"Not sure why this book is so expensive. It's in pretty bad shape too. But hey, I don't price 'em."

She took his money and gave him back his change. He wasn't interested in small talk. Not here, not with this woman dressed all in black, with the tattoos on her arms and neck.

She studied him. "You a fan of horror novels?"

He wasn't about to tell her that yes, of course he was, and that yes, he was writing his very first novel.

All he did was nod, staring at a trio of jars near the cash register that contained animals suspended in liquid. A coiled-up snake, what appeared to be a mutating squid, and a floating monkey head.

"Like those?" the woman asked again, prying. "Got a guy who comes in every few weeks with more."

The big woman reached behind the counter and produced a hardcover book. "Here—I have a few of these. I just finished it. You might like it. You paid enough for that book."

He looked at the all-black cover, the ghostly white letters spelling out *Breathe*.

"If you like Stephen King and Dean Koontz, check this guy out."

He nodded at her but didn't bother saying thanks. He doubted he would read much of the novel.

Cillian Reed had very discerning tastes.

The Stranger

1.

"Where do your ideas come from?"

This was the question he feared the most, the question he least wanted to hear, the question that was always asked. Perhaps it was prompted by the fact that he was one of the country's premier writers of horror. "How do you come up with such terrifying tales?" people always asked, obviously hoping to get some sort of response like, "I was abused as a child" or "I met the devil when I was seven." He had his standard quips and comebacks, and usually it was all in good fun. But nothing about this trip to New York was fun. Answering that question when it came up this time would be impossible.

And Dennis knew exactly why.

Walking back to the hotel, feeling light-headed from the wine shared with his agent over dinner, Dennis felt watched. Everyone he passed seemed to be staring at him. And not because he had a recognizable face. All sorts of celebrities walked this part of New York all the time. It was as if these people knew.

At least that's what his imagination made him think.

It had been this way during the whole trip. They watched him. Strangers in the terminal. Their leery faces followed him as he walked past or sat reading or boarded the airplane. People on the street and in passing cars and through store windows.

They all watched him with eyes that knew.

Dennis spotted the glowing red sign that signaled his hotel in this part of Gramercy Park. It was a small boutique hotel that probably cost the publisher some ridiculous amount. Nestled amidst a lush park, Hotel 42 was new and certainly impressive, feeling like a cross between a modern art exhibit and an Asian painting. Lucy would have hated it, all its ornate excesses and its cold, dark colors.

Entering the lobby, stepping on crimson carpets with patterns that swooped and showcased the hotel's emblem, Dennis noted that this hotel was a perfect reflection of this trip.

New York felt different.

The cab drivers seemed crabbier, the drivers more dangerous, the streets more crowded, the busyness more annoying. It had been almost exactly a year since his last visit. A year ago had been the last trip Lucy and he ever took together. Nothing much had mattered then except staying in the moment with her. But the moment was gone now, and Dennis was stuck by himself in a big city he'd be happy never to see again.

If only he could have persuaded Maureen and James and the rest of them that he didn't need to come here for the launch of his new novel. But the advance buzz on the novel and the news about the loss of his wife a year ago made the trip necessary. Dennis had spent a career saying yes, and this would be no exception. He'd play the game and go through the motions and ensure another home run. But secretly he hated being here, hated answering the questions, hated being treated like he was special. Lucy *was* special. He was just a guy who made up strange stories that spooked people.

Dennis stepped into Hotel 42 where a man in a suit stood behind a small desk, the wall behind him adorned with a massive-sized image of a Kyoto-style woman gazing sadly off to the side. The man simply nodded, acknowledging that

Dennis could pass. The sound of bells echoed as he walked down a narrow hallway lined with wallpaper that looked to him like rivers of blood.

Mystique and expense aside, Dennis couldn't figure out why they had put him here versus the Marriott or the Hilton or one of the big guns. He wondered how expensive it was for one night's stay and felt glad that he didn't have to pay for it himself.

Money hadn't been an issue for a long time. But that was just one of the many things Dennis had been left with after Lucy passed away.

He entered the elevator and punched his floor number. It was close to ten o'clock, and he had a very full day tomorrow, starting with his annual visit to *The Today Show* early in the morning, then a host of shows before his late afternoon book signing at Barnes & Noble. Just like his usual September visits, except for two things: Lucy wasn't there and that other thing.

That other thing.

He pushed the thought out of his mind. He was good at that. Like when he started to dwell too much on Lucy's absence. He had mastered the art of not thinking about her. At least he liked to believe that.

As he approached his hotel room, Dennis slowed down on the brand-new black-and-white plush carpet. He could see the door to his room was slightly open, light peeking from inside.

Dennis edged the door open, looking to see if someone had come to turn down the bed perhaps, give him a special late-night treat. In a place like this, it might be a fortune cookie dipped in blood with a fortune that said something like, "He who steals is he who dies." But as he entered the room that looked like a scene from the Renaissance, with its deep rose and mahogany colors and its ornate but uncomfortable hand-made furniture, Dennis couldn't find anyone.

"Hello?" he asked.

The room felt cold, silent. It didn't look like anybody had

been in here. And the only thing worth taking—his laptop, nestled in his faded leather carrying case—was still there.

Dennis checked the bathroom, the closet, but found nothing. And as he finally sat on the edge of the velvet bedspread, staring at a painting of a girl running from some unseen attacker, the sky above her ominous with its gray swirls of clouds, he finally noticed the small envelope next to him.

It was a white envelope with *Dennis Shore* scrawled across the front.

He opened it up and read the short card, immediately tossing it to the ground, jumping off the bed, and searching the room again, checking under the bed and in the closet and anywhere someone might hide.

Nobody was there. But that didn't mean they hadn't been there earlier.

The note was clear enough.

He read it again, then shivered as he tore it up and flushed it down the toilet.

2.

"Lucy was the one who told me to write a ghost story," Dennis said to the interviewer. "After my first two books came out and sold nothing, she encouraged me to write in a genre she'd never actually read. She knew my penchant for telling a good ghost story and how I enjoyed watching and reading them. So I tried it. I guess it worked."

He had told that story before, but now the anecdote carried more weight. He was a *New York Times* bestselling author of nine novels, soon to be ten. His first bestseller, *Breathe*, was a simple little ghost story about a mother and father who lost their only child and started being haunted by her. The fact that Lucy, now gone, had told him years ago to try something that had turned into huge success—*that* was the story, not the fact that Dennis was here in New York hawking another book.

So during the day, starting with the fine folks at *The Today*

Show, Dennis obliged his interviewers with personal stories. He'd rather talk about Lucy then about the newest book, *Empty Spaces*. Of course, the interviewers always felt like they needed to focus on the book at least a little, but Dennis did his best to veer off the subject as quickly as possible.

Hovering in the background all day were two very important people: his agent, Maureen Block, and his editor, James Wilcox. They had remained through the interviews and a fine-dining lunch and now watched the mob that filled the Barnes & Noble bookstore in Greenwich Village. People of all ages filled the bookstore, from teenagers to seventy-year-old men and women.

"Looks like a bigger crowd than usual," Maureen had said earlier as they prepared to greet the nervously eager manager of the bookstore.

The crowd didn't surprise Dennis, not with the strange buzz going on about this story and about him. His name had been in the papers a lot more since his wife's passing, and Dennis knew people felt a connection to his loss. The fact that this book dealt with a man grieving—it was purely coincidental.

If they knew the truth, they would know how coincidental it really was.

During the book signing, he heard all the usual things.

"My favorite movie of yours is *Sorrow*," a young man said, as if Dennis had any part in that movie besides signing the agreement to let his novel be adapted for cinema.

"Are you going to write a sequel to *The Thin Ice*?" a round-faced woman in her fifties asked about the novel that came out last year.

"I can't read your books late at night."

"I thought *Scarecrow* was a little too gory."

"Do you ever scare yourself?"

"Are you getting writer's cramp from signing?"

"What's the next book about?"

And then, of course, it came.

"Where'd the idea for this book come from?"

He had probably already signed a hundred copies of *Empty Spaces*, the cover mostly black with his name prominent in red right above a simple image of a path forged through a cornfield. Dennis looked up from the table near the back of the bookstore and his vision caught on a tall, lean guy maybe in college, maybe a few years out of it. The young man wore a worn tweed jacket and faded jeans. An aggressive smile hung on his long, pale face, marked only by the faintest scribbles of facial hair. Looking into his eyes, Dennis noticed something absent. The dark brown eyes stared at him blankly.

"I get my ideas from lots of places," Dennis said, scrawling his signature with his black Sharpie.

"Sure, but where?"

Dennis closed the book cover and looked at the young man who had spoken. Something in his tone was just like his glance—off.

"I have a vivid imagination."

"Do you?"

The stranger didn't smile after the question. It sounded as though he was really asking.

"Yeah, I do," Dennis said, shifting nervously in his chair. "At least that's what everyone tells me."

"So tell me what this story is about."

Every now and then one of the fans at these book signings wanted to talk at length. It was hard for him to deny them that, especially since they had made the special trip to wait and stand in line to meet him.

"It's about an evil that takes over a town and about one family that tries to prevent it."

The stranger holding his autographed Dennis Shore book laughed. "Really?"

"Really," Dennis said, surprised and a little annoyed.

"I wouldn't exactly describe it that way."

"Well, you probably need to read the book first before describing it in any way."

"You're smug, aren't you?"

At first Dennis wasn't sure he even heard the question. A woman behind the tall man heard it, however, and she looked as baffled as Dennis felt. "Excuse me?"

"Why would I need to read something I know by heart? Authors should know their own writing, shouldn't they?"

A wave of dread washed over Dennis. He couldn't move, couldn't speak.

Maureen was talking with the bookstore manager too far away to hear what was happening. The line behind the young man was waiting and not paying attention, except for the woman who seemed irritated and impatient. She seemed to be the only one aware of what was going on.

"You don't remember me, do you, Mr. Shore?"

Dennis shook his head, afraid of where this might be going, afraid of this.

The young man smiled, revealing strangely crooked teeth that gave him a wild, untamed look. Dennis noticed the beads of sweat on the man's forehead. The stranger wiped them away and brushed his hand through long, stringy brown hair.

"It's Cillian Reed."

Once again, Dennis shook his head, the forced smile on his face giving nothing away, even though something grated on his insides. It sounded as though the words had been uttered behind a locked door, that the name had been spoken but not fully heard.

"Excuse me, but there are a lot of us in line . . . ," the woman said.

Cillian turned and gave her a look that shut her up. His eyes smoldered, the gaze ticking, boiling, frightening. He held the hardcover in one hand and turned back, waving it at Dennis very slowly.

"This," he said deliberately, his dark eyes glancing at the book, then back at Dennis, "is mine. And you know it."

The bookstore manager stepped behind Dennis. "Is everything okay?"

For a second, those brown eyes narrowed, lips tightening; then the unsettling smile filled his face. "See you later," the stranger said.

And he slipped out of line and was gone.

3.

"This is possibly your best reviewed book since *Breathe*."

"That's great," Dennis told his editor.

They were finishing up a dinner celebrating the successful launch of his tenth horror novel. The book signing could have gone on all night, but they had stopped at eight o'clock to get out of there. After meeting Cillian, Dennis had little desire to sit around and meet more quacks like that guy. Everything the young man said stuck with him.

"You didn't eat much tonight," Maureen observed as the server took away his mostly untouched plate.

"Probably just nerves," he said, working on another glass of Shiraz.

"Nerves over what?" James asked, still polishing off a steak. "You know you got a home run this time."

James was about the same height as Dennis—right around six feet tall—but he was lean and could put away food without ever showing it. James was approaching forty, but still very much a kid in Dennis's eyes. He had been Dennis's editor ever since acquiring *Breathe* and helping Dennis work on making it creepier and darker. But one would never know James had a dark creative side to him since he was so amiable and quick to laugh and fun to work with.

The successful ride Dennis had experienced for the last nine years could be attributed in many ways to the man sitting next to him. Dennis was the one telling the stories, but

James was the one pushing Dennis to dig deeper and cut when necessary or change when required. They had a great working relationship, one built on trust and honesty.

Trust and honesty.

Dennis shrugged at James's comment. "Maybe it's just the introvert in me that's exhausted from meeting three hundred fans."

But Dennis knew that was a lie. He wasn't tired from meeting three hundred fans. He loved meeting them. He was anxious about one particular fan. And nervous about who that fan might be.

"So, speaking of the fans," James said, shifting gears, "how's the next book coming along?"

"It's coming along well."

Another lie.

"Are you going to give me anything other than 'another scary story from Dennis Shore'? Everybody's asking me, and I'd like to offer them something."

"The scariest story yet."

James and Maureen laughed. "If it's scarier than *Empty Spaces*, I don't think I want to read it."

Dennis forced a smile.

"Any chance you might be able to hand the book in early?"

"We'll see," he said.

James shook his head, looking at Maureen. "Boy, he's being really evasive this time."

"Maybe I'm nervous over the fact that everybody loves the new book. What if the next one is a flop?"

"You haven't had any flops," James said, grinning in the subdued light of the Italian restaurant.

"Critically or commercially?" Dennis asked.

"Critics always target authors who write popular fiction," Maureen said.

He nodded at the composed New Yorker with her narrow, stylish glasses and her dainty frame.

"Give me a sound bite at least," James said.

Dennis shook his head. "I already gave you one. It's about a man with a dark secret."

"And what would that secret be?"

"I swear," Dennis said with a laugh. "You publishing people."

"What?"

"The new novel's not even a day old, and you're already talking about the next one."

"We're always looking ahead to the next big thing."

"I know. And it drives me crazy."

"Yes. But it's also very good for you. It pays for expensive meals like this."

"I'd be happy with Taco Bell every now and then."

"Whatever you want," James said. "You're the talent. Just tell me what you want. As long as you give me that next book of yours."

There was pleasant laughter and easy conversation for the rest of the evening. Dennis was thankful there was no more discussion of the next book. He couldn't tell James the truth. And even if he could, James and Maureen wouldn't want to hear it. Nobody liked the truth when it was bad.

So Dennis remained silent on the issue.

He'd figure something out.

4.

There had been no way to do it. He wasn't sure how to pull Maureen aside and tell her during dinner. He wasn't sure how to tell her or exactly what to say. All he knew was that he was in trouble, and time was truly ticking away.

As he sat in the cab heading back to his hotel, the irony of all this pampering from his publisher gutted him.

Just moments earlier he'd received a text message from his phone service reminding him that if he didn't pay the bill that was overdue by two weeks, they would shut off his service. Sure, it was just a hundred dollars or so. No big deal, right? Not for someone like Dennis, some big-name bestselling author.

But the text was a symptom of something much bigger.

It wasn't his negligence in paying a stupid cell phone bill. It was his avoiding paying any bills—which would force him to think about his financial situation, which would force him to think about the novel he was supposed to be writing and handing in to get his next check.

All of this would speak the truth, a truth he didn't want to hear.

As he climbed out of the cab and headed into his swanky hotel, thoughts of his unpaid bills hung over him like vultures waiting for a carcass, circling and hovering. Just a few years ago money was not an issue, and it was easy paying for a cabin in Beaver Creek, Colorado, or paying Audrey's college tuition outright.

But then Lucy got sick. And their family insurance didn't turn out to be as helpful as he had hoped.

None of that mattered the moment Lucy told him. But it mattered now. He had Audrey to think about, and he couldn't lose their house in Geneva.

It meant too much to Audrey to lose it.

He decided to go to the hotel bar to have a drink. Not to think about things but to *not* think about things. He didn't want to think about the book he wasn't writing, the book he wouldn't be handing in, the advance check he desperately needed but wouldn't be receiving anytime soon.

He didn't want to think about the cabin in Beaver Creek that had been for sale for the last year and a half.

Dennis didn't want to think about any of it because it always came down to the same old thing.

The bitter reality that Lucy was gone.

5.

The telephone rang. Dennis knew he was dreaming because it didn't sound anything like the telephones in his house. Not the one in his bedroom nor in his office nor in the kitchen.

He opened his eyes and saw nothing but darkness. The phone continued ringing.

I'm not at home.

His hand waved through the black to find the phone.

"Hello?"

"I hope you appreciate the fact that I spared you from embarrassment and humiliation tonight in front of your agent and your editor and your adoring fans."

Dennis opened his eyes, looking at the clock on the dresser. It was 3:15.

"Who is this?"

"You know who it is," Cillian Reed said.

"Why are you calling?"

"Because our conversation is not over."

"Yes it is."

"No, Mr. Shore, it's not. You stole something of mine."

"I didn't steal anything."

"I think we both know that's not true."

"I don't know what—"

"You know exactly what you did. And you turned pale as a ghost earlier because you were afraid I was going to tell them, weren't you? But I didn't."

Dennis didn't say anything, wondering if he was dreaming.

"What did you think—that I would never find out? That you could slap another one of your appallingly unoriginal titles on a hardcover and go completely unnoticed?"

"Look—"

"Granted, we all lead very busy lives, and mine in particular has been quite thrilling these last—well, who keeps track of time anyway? But did you really honestly think I would not find out?"

"What do you want?"

"What do *I* want? What do *I* want?"

The words were spoken slowly and quietly, as if the guy who said it had a bomb strapped over his naked chest.

"It's the middle of the night. . . ."

"And what? You don't usually stay up this late? You're a writer, Mr. Shore. At least you used to be."

"What do you want?"

The cackle of laughter made Dennis shiver.

"It used to be praise, recognition, thanks, acclaim. People don't write for money, do they? You've said that yourself even though you said it all the way to the bank. People might say they write for themselves, but we all know what writers want. They want to be admired. They want *credit*."

"Look, it's late, and I just think—"

"What do you think, Mr. Shore?"

"I think I don't like a moronic juvenile harassing me in the middle of the night. That's what I think."

"You have a lot of gall."

"So do you," Dennis said.

"A boy sent you that manuscript in the mail a long time ago. You don't even remember getting it, do you? So long ago. Almost seems like another life. All I wanted, all I asked for, was input. But I heard nothing. Nothing. Nothing!"

Dennis didn't say a word. He rolled over on his side in the bed.

"I just wanted a chance."

"A chance at what?" Dennis asked.

"A chance to have what you have. Your career. Your success. And now—after all that—you had to go and do this. It's interesting. I'm curious why."

Dennis cursed at him.

"Ah, that's nice, but that's not a reason," Cillian said.

"What do you want?" Dennis asked again.

"You never answered the note I left you."

"You broke into my hotel room?"

"You never answered the question."

"What? The note asking where I get my ideas from?"

"Exactly."

Dennis didn't respond.

"You're silent because you don't want to answer. I know where you get them from. You steal them. You've always stolen them, and this time you stole from me."

"Why don't we—"

"Why don't you just shut your face, high and mighty author man."

"Why did you come to the book signing? Why not tell them? Huh? What do you want?"

"Soon enough, you'll know. And by the time I get finished with you, you're going to get on your hands and knees and wish to God above that you never met me. But for the time being, you'll have to do something you forced me to do."

"What?"

"Wait."

The phone clicked off, leaving Dennis holding the receiver in silence.

He couldn't believe what had come in the package. Its contents lay scattered on the mail-room table. He stood for a few moments just staring, ignoring the other customers waiting to use the table.

Every day he checked his post office box, which he had gotten six months ago. He needed a P.O. box if he was going to be a bestselling author. It would look more official, more businesslike. This packet marked *Cillian Reed* was the only piece of real mail he'd received besides flyers and coupons and church brochures.

When he initially saw who it was from, he was excited, ripping open the envelope. Finally some contact after the five e-mails he had sent.

But what he found inside incensed him.

The letter was a fake. Nothing but a form letter. He'd bet the author hadn't even signed it himself.

It was short and sweet.

Dear reader:

There was no *dear* about it, he thought, because there was a *reader* after it, meaning this was the standard letter sent to *anyone* who wrote. Anyone.

He was not anyone.

Thank you for your recent contact.

Again, the impersonal tone of the letter galled him. "Recent contact." That could mean e-mail, snail mail, phone, fax, or personal in-house-upstairs-in-the-shower visit. It could mean a conjugal visit or an SOS from space. Anything.

I'm glad you enjoyed my first four horror novels. I'm busy on my fifth, which I'm calling Run Like Hell and will be released September of next year.

First-person narration even though the author surely isn't the one writing, he thought angrily. He wondered if the author truly was glad.

I've enclosed a few items I thought you might like. I'd love for you to be part of my street team, spreading the word about my books.

"Street team?" he asked out loud. "Street team?" He cursed and tightened the letter in his hand.

"I'm sorry, can I help you?"

He glanced at the silly person dressed in a silly outfit and clenched his teeth, shaking his head. She quickly got the message and left him alone. He kept reading.

Here are some autographed bookplates along with a bookmark and sticker for Breathe. The marketing department does a great job on these things!

The bookplates were square, colored strips with the author's signature on them. But a bookplate with a signature did not equate to a signed book. A signed book meant you met the author, meant you *spoke* to the author, meant the author had some idea you were alive. The sticker had the cover of *Breathe* on it with additional gratuitous splashes of blood, along with the author's Web site address. The bookmark was cheap and flimsy. Cillian would never use it.

```
Sign up for my regular newsletter and stay tuned
for details related to my novels. As always,
thanks for your interest! Keep in touch.
```

And then signed (but signed by whom was the question) at the bottom:

Dennis Shore

His hands balled up the letter, then let it go.

He left the post office with the wrinkled letter, the book plates, and the sticker all sitting on the table.

He didn't want to have anything to do with them, or Dennis Shore, ever again.

Discoveries in the Dark

1.

I'm finished.

He wished he was finished with *One of These Days*, the tentative title for his current work in progress. But the title wasn't the only thing tentative in his novel. *Everything* was tentative—the words, the characters, the story. . . . So tentative, in fact, that he hadn't even started.

Dennis Shore, bestselling novelist soon to have the number-one selling book in the country, was lost for words. And he hadn't been able to find them in some time.

He just got back from New York last night. He wasn't sure what time it was, but it was late. After going through e-mail and voice mail and reading through his favorite Web sites and blogs, Dennis tried to write. But he wasn't sure what to write about. He had vague ideas, but they all seemed so random.

"It's about a man with a dark secret."

Yet he hadn't met the man, nor did he know exactly what shade was his secret.

He had a little over a month to hand the book in.

But the deadline didn't matter as much as the fallout from his latest novel if anyone found out the truth.

Thinking about it made his head ache, along with his heart.

Empty Spaces sat on the corner of the massive oak desk in his office, seeming to pulse like a wounded, bleeding animal taking its last few breaths. The book had never been his and never would be.

He wasn't sure how everything had gotten this far.

Grief, my man. That's what grief will do to you. It will make you do things you once thought were unthinkable. And you can think of everything, can't you?

Dennis had never thought the words would leave him. But much worse than that, he had never thought Lucy would leave him either. Lucy encouraged and motivated him and helped him along. And always, always, the writing came. She would give him random ideas or read bits and pieces and give him glowing affirmation or tell him to change gears and go down another path or try again. Lucy was his biggest fan and biggest critic. She was also the love of his life whom he had lost to colon cancer on October 30, 2008.

Six months before Lucy passed away, the block started. But of course it did. Because his whole life was suddenly blocked. There wasn't a God above to pray to no matter how he wished there was. Not that he wanted help now—no, if there was a God, he wanted to curse him. But cursing the air did nothing.

He tried to write. Writing used to be cathartic, especially years ago when he first started *Breathe* after Lucy's miscarriage. But in the midst of everything with Lucy's cancer last year, the deadline approached and he had absolutely nothing. Rather than admitting guilt and lack of control, Dennis had tried to control the situation.

And now, nearly a year later, with glowing reviews celebrating a whole new level of success for Dennis Shore, he didn't know what to do.

Especially since the inevitable had happened.

Cillian Reed had come knocking on his door.

The truth was that he had buried Cillian's name along with a hundred other memories and details, hoping they would all just leave him alone. But Cillian was right—Dennis had stolen something from him. There was nothing subtle or clever about it. It was during the maelstrom, and he had simply sent off the manuscript doctored up with a few changes. Like the title. And the byline.

I didn't think things through at the time because I didn't care.

He knew it was all over. And part of him still didn't care. Audrey would always be loved and taken care of, and the only thing she might have to suffer would be jokes about her father. Dennis, on the other hand, would be ruined. It would be over.

I can deny everything. Every single thing. And I can beat anyone in court simply because I have money.

But that was wrong. He had needed the money when he handed in *Empty Spaces*. And he definitely needed the money now to stay on top of his mounting bills.

And what about taking care of Audrey? How do you expect to do that without continuing to work, without continuing to write?

All of this made his head swim, and his head was the one tool he needed in order to write. Once again he was approaching a deadline, and he had nothing, absolutely nothing.

Dennis sat back down at the computer and looked at the screen. Nothing but white. Nothing but emptiness. Nothing at all.

That's what his career would look like.

That's what his life would become.

He wanted to burn every copy of *Empty Spaces*. He wanted to delete every e-mail about it and every review and every word of praise and acknowledgment.

Yes, he had stolen the book.

And yes, its author had stepped out of obscurity to introduce himself.

The lack of words . . . the mounting bills . . . the imposing deadline . . . the danger of losing his career . . . none of these scared him as much as one thing:

Cillian Reed himself.

2.

"Hey, Dad."

Even though he'd heard this phrase a thousand times, it still warmed him like the morning sun. It had been a few days since he had spoken with Audrey. There were no rules or even mild suggestions from him as to how often she should call. But if it were up to him, it would be daily.

"How's your week going?"

"Oh, it's been crazy. My roommate, Nicole—she's a lot like me and we haven't been getting much sleep lately, but it's been a lot of fun—"

One long run-on sentence—that was Audrey. As he listened to her, not worried about getting a word in, Dennis thought of what Lucy used to say: "She takes after you so much it's scary." He remembered asking his wife what she meant by *scary*. Who knew years ago that that single word would be used so often alongside his name? *Dennis Shore* equals *scary*. But Lucy just laughed. "She actually enjoys reading your novels. Now *that's* scary."

College seemed to be going well. It already sounded like Audrey had a whole dorm full of girlfriends along with a slew of guys who were interested in her. And that was no surprise. They should be interested in her.

"Just tell those fellas that your father's slightly demented and that he's been off his medication for a while now so he'll gladly come up there and kick some collegiate tail if he has to."

"*I'll* kick some collegiate tail if I have to," Audrey said.

"Yes, I believe you will. Just—you know what I always say."

"No, what do you always say?" she asked in her full-on sarcastic voice.

"Be safe, and be smart."

"I've never heard you say that."

"I didn't say be sassy," Dennis said.

"You know I'm safe, and I take after Mom in the smarts department."

"Thank God for that."

"Don't say that if you don't believe it."

"Don't start sounding like your mother," Dennis teased.

"Someone needs to."

Audrey went on to talk about her classes. She knew she wanted to do something in communications—possibly publicity or marketing. Audrey did take after him in a lot of ways, including getting her writing talents from him. Lucy had never indulged in the arts—literature or music or film—not like Dennis. His wife liked to say he didn't know anything about literature either. And he couldn't deny the fact that even though he read a lot, he didn't write deep, thinking-man's prose. When you wrote a book that actually featured possessed rodents on the rampage, well, you weren't going to be considered for the Pulitzer.

Audrey takes after Lucy in one big way, a way I'll never know or understand.

After half an hour of talking about her classes and friends, Audrey asked him how his writing was coming along.

"Oh, little by little," he said.

Little was definitely an exaggeration. That implied he had written *something*.

A title didn't constitute writing.

"I bet you're bored there all alone."

He thought back to the days since dropping her off at college. A creepy, bruised girl had shown up, warning him about the book coming out, then had just walked away and seemingly disappeared. Then a guy named Cillian Reed accused him of plagiarism, a charge Dennis couldn't deny. Now he waited and wondered when the stranger would contact him next. When, and how.

GHOSTWRITER

"Yep, I've been quite bored."

He could see Audrey's innocent eyes staring him down if she knew the truth. Dennis wouldn't know what to say. There wasn't anything to say except that he had done something very wrong and very stupid.

"Well, don't get too stir-crazy without me," Audrey said.

"I won't. Take care of yourself. And make sure you stay away from strangers, okay?"

"You too, old man," she said, adding an adorable "I love you" that made the world temporarily stop and the stars fall from the sky.

After saying good-bye, Dennis walked back into his office.

The sun came in through two different sets of windows, illuminating the walls that showcased his writing career during the last decade. There were movie posters, framed album covers, a couple of photos with famous people, some book awards. But he ignored all of them and glanced at one picture on the wall. It was a shot of him and his wife, one of the last pictures taken before she passed away.

He was sitting at the dinner table making a joke, and Lucy sat next to him, laughing, her head turned slightly to the side, her face unable to contain the joy inside.

It wasn't posed—not like some of those dreadful shots taken in front of colored backdrops, where some dull photographer went through the motions only to try to get you to buy overpriced sets of fifty pictures. Nor was it one of those where husband and wife wore matching outfits and happened to be strolling through a picturesque park. No, this was completely candid and real. This was how he liked to remember Lucy. This was how he liked to remember both of them.

I was probably making some sort of crass joke, knowing me.

He didn't want to sit back down. He didn't want to hear the silence pounding in his ears as he stared at an empty screen.

Sometimes he wished he had a full-time job again, a full plate of responsibilities that didn't allow him the room to grieve, that didn't allow him the time to break down. It was strange to long to be stuck in traffic, to be stuck in a cubicle, to be stuck in meetings, to be stuck in the corporate world. But maybe that would be better than simply being stuck in life.

Dennis sighed and left his office.

3.

It had started with a simple phone call.

It was close to a year ago, a month before Lucy passed away, when Dennis picked up a phone call from New York, assuming it was his editor. Just like now, and just like always, the deadline approached. Dennis hadn't spoken with James for some time, so he assumed the call was a gentle checkup on his progress.

Instead some woman who acted like she knew him greeted him. He recognized the voice. But he couldn't think of a name. "Yes?"

"This is Tara Marsh. Is this a good time?"

"Oh sure, Tara. How are you?"

"I'm fine, busy as always, getting ready for another crazy fall."

He neglected to add that his wife was terminally ill and had only weeks left to live. Ms. Tara Marsh didn't need to hear that.

Tara was one of the three people who worked on publicity for his books, and even though she never talked about her other authors or projects, Dennis knew her plate was quite full.

"I wanted to touch base about next week's fund-raiser."

"Sure," Dennis said, having no idea what next week's fund-raiser was about.

And then, even as she spoke about the details and his flight and the hotel arrangements, Dennis suddenly realized what she was referring to.

The fund-raiser.

With all the big shots in New York.

Where I have to read.
From my work in progress.

He gritted his teeth and went to his computer, opening his calendar. Yep, there it was, right in front of him.

```
Fund-raiser, Times Square, Saturday,
September 13, 2008, 8:00 p.m., details
to come.
```

"How does that sound?" Tara asked him.

"Great, thanks. Hey—can you e-mail me those details?" Even as he said it, he knew details were the least of his problems.

"I'll plan on meeting you in the hotel lobby around six," Tara continued.

Dennis thought with a sinking panic: *I have to stand in front of a room full of—how many people?—and read from my next novel.*

"And don't worry about how rough the section you'll be reading is," Tara said. "No one will remember how different it is when the actual book comes out. I've already talked with James, and he's fine with it, though he would like to see the section you plan to read ahead of time."

Yeah, me too. "Thanks Tara."

She continued talking, but Dennis didn't say much. All he could do was look around his desk, which happened to be clean. Far too clean for his liking.

Cleanliness wasn't next to godliness, not in his book, not for a writer. Cleanliness only meant he was blocked.

And he had one more week to get unblocked.

But in the midst of Lucy's battle with cancer, his battle with writer's block seemed lame, almost ridiculous. He refused to let it affect him or them.

And that's how it started. That's how it had come to this a year later, a book later, with still no words of his own accounted for.

4.

One sentence.

A whole morning and afternoon and evening and all he had managed to come up with was one sentence.

It was the opening line of the novel, and it wasn't even very good.

Despite what everybody told him, Jackson refused to believe she was gone.

He didn't have to come up with "Call me Ishmael" or "It was the best of times, it was the worst of times" or anything that great. He didn't even have to get this past an editor's eyes. Greatness only came when the following three hundred pages of sentences built into a crescendo that served to magnify that opening line.

It was eleven at night. And even though he sat in a four thousand square foot home, he felt trapped, crammed in, stifled.

The rock music from his iMac blared, tunes no longer helping to inspire, just serving to block out this silence. He glanced at the sentence on his computer again. It looked as bare and lifeless as a skeleton in snow.

Refused to believe she was gone.

He looked at the photos on his desk. A wedding shot of Lucy. Pictures of him and Lucy with Audrey, one when she was a newborn, another when she turned ten. All around him were memories of Lucy and her life and her loveliness.

Refused.

She.

Gone.

Dennis shut off the music and set his computer to sleep mode. He shoved away the thoughts. They were ludicrous.

I know she's gone, and I'm not going to write about her.

He went to the kitchen to get some milk before going to sleep.

This isn't life imitating art or art imitating life or any of that. I just can't start it up this time.

Standing in his kitchen, he refused to believe that his block was solely based on losing Lucy. There was more to it. He just had to figure out what.

As he rinsed the glass in the sink, looking out the window that overlooked the lawn and the river, something caught his eye.

In the darkness, somewhere over the river, straight down from the house, something . . .

What was the word?

Glowed, he thought.

He rubbed his eyes and kept looking, but the image didn't go away.

Dennis headed to the back door.

5.

The wet, recently cut grass stuck to his feet and ankles. It was still warm enough to wear shorts, which was fine by him. If heaven existed, though he knew it didn't, it would be a place where you wore shorts and flip-flops all the time. Wait a minute—that was Margaritaville, Jimmy Buffet's version of heaven. Either one was fine with him.

The wide backyard sloped downward, flanked by trees on each side that served as privacy barricades for the neighbors. The family who lived on the south side of his house was a friendly gang with three children ranging in age from junior high to high school. On the north side, however, he wished there were a few more trees and perhaps a few more miles between houses. He didn't know the full story on the elderly couple living in the small, run-down house, but he did know they were unsocial and had a knack for littering their lawn with garbage that often blew over into his yard.

The sky was clear, and he gazed up as he often did when walking down toward the river. He remembered similar nights when he had taken Audrey down to the river's edge and looked up at the stars with her. It was a cliché, but it was so utterly true: time did flash by. You *do* blink, and they're grown up. When he was in his thirties, still changing diapers and getting up to soothe cries and finding Cheerios in the strangest of places, Dennis never thought it would happen. Everybody told him he'd blink and she'd be grown up and gone, but he never truly believed it.

There were other things I wouldn't believe too.

He didn't come out here at night to get caught up in the melancholia of life. He didn't have any room in his life for that. Yes, he missed Audrey and Lucy, and yes, it was a normal emotion. But he knew how to control those feelings, right? He told himself this over and over even as he found himself pining away for his deceased wife and grown daughter every single time he saw a sea of stars.

I came out here because I saw something.

At the edge of the river, he tried to spot what had been glowing. There was nothing. He waited and watched for several moments.

Someone on the river perhaps? Occasionally someone decided to take a boat down the river at nighttime. It wasn't all that dangerous. There were spots that were tricky and certain places you couldn't pass. But he doubted someone was actually out there at this time of night.

There were no sounds, no teenagers with flashlights, no helicopters hovering above.

I know I saw something.

Dennis waited. They had moved here back in 2002, a couple years after the publication of *Breathe*, when things were really getting interesting with his publishing career. It had always been Lucy's dream to live in Geneva along the Fox River, so Dennis surprised her with this. He knew the house was one of those she loved to look at when they drove by. You could just see the top of the Victorian house back then; now, because of the trees and landscaping, not to mention the fence, you couldn't see their house at all from Route 31.

Seven years should've felt longer. But it felt like they had moved into this house just yesterday. And now it was just him, outside trying to find what he had seen on the water, trying to make sure he hadn't imagined it.

Give me another ten, fifteen years, and that's when I'll be going senile, he thought as he turned back toward the house. *But not yet. I'm not crazy just yet.*

He heard a shuffling in the bushes and walked over to see what it was. A cat jumped out and scampered across the lawn. For a second he thought it was Buffy, the cat Audrey had brought home a month after Lucy passed away, the cat she had left behind after going to college. But the color told him otherwise.

This cat was white and seemed to glow in the dark.

It must belong to his elderly neighbors. They probably hadn't fed it in a week or two.

Maybe it was walking on the water, Dennis thought. *Right. That would explain it.* He stared up at the heavens before shaking his head and gritting his teeth.

He'd give anything to know she was up there watching him.

Anything.

6.

It had been last year, the night before the benefit in New York, when Dennis found the novel.

He still had nothing of his own to read to the gathering, not even a brief section of a chapter. And his conversation with Maureen earlier that week still resonated in his head.

"Who's going to be there?"

"Spielberg, for one."

That's just perfect. Is it possible to option a book that doesn't exist?

"Any other big names?" Dennis asked the familiar voice on the other end of the phone.

"Lots," Maureen said, rattling off a list of who's who that would be attending the fund-raiser. With each name, Dennis winced, glad he wasn't talking to her in person.

It was around lunchtime, and Maureen was returning his call. He hoped she would have some kind of solution for him when he told her he had nothing to read, but the literary agent was unusually silent and offered no ideas to help him out.

"You can read just a portion of it," she eventually said, her tone asserting that surely he had a portion to read.

"I don't think I can," was all he would reveal.

Again, Dennis got the silent treatment. He could tell Maureen was alarmed. Finally she cleared her throat and seemed to regain her composure.

"Just read anything—they'll enjoy it," the New Yorker said. "Don't you have an old short story laying around? The start of a novel you never finished?"

"Lots of literary crap," Dennis said, "but nothing like my last nine novels."

"You have a few days—you can do it."

I don't think you understand, Maureen.

As with the last three books he had written, Dennis had not given the publisher an outline or a synopsis. That's how much they trusted him. They knew the story would be in the same vein—that's what they wanted and cared about. No creative diversion. Readers wanted something to scare the snot out of them, to keep their eyes open after slipping under the covers, to give them second thoughts about opening a closet or going down to the basement or even turning off the light. Even if it made them terrified of what was under the bed, readers still wanted something scary to put on their bed stand at night.

"What's this one about again?" she asked.

"Oh, it's a romantic comedy," he joked. "About a man searching for his missing wife and discovering this whole underground . . . *thing*." Dennis laughed.

"Thing?" Maureen asked.

"Yeah—you know, cults, witches, all that fun stuff. Evil."

"Sounds perfect."

The two of them often laughed about the amazing success of his books and the reading public's appetite for horror. He had done everything, from his haunted house story to his ghost story, even to his demon-possession story, which people often said should have been another sequel to *The Exorcist* because it was so frightening and disturbing. This was his missing-persons story. And as much as he might have liked to do something else, to tell a story that didn't have severed limbs and evil spirits and lots of blood, he had to take this idea and weave it into the Dennis Shore world. So that meant it wasn't *just* a missing-persons story. Evil rested at the heart of the book, at the heart of each of his books, and readers would be sucked in and become too invested to stop reading when the horror got turned up.

"What are you calling this again?"

"*Empty Spaces*," he said.

"Is that another Floyd song?"

"Yep. Keeping the chain."

"It's worked this far."

"The writing's not working. Nothing's coming. Nothing at all."

"When you say nothing, Dennis, do you mean—"

"Yeah, I mean nothing."

"Okay. Let's see." Maureen was quiet, surely thinking through the ramifications of what "nothing" meant. "So you write a scene between now and Saturday. No problem. It doesn't even have to be the beginning."

"Yeah, I'll be fine."

"And that chapter can jump-start the writing. That's all you need."

"Sure."

"You can do this in your sleep. It'll be great. Now, how long are you going to be in New York? I have a few people who want to meet you, and I was thinking we could go to this great restaurant—"

Reliving this pep talk from the previous week did him no good now that it was the night before he was supposed to go to New York. Those who sold and marketed art didn't know how difficult it was to actually create it.

Dennis sat in the squeaky writing chair he had owned for fifteen years, ever since he started writing. He had penned four unpublished novels sitting in this chair, those dreadful things that still sat in his closet and that truly were unpublishable. He had tried too hard to be the next Hemingway or Faulkner and failed on all accounts. All four of those books were terrible. He had written his first two published literary novels in this chair too, the two novels that garnered his best reviews . . . and that sold under five thousand copies each. And that's when he had made the fateful decision, again in this chair, to do his best Stephen King impersonation. And what happened was *Breathe*, a ghost story that sold millions and made him a household name.

As he sat rocking back and forth in the chair, he stared at the words he'd scrawled after talking to Maureen: *One chapter. One scene. Any scene. Several thousand words.*

He looked at the words, then added an exclamation point at the end.

In only eight hours he would be boarding a limo to go to O'Hare and fly to New York, where he was supposed to give a reading to a special VIP dinner of more than five hundred people.

Like Jerry Seinfeld and Oprah and a hundred different big-name actors, actresses, musicians, athletes, and authors.

That's all. No pressure.

"*Spielberg for one,*" the voice of his agent said again.

Standing in front of people didn't bother him, and celebrities didn't intimidate him. But reading something that wasn't entertaining—that horrified him.

I could just read them something from one of my older novels. Stephen King loves to read the puking scene from Stand by Me. *I've been in the audience twice when he's done it.*

But people wanted something they hadn't heard before. Something exclusive to make it worth their while.

He had made a promise. And he had his agent and publisher to think about, both of whom would be there, sitting at the table with him.

That's why it was nearly two in the morning, and he was going through his closet, searching for something, anything.

A scene never seen before. A chapter never typeset. But Dennis knew it was impossible. He wasn't going to find anything.

Seinfeld would deliver hilarious one-liners and Oprah would talk about saving the world. Would they really care what Dennis Shore the horror novelist was writing about? Why should he care what he read out loud?

Why is it so hot? Why am I sweating?

The stereo pumped in the loud rock music. He went by his desk and finished off his Diet Coke. It didn't matter what time it was. It felt like it could be ten in the morning or two in the afternoon. He was wide awake, and he suddenly felt like he couldn't breathe.

I'm in serious trouble.

Horror wasn't somebody chasing you with a chain saw. It was standing in front of a room full of somebodies, feeling like you didn't belong there, having to deliver something you didn't believe in, reading something that didn't impress anybody.

The stacks of paper in his closet seemed endless. One day he would organize everything. He had said that five months ago to Lucy, who had told him she would help him. But she was running out of time to help him with this project or any project.

All of his writing was in here. He even had a filing system which used to work but now was overloaded and disjointed.

There was everything from folders and files of previous novels to book ideas to works in progress to interesting articles to his massive, stuffed contracts file folder.

There was a hard copy of *Sorrow*, his fourth horror novel.

There was a photo album next to it.

There were a handful of foreign editions of *Run Like Hell*.

Dennis sucked in a breath. Tried to figure out a plan.

Tell them I'm sick.

That was a horrible idea. So were the other ten he had.

No, I need to sit my butt in that seat and write, advice I've given a hundred, maybe a thousand aspiring novelists who want to see their name in big print on a book cover and want to be one of the headliners at a big-name gig in New York.

Just then something in the closet caught his eye.

It was colored paper. Orange paper in fact.

It was under another thick manuscript—some early draft of one of his unpublished novels. He didn't remember ever printing anything on orange paper.

It was a manuscript printed in very small handwriting. There had to be at least 250 pages, maybe 300.

The title was one word that didn't ring a bell.

Reptile.

Neither did the author's name.

Cillian Reed.

Dennis turned the page and started reading. He couldn't remember reading this before, and he knew he would have remembered.

The opening sentence was good.

Chilling and creepy and good.

The first person he killed didn't scream and didn't cry because she was too surprised that her son could do such a thing.

He continued reading, walking across the office to the leather love seat against one wall. He sat down, turning the first page.

The actual killing was on page two, and it took his breath

away, surprising him, making him want to know what would happen next.

He devoured the next thirty pages in perhaps fifteen minutes. He got goose bumps. Glanced over his shoulder. Felt a bit panicky.

For the first time in a long time, he wanted to keep reading, he wanted—needed, in fact—to see what happened to the young woman, the girlfriend at the center of the story, to see if she got out alive.

Where did this come from, and who is Cillian Reed?

He looked for anything else in the manuscript—an address or an e-mail or even a date—but he couldn't find anything.

Dennis searched his closet for half an hour. It was almost three thirty in the morning.

He couldn't find anything else. No more orange sheets, no more pages with typewriter imprints, nothing else connected with this. Just a manuscript that appeared out of nowhere.

As he returned to his computer, the screen sleeping the same way he should have been, the orange pages lying on the edge of the couch, Dennis suddenly had an idea.

2004

The creak in the door awoke him.

One hairy finger wrapped around the edge of the door, then another, then an entire spider scurried across the carpet toward him.

He had never seen a tarantula before, but it fascinated him. It crept closer.

He stared in front of him at the pages, so many pages, all written with black ink on orange paper.

He looked at the last page he had written.

A rustling near the door brought his attention back. Another spider. He wondered where they were coming from.

Then another, another, one more.

The first furry creature had made it to his desk and now rounded the edge to go underneath, to his bare feet. When it made its way over his feet, onto his toes, he wasn't surprised. It felt odd, itchy, but he didn't move, not even when he felt the bite.

The tiny teeth dug into his skin and made him wince, but he remained still.

He wrote another page, then looked up again. There were spiders crawling up the walls. One crawled up his leg, toward his lap.

He looked at the bottle on his desk. Then at the pills next to it. But that was just liquor and speed, nothing crazy, not enough to make him hallucinate.

It might have been some of the other things he took. He couldn't remember the day, the time, the year, anything, nothing but the story.

He was almost finished.

Ten—eleven—twelve?—days ago, he had started this. Writing in a mad, desperate, frenzied state, letting the drugs and booze keep him going. Going going going.

"Gone," he said to the tarantula that crawled up his belly toward his face.

Now they were dropping from the ceiling too.

Onto his head, his arms, his hands.

He kept writing.

The music played, and it helped him too.

It was so loud.

In his head, everything was loud.

And the words kept coming, like yesterday's lunch you couldn't help puking, like a deep, dark secret you couldn't help telling, like a deep, dark hole you couldn't help falling into.

"The lunatic is in my head," someone sang, and he agreed.

Tarantulas were everywhere, and he brushed them away, his pen running out of ink.

"There's someone in my head, but it's not me."

He was running out of adjectives, and the sentences were running out of structure, and finally finally finally he finished.

And he wrote the words, "The End."

And then, covered in spiders, furry, hairy, thick spiders, he rested his head on the book, his first, his masterpiece.

This will get Dennis Shore's attention, he thought. *This time he won't simply send me a generic form letter. This time he'll take notice. He will have to.*

The words went around and around and around.

Scared

1.

Dennis.

He stopped typing for a moment, the voice a whisper but somehow heard above the music blaring from his computer. He could see the word count on the bottom of his document, the number continuing to get higher and higher. It already read 35,000 words. He was soaring.

Dennis.

He turned around but knew the only things behind him were bookshelves. Dennis muted the song, waited.

I'm not far.

His head jerked left. Toward the closet.

Don't stop looking.

He stood and walked over to where the voice seemed to be coming from. It was her voice. He could picture her and sometimes smell her and could even sometimes hear her when he was trying, but not like this, not this way.

It's time.

The door was closed. He turned the handle.

The faint light spilling into the closet from his office showed him enough. He saw the bare legs, so long, and the ankles. She was wearing shorts and a T-shirt. The shirt was wet with blood, as was the carpet next to her. A fresh wound bled from her head, her eyes closed, her mouth caked in blood.

And just as Dennis was about to go to her, her eyes opened. A bloody cracking mouth spoke.

I will always love you. Always. Forever.

And then a ping sounded, the ping of an incoming e-mail, the ping awakening him from this deep sleep at his computer.

The music had stopped. He checked the time. In half an hour it would be midnight.

Dennis looked over at his closet door and saw it was closed. His head hurt. He rubbed his eyes and yawned. For the first time in—well, maybe the first time ever—the thought of that door and what lay on the other side of it scared him. The stillness of the suburban night and this empty house and that horrific vision and that door . . .

Come on, Den. Get a grip.

He jogged his mouse to wake up his computer, which he was sure wasn't dreaming about his dead wife. The empty page on the screen was the first thing he saw.

He hadn't written 35,000 words. He didn't even have 3,000 words.

Dennis shook his head and cursed. He decided to open up his e-mail, which probably wasn't the best idea but there was nothing else to do.

Except write.

Or sleep.

Or bury the corpse that was decomposing in his closet.

2.

The e-mail was from Cillian.

He'd known he'd eventually hear from the guy again. It had been a week since the creepy young man had approached him at the book signing in New York. He was surprised Cillian's next step was a harmless e-mail. The address was interesting: Demonsaint4424@gmail.com.

Dennis wasn't sure what *Demonsaint* meant and wasn't in the mood to ask. The e-mail was short.

Dear Mr. Shore: Do you remember what it was like when you first wrote *Breathe*? Did it come easily? Will you ever recapture that energy? Cillian

That pompous little jerk. He's goading me now. Taunting me.

He started to write a reply, something along the lines of "Get lost" except far more creative, but stopped and canceled the e-mail.

That's what he wants: a response.

A few moments later, an instant-messaging box popped up on his screen, full of text.

I know you're there. And I know you want to respond. I'll ask my question again. Do you remember what it was like writing a book that would go on to sell several million copies? Do you remember when you didn't have the pressure of a name, of a slot to fill on the *NY Times* list, of a thousand mouths to feed at a publishing house?

Dennis didn't answer, instead turning up the music and trying to get some writing done. He clicked off the box in the corner of his screen. But it burst back almost instantly.

You don't remember, do you?

Then another.

You can never recapture what it was like, can you?

Then another.

You're afraid you've lost it. And this is the thing, Mr. Shore. I believe you have too.

Then another.

You can't *begin* to fathom loss, or hurt, or pain.
But you will.
You will, Dennis.

Dennis gritted his teeth and cursed, picking up a paperback on his desk and hurling it across the room. He would've done that to his iMac, but he needed it. He shut down his computer and left the room. On his way out, he decided to open his closet door. Just open it. Just in case.

The door sounded like it hadn't swung open like that for some time. Dennis turned on the light.

There was nothing and nobody there. Just a lot of books.

He turned off the light and closed the door.

Tonight the house felt very still, and very empty.

3.

The old brick church in downtown Geneva had stood there for more than a hundred years. It had character, the kind of church couples put their names on waiting lists for their weddings, the kind that would probably still be there even if someone proved God didn't exist. Lucy went there with Audrey the last few years of her life. Dennis had gone a few times after constant urging, but not enough to consider it routine, like going to the dentist. At least going to the dentist accomplished something.

Throughout the years, as Dennis and the girls passed by the church, he often remarked at the weekly sayings on the sign outside the building. Whoever put these up had a good sense of humor.

"Why can't the preacher have a sense of humor like those signs?" Dennis asked his wife one summer day. "That's the kind of church I want to go to."

Some of the more classic ones Dennis remembered included

"We are not Dairy Queen, but we have great Sundays!", "Have you read my #1 bestseller? There will be a test. God" (that one in particular made him laugh), "Stop, drop, and roll does not work in hell" (which he said was inspiring—giving warnings about impending fire and brimstone to an entire city), and then the whole series of *God is like* . . . including the classic "GOD is like ALLSTATE. . . . You're in good hands with Him."

Even Lucy had laughed at some of the church signs. Dennis, meanwhile, just went off about them.

"Okay, so what's that trying to say then?" he asked one day after passing a sign.

"Yes, I know."

"You know what?" Dennis asked, smirking.

"That one was—interesting," Lucy said.

"'Interesting'?" Dennis had laughed at her. "'Try Jesus. If you don't like Him, the devil will always take you back.' Well, that's comforting. I would love to know what they teach the kids in Sunday school."

"Those signs are just meant to get people's attention."

"And tell us we're on our way to hell. I already know that based on some of the things my book critics have said."

"I picture some eighty-year-old janitor putting up those signs," Lucy said with a gleam in her eyes. "One of those old-timers who always has a saying and a quip."

"Exactly," Dennis said. "And I bet the pastors scratch their heads and go 'Oh boy.' But it's Vernie's job."

"Vernie?" Lucy asked.

"Sure. Seems like he'd be a Vernie."

Lucy shook her head. "No. I see him as a Walter."

"This is why I don't give you early drafts of my novels."

She nudged him. "No, it's because I don't read your books. I don't want nightmares."

"'You think it's hot now. . . . God.'"

"Stop," Lucy said.

"I think one morning the pastor should just read a list of all the church signs. I'd go to that service."

Passing the church the morning after his online contact with Cillian, Dennis recalled a host of memories. And it felt like brushing by a cactus.

This was how he grieved. He hadn't wept bitterly after Lucy's passing because they had known it was coming. He hadn't been prepared; one can never prepare to lose a loved one. But he had remained strong for Audrey. And he had immersed himself in work. Or the illusion of work, however unproductive it might be.

But every now and then it came. The stinging barb of memory.

The way she laughed at his jokes, even if they were sometimes terrible. The way she talked. The way she lived her life.

Her name and her face and her touch and her life were all easily conjured up by the smallest or most simple or even the craziest thing.

Like a church sign.

And today he remembered this as he passed. And he noted the sign: "God knows you well and loves you anyway." Dennis thought about that for a minute. So the implication was that God shouldn't love him? Because what? Because he was such a sinner?

He suddenly wanted to punch whoever put up that sign. He didn't want God's love. In fact, he didn't want anything to do with God.

Just send her back to me if she happens to be around.

He looked over at the empty passenger seat in the large SUV. He wished Lucy were there. She would have said something uplifting or encouraging. All he could think of right now were profanities.

Staring at the grooves outlined in the leather seat, Dennis sighed.

4.

It was three in the afternoon when Dennis saw him. The figure lurking behind his house.

He first saw the man by accident. Dennis was getting a glass of water in the kitchen and sorting through a stack of mail. It seemed like Audrey's mail was only increasing. The credit card companies sure wanted her. Occasionally a piece would come for Lucy. He liked seeing mail come to her attention. It made it seem like she was still a part of his life in some way. Today there was nothing but junk. And as he prepared a pile to throw into the garbage, he saw a towering block amble by his window.

Dennis ducked before he had time to think. He went around to the window and caught a glimpse of the stranger's back.

Too big to be him.

But this still could have something to do with Cillian. Maybe it was a friend that he sent to do the dirty work for him. To vandalize the house or trash the lawn or scare the snot out of Dennis.

Dennis thought about calling the police. But he put the phone down, knowing he couldn't involve them after what he'd done. Another thought raced through his head. He should grab something to protect himself with. Dennis watched the man through various windows. At one point he lost the trespasser and rushed upstairs for a better view.

Maybe he's inside. Maybe he found a way to get inside.

The doors were unlocked. Dennis never locked them. Why should he?

He went to his study and got a baseball bat—a memento from his college days. It felt sturdy, and he knew it would do quite a bit of damage against an intruder's head.

Halfway down the staircase, he froze.

It was the doorbell.

The door was right in front of him, in front of the stairs.

His heart pounded, his hands throbbing as he gripped the smooth wood of the bat. For a second he thought about not answering, but it rang again.

Hello? Any plagiarizers home?

They had to know he was home.

They? As in the group of them? Are there more outside?

He went to the door and opened it to see immense shoulders, a thick neck, a square jaw.

And death.

"Mr. Shore?"

Dennis nodded, the bat still in his hand.

"Just wanted to let you know I checked and things should all be good."

"Checked what?"

"Your cable. I'm from Comcast. You called on Friday."

"Oh, right," Dennis said.

The bat suddenly felt heavy. The big guy glanced at it, then back at Dennis, then smiled.

"Well, if there's anything else you need, just give us a call."

"Sure," Dennis said, closing the door, looking at the bat, and shaking his head.

5.

That night Cillian e-mailed him again.

It was another simple question.

Scared yet?

For a long time, Dennis just looked at the two words, wondering what Cillian was referring to. He finally broke down and e-mailed him back.

Scared of what?

The reply came swiftly.

Scared of me. Scared of what you've done. Scared of what you *haven't* done. Scared of tonight. Scared of tomorrow. Are you scared, Dennis?

Dennis typed a response: NO. It was a lie of course.

You will be. I haven't even started to mess with you and your life, but I will. And I will very soon, Dennis.
Sweet dreams.

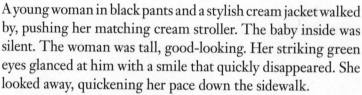

2005

A young woman in black pants and a stylish cream jacket walked by, pushing her matching cream stroller. The baby inside was silent. The woman was tall, good-looking. Her striking green eyes glanced at him with a smile that quickly disappeared. She looked away, quickening her pace down the sidewalk.

Cillian had been sitting on this stone bench for an hour now. He had already finished reading two newspapers all the way through. He was getting tired of looking at his watch.

In another fifteen minutes he would leave.

Behind him sat the courthouse with its cannons on the lawn. He sat on the edge of Third Street, watching a sea of wealthy strangers walk past carrying bags from the dozens of local niche stores. A week ago, on this very same street, he had gotten lucky. He had driven past and seen the author getting into his car. He had tried turning his own car around but hadn't been able to do it quick enough to follow him.

He asked a few people; they said Dennis Shore came by the post office once a day.

It was easy finding out where Dennis lived. Geneva, Illinois. But his home address was unlisted, as was his telephone number. So Cillian had decided to come down and wait. It was close to the time he had seen him in passing last week.

Seven more minutes. Seven more minutes and he'd leave.

The summer day was hot, his forehead probably already sunburned.

An older woman in a wide flowery hat walked by and said hello. He didn't reciprocate. His eyes peered through sunglasses at the revolving strangers sending out mail.

And then the car pulled up.

It was a silver four-door Volvo SUV. The same one he had seen the other day.

And out stepped Dennis Shore, wearing cargo shorts, flip-flops, and a red T-shirt. He wore sunglasses and looked unshaven.

Cillian wondered if this was how Dennis Shore always dressed up when running errands in town. He couldn't help smiling. He stood and walked to his car. In the hot leather seat, the air conditioner cooling him down, he waited to see the author again. Ten minutes later, several items of mail in hand, Dennis Shore climbed back into the Volvo. Soon the silver vehicle passed directly in front of him.

He turned his car right to head down Third Street, following. And in less than ten minutes, maybe even five, he watched the silver Volvo pull into the street flanked by walls and trees and bushes off of Route 31.

A sign said Private Property.

He slowed but sped up as the car behind him pulled up to his bumper. He drove down 31 for a few minutes, then turned around, driving past the driveway again.

The private dirt road headed down toward the river. He could barely make out the two houses down there because of the tall, aged trees. One was a stately Victorian house, another a lackluster two-story brick house.

He guessed which belonged to Dennis Shore.

And he smiled, knowing it wasn't private property anymore.

Breathe

1.

The doorbell rang and someone tromped in before Dennis could get to the front entryway.

"Hey, man, your neighborhood having a cleaning day or what?" Hank McKinney always came over on Sundays during the football season. He was a jock who used to play hockey and had a face that proved it. His muscular arms carried a box full of food and beverages.

"Why do you say that?" Dennis asked.

"'Cause the Addams Family next to you has a lawn full of garbage that's blowing over into your yard."

Dennis stepped through the front door as Hank headed toward the kitchen. There were newspapers scattered over his lawn, stuck in his bushes, even somehow lodged in his trees. Then he noticed other things. A sock. A cardboard box. A couple of milk jugs. And sprinkled like snow all across his yard, shredded Styrofoam. He shook his head and shut the door. He'd deal with this later.

In the kitchen, the stout guy wearing the Bears jersey was almost finished unloading everything he'd brought.

"Expecting company?" Dennis asked as his friend finished putting the beer in the fridge.

Hank just grunted. "What's the story on those neighbors?"

"I have no idea," Dennis said, stacking dirty dishes in the sink. "They've been there since we moved in. They're reclusive—they never have the lights on. Sometimes I see the old man using an ax in his front yard, chopping something—I don't know what. It's strange."

"Yeah, they're weird all right."

"Every time I try to make conversation they either act like they don't understand English or simply are completely unsocial. Yet then I see them talking to the mailman, so I have no idea."

Hank uncapped a beer and offered it to Dennis.

"I still have a stomach full of coffee," Dennis said.

"You suck at tailgating, you know that?"

"We're not twenty-five anymore."

"Yeah, yeah, whatever. How's the bachelor life?"

"Quiet," Dennis said.

"Any more strange girls knocking on your door?"

Hank was one of the few people he'd told about Samantha.

"Yeah, this time a trio of beauties showed up at my door. I sent them away."

"Send them over to my pad."

They went to the family room where Dennis's state-of-the-art television hung against the wall. He had bought an entire package—the high-definition television, the Bose surround sound system, the *one remote to rule them all*. Lucy would never have allowed him to spend that much money on technology, no matter how big his savings account was.

As the announcers blathered on about how the Bears were sure to lose today, Hank quickly polished off his first beer.

"Nervous about the game?" Dennis asked.

Hank had a few days' worth of reddish beard, deepening the color that was already there from so much time in the sun. He rubbed his chin and shook his head. "Nah. Julie came over."

"To your apartment?"

"Yeah. Must be the apocalypse if she came over, right? That or the fact that she's getting married and moving to Santa Barbara or Santa Ana or Santa Claus. Somewhere in California."

Dennis watched as Hank sucked down half of his second beer, his eyes glued to the television. He'd seen Hank before when he was in this mood, and he was like a loaded gun. Eventually he was going to go off.

"I mean, I knew she was dating, you know, but I didn't think it was that serious. And maybe it's not that serious. Maybe it's a serious rebound from us being official six months ago."

Hank and Julie had been married for eight years. It was Hank's second marriage and her first. Part of the issue, an issue that had always been there, was Hank's first go-around and the three children he had with his first wife. Dennis was glad there had been no children for Hank and Julie. He wasn't sure what to say.

"Tell me you were right," Hank said, cursing as he looked at his friend. "You can say it. Go ahead."

"I think I might go ahead and have a beer," Dennis said.

"No, come on. I mean, you were the best man. A guy's supposed to listen to his best man, right? And what'd you tell me—Lucy and you in fact." He cursed again. "What'd you guys tell me before I proposed, and then again before the wedding?"

"It's done now."

"You were right."

"Life happens," Dennis said. "We're both alone and neither of us expected it or wanted it."

"Yeah, but for you—I mean, women like Lucy don't come along. Ever. And I mean—she was something else, you know? What she went through, that's just not right. For me it was my own stupid fault, you know, but not you. It wasn't your fault Lucy died. You didn't have me telling you the night before the wedding not to go through with it."

Dennis laughed. "I wish she could hear you say that. She used to argue with me sometimes about friends like you."

"Yeah, I know. Bad influences. I still am, huh?"

"Think the Bears are going to win?" Dennis asked.

"I don't know how you've done it."

Dennis studied the ruddy-faced man across from him. "What do you mean?"

"How you've managed to stay—to still be you—after she died. I mean, I think *I* fell apart more than you did when Lucy died."

Dennis nodded. He had heard it before. "I couldn't afford to fall apart," he said. "Not in front of Audrey. She was going through enough pain."

"Audrey's a great kid. She has Lucy's genes."

"Thanks. But she's got a lot of mine too."

"You know, man—everybody needs to grieve."

"Yeah, I know," Dennis said. "But everybody grieves in different ways."

"So what's your way?"

"Trying to control as much as possible."

"Control's an illusion, man."

Dennis forced a smile.

2.

"Can you make it to your apartment?"

Hank cursed. "I only let you drive me home so you could sleep well. Didn't want to give you any *nightmares*." Hank stressed that last word, something he joked a lot about since Dennis specialized in writing books devoted to giving others the very same thing.

"What a game, huh?"

"Ninety-five yards in less than two minutes," Hank said.

"And they say miracles don't happen."

"At least not to the Bears. But it happened today."

"Want me to pick you up tomorrow?"

"Nah. I'm calling in to work. I'll get Stan to drop me off to pick up the car tomorrow."

It was close to eleven. They had spent the entire day watching football. First the Bears game, then the Packers (cheering on Philadelphia to win but to no avail), then the Sunday night game which wasn't that interesting but provided background to make jokes and continue to eat bad food and, at least for Hank, continue to drink beer.

The big guy usually was pretty good to go after a game, but today he was completely soused. He talked as though he were in slow motion. It took him a few minutes to find the door handle before he added, "I'm fine. No problem."

"Call me when you wake up."

Hank laughed, standing on the curb. He didn't seem to mind that it was drizzling. Dennis faced him through the open window. "Sorry about Julie," he said.

Hank held up his middle finger in response to what he thought about all of that. But that was a twelve-year-old's response. Dennis knew his friend still loved this woman who had broken his heart but had nowhere to go with his wound.

Nowhere to go with his grief.

Dennis understood that all too well.

Waiting at a light right before the bridge, Dennis thought about Hank. They'd been friends since their college days at Northern University. He only had a couple other friends from his younger days, and he only saw them when he had tickets to play-off games. He was struck by how you might choose your friends, but you didn't choose who would become part of the fabric of your life. Most of the time the unlikeliest people stuck around. When he first met Hank, they hardly had anything in common. Little did he know at the time that Hank would become his closest friend during the course of the next three decades.

He drove along Butterfield Road as it wound past the police station down toward the Fox River and over the bridge, the drizzle becoming heavier. He flicked on his windshield wipers as his eyes caught something strange ahead.

At the edge of the sidewalk lining the concrete bridge, a small bike leaned against the short wall. And there, in the rain, was a girl. He noticed the blonde hair. The pigtails.

She stood on the railing overlooking the well-lit northern side of the bridge, the dam fifty yards away.

Just as Dennis slowed his car down, staring through the blurry glass, not believing what he was seeing, he saw the little girl step off the railing and drop.

What the—

He jammed on the brakes and jumped out, running around his vehicle and vaulting over the stone barricade between the road and the sidewalk.

Wind blew the rain sideways as he stood at the railing, disoriented and dizzy. For a second he thought about diving in and saving her. But he second-guessed what he saw.

The railing was lower than he remembered. A car passed his waiting SUV, slowing down to see what was going on. Spotlights beamed down on the river below, facing the dam and its steady stream of pouring water. The dam itself wasn't too high, and the water levels seemed fairly low. He could see the moving water below him, the eerie glow of the lights on the rising foam.

"Hey—you okay?" he called out.

He heard a howling sound, a high, piercing cry. Not a cry of anguish, but one of fear.

"You down there?" he called out, unable to see anyone. "Hello? Hello?"

A car honked its horn behind him. He turned around and waved it on, his forehead wet, his hair damp. Dennis watched the car move past, then sprinted toward the other end of the bridge. Dark trees guarded each side of the river, shadowed and sinister.

"Hello? Anybody down there? Hello?"

Another car stopped behind him, waiting, then passing.

Dennis peered over the edge and again felt a dizzy foreboding. The darkness seemed to call him, enticing him, urging him to jump.

He shook his head to get out of the slight trance.

The water looked calmer on this side, but he could barely make out the surface.

Someone on the bridge blared their horn to make him move his car. Dennis jumped back over the median and climbed into his SUV, driving ahead to the small parking lot on the darkened south side of the bridge.

He rushed back out of his car and down a small incline to the edge of the water. A biking trail wound near the river, under the bridge. The sound of trickling water falling off the bridge and spattering onto the sidewalk below caught Dennis's attention.

Maybe she got out of the water. Maybe she's under the bridge.

Dennis called out a few more times, scanning the water. He walked closer to the bridge that loomed above him. He squinted in the misty rain as he edged closer, entering the bridge's shadow, still unable to make out anything.

"Is anybody there?" he called, wondering if he had really seen the girl jump into the river at all.

He paused partway under the bridge. He heard something. A heavy, distorted, wet sound. Not from rain or from the river, but from something else.

Breathing.

Someone was breathing, the haggard, sick panting of someone not well.

"Who's there?" Dennis asked.

The sucking sounds continued as he edged farther under

the bridge. He stopped for a second, his eyes watering. There was stench unlike anything he had ever smelled. Something rotten. Something dead.

I'm smelling death. That's what I'm smelling. That's what I'm hearing. No . . .

Two flames glowed at him.

Demon eyes.

He turned and sprinted out, never looking back. He ran up the hill, almost slipping on the muddy bank as he neared his car. He tore into the car and revved the engine, locking the doors and putting it in reverse even before catching his breath.

Those eyes from the pit of hell. Red glowing embers pulsing with rage and fear.

I didn't see anything. It's just my imagination.

As he pulled back onto the road, he looked back at the bridge where the bike had been—where the girl had stood on the edge and dropped—but saw nothing. He thought about calling the police. But what could he say? The bike was missing and the girl was gone and whatever was below the bridge . . .

"No," he spoke out loud to get some sense of balance and reality. "No way."

What could he tell the police? After a day of watching football and drinking and taking his drunk buddy home, he saw a girl hop over the side of the bridge and jump into the Fox River? They'd probably assume he was drunk as well.

Am I?

He took a deep breath and knew he'd seen something. He hadn't made this up.

The images came back to his mind. The girl was one thing. But what had he seen under the bridge? What had he imagined?

"I'm just tired," he said out loud, speaking for the sake of his sanity.

A drop of sweat lined his cheek. He opened his window and

let the breeze cool him. As he replayed the events that had just happened, Dennis couldn't shake the feeling that they had happened once before.

It took just a few minutes to realize the truth.

He hadn't experienced the events that had just happened.

He had written them.

The big guy staggered out of the car, looking up and down the street. This was surprising. Why would this disheveled, bulky, anxious man in his thirties think he was being watched?

Cillian wondered what secrets the man held.

The guy wore khaki pants—he always wore khakis. They looked like they never got washed. They were loose except around his gut, which stuck out past his button-down, un-tucked, short-sleeved shirt. His cap and black glasses made him look ordinary, forgettable. He walked with a slight limp in his right leg.

Cillian watched the big man go inside and found it interesting that a guy living in Geneva would drive twenty minutes to this hole-in-the-wall bar. There were plenty of others between where he lived and here.

The tavern smelled like peppers. Peppers and body odor. The air was thick with smoke, the lights dim, a television in the corner playing an old movie. The bartender appeared bored as he took a long drag from his cigarette.

Cillian ordered a beer, then sat a couple stools down from the big guy. On his second beer, he tried to strike up a conver-sation. The man was pounding Budweiser. He noticed the big guy's right hand shook whenever he picked up the bottle.

"You smoke?" Cillian asked.

The guy looked at him, his flat eyes curious. He nodded but didn't offer him a cigarette.

"Here," the bartender said, handing him a pack and giving him a glance that seemed to say, "Don't mess with that guy."

Cillian took a drag from his cigarette, doing it for show. He sometimes smoked but didn't really like it. The beer tasted worse with the Marlboro in his mouth. He wasn't here for this anyway. He was here to make a connection with this stranger.

A stranger who provided him a link to Dennis Shore.

"Where are you from?" he asked.

The big guy stared at him intently for a long minute. "Why?"

Cillian shrugged, inhaling the cigarette for effect. "Just a friendly conversation."

The guy looked ahead, picking up his beer and draining it, hiding his shaking hand.

It looked like he hadn't shaved in a week or more, his blond and gray beard speckled all over his pudgy face. Oily white hair curled up from the back of his cap. Bumps dotted his neck around his patches of whiskers.

Cillian finished another beer and waited to order another. When he did, he told the bartender to give the big guy one as well.

The guy looked at him again. The look had a dead quality about it—something missing, something blank. The eyes were cold, dispassionate, the glance appearing slightly off, as though he was thinking of something else.

The guy leaned in toward him. "What do you want?"

"Nothing," he said. "Just bored, chatting."

"Never seen you here."

"That's 'cause I followed you."

The big guy turned even more white than he already was. "You what?"

"I followed you here. From your house in Geneva."

"That's not my house."

"I've seen you there quite a few times."

"And why were you looking?"

"'Cause I've been spying on your neighbor."

"What neighbor?"

"Ever hear of Dennis Shore?"

"No."

Cillian told him the truth, all of it. He talked about being a Dennis Shore fan, then being disappointed by the silence and the treatment. The big guy continued to stare, looking ready to pounce on him if he moved.

"So why do you care what he does?" the big guy asked.

"I'm just curious," Cillian said. "I'd like to know how he writes, how he gets his inspiration."

"Inspiration for what?"

"Writing his horror novels."

"I don't like curious people."

"Yeah, me neither." Cillian paused. "Speak with your neighbors much?"

The big guy shook his head and lifted the bottle to his mouth.

"If you don't live there, you certainly visit quite a bit."

"My parents live there."

"And you?"

"What do you want?"

"I want to watch," Cillian said. "I want to know."

"Know what?" The big guy coughed, clearing his throat, his eyes watering.

"I've seen some interesting things," he said.

"Like what?"

"Just—interesting things."

The big guy licked his lips and lifted his beer. It shook. Sweat dotted the man's forehead, just above the eyebrows and below his cap. "What things?"

"All I want is a chance to watch, to spy on your neighbor, to get close to him," he said. "That's all I'm interested in. I won't bother anyone."

The big guy looked at him for a long time, saying nothing. "So now—what sort of things are you interested in?"

The smile on the big guy's lips made Cillian shudder.

The Blood-Smeared Note

1.

Dennis held his wife's hand on that long drive back from the hospital. They rode in silence, the stereo off, the whisper of air slipping through the window cracks. He felt like he was in a daze, without anything to say, without anything left to feel. He needed to be strong for Lucy, but he wasn't sure how. All he wanted was to take back the last few hours, to rewrite them with a happier ending. But he couldn't.

Pulling into the driveway, the garage door whining open, Dennis stopped the car prematurely when he felt Lucy's hand grip his and then heard her crying.

"Don't—I don't want Audrey to see me—not like this."

"Okay," he said, putting the car in park and wrapping her in his arms.

For several minutes, a small chunk of eternity, Lucy wept against him. It was impossible for him to remain strong and fearless. Tears brushed down his cheeks and fell against Lucy's thick hair.

"I'm so sorry," he told her over and over again.

When Lucy's swollen red eyes glanced back at him, she seemed lost.

"I don't know why. Why? Why would God let something

like this happen? Why, when I prayed? Why, when it was so close? When we were so close? Why, Dennis? Why?"

But he didn't have a clue. He had no answer. He only shook his head.

"Do you want to know the name I picked out for her? I wanted Abigail. Abby for short. Audrey and Abby. That would have fit, you know? Audrey would have liked that."

"It's a perfect name," Dennis said.

"She lived eight months. Eight months. Why, Den? Why so short? Why couldn't she at least have a chance? Why couldn't she have been born?"

Lucy clung to him and continued to weep.

Dennis thought about holding his little baby girl in his hands after the premature delivery. He would never forget her tiny hands, her little face, the strands of hair on her little head.

She would be part of him for the rest of his life.

Dennis remembered seeing the brilliant orange sunset when they finally climbed out of the car to go inside and tell Lucy's parents and their eight-year-old daughter the news. It haunted him with its beauty.

That was the day he decided there was no God. That there was nothing more than what he could feel and touch. There was nothing else in this world, not a single thing.

2.

On a quiet afternoon walk, Dennis couldn't help thinking about Abby. Eleven years still felt like yesterday, the void in his heart still empty. As he walked along the trail lining the tranquil Fox River, Dennis knew that this life of his—the house and the books and the fame and fortune—had all started because of that momentous event.

With his first book already out at the time, his second finished and soon to be published, Dennis had found himself lost without a story to write. Every time he tried, nothing came.

And then he started to write about a couple that went through a miscarriage, whose lives fell apart after that. And what he thought was just going to be a drama took a left turn into horror as the couple began to be haunted by a young girl they assumed was the daughter they lost.

It was creepy and chilling and extremely cathartic. And even if it had never gotten published, Dennis had needed to write that book. The story became *Breathe*, which went on to sell several million copies.

I'd take back every single copy sold to still have her with us.

He thought of what happened the other night, the image of the girl jumping off the bridge. It had been a pivotal scene in *Breathe*, one of the first scenes where the protagonist started being haunted.

Dennis knew he wasn't being haunted and there had been no girl on the bridge. It had been purely his imagination. That was all. His imagination and stress.

He passed a couple of joggers and nodded at them. If he got paid by the hour, Dennis would record his walks on his time cards. They were an invaluable part of the writing process. At least, they always had been before this bout of block seized his fingers and his soul. The strolls had always given him time to let ideas germinate. Sometimes all an author needed was time. A premise could turn into a character that turned into a scene. And scene after scene turned into a novel.

As if on cue, his cell phone vibrated. He glanced at the caller ID.

"Hi, Maureen," Dennis said.

"Just checking in to see how you're coming along. I sent you a couple e-mails."

"I'm out walking."

"Coming up with some great ideas?"

"You know me," Dennis said, avoiding the answer.

"I just got off the phone with Random House. You're going to laugh at this."

"They're bankrupt?"

"They're already in their fourth printing for *Empty Spaces*," Maureen said. "Making 2.5 million copies in print."

"The shredders are going to be busy."

"The sales they're tracking are going extremely well. And publicity is just starting to kick in too—"

As Maureen spoke, Dennis stopped and stared at the peaceful water reflecting the fading sun. For some time he heard her words but didn't really hear a thing she said. Because as she spoke, another thought ran through his head.

Actually, it wasn't a thought. It was a face.

Cillian Reed's face. Those eyes.

"Dennis?"

"Yeah?"

"What do you think?"

"About what?"

"Us doing dinner when I'm in town."

He remembered her saying something about a trip to Chicago, about coming out to visit him.

"I'm up for anything that'll get me out of the house," Dennis said casually. "Just let me know when."

Maureen laughed and told him she had already e-mailed him when she was coming.

After hanging up the phone, Dennis felt a dread hanging over him. He didn't want to see Maureen. He didn't want to talk about the novel that had just been released and oh yeah, by the way wasn't his. And he didn't want to talk about the novel that he should be writing because oh yeah, by the way he hadn't even started it.

And maybe Cillian would show up to crash their dinner.

As he stepped through the trees at the edge of his property and back onto his lawn, he noticed something on his deck near the sliding glass door.

The closer he got, the more he expected it to fly away or scamper off. But it didn't.

And then he saw why.

The body of a Canada Goose lay on its side next to the door, but its head and neck were somewhere else.

And the glass door . . .

Dennis cursed out loud, wondering if he really saw what he thought he was looking at.

It looked like something had been smeared across the glass. Something bloody and wet with clumps in it.

As he walked up the steps to the deck, he saw where the head and neck had gone.

They were resting on the wooden table. Right next to a blood-smeared note.

Dennis froze. He scanned the lawn, the tall trees on each side, the river, even the sides of the Victorian home. He listened to see if anybody was around, but he was alone.

Just him and this dead goose.

3.

He flung the note across the kitchen, and it went flying better than most paper airplanes, shooting upward until it hit the small chandelier above the round breakfast table. It dropped down and seemed to rest, waiting, beating like a just-removed heart.

This time he didn't hesitate. He grabbed the cordless phone on the counter and dialed a familiar number. A cheery voice answered.

"Hey, Ryan, it's Dennis."

"Oh, hey," the deputy replied. "I just passed your way not long ago."

"I have a situation I need a little input on."

"Did that young lady come back around?" Ryan joked.

"No. It's along those same lines, but this time I'm a little worried."

"What happened?"

"Somebody left a dead goose on my deck, along with a note."

"A dead what?"

"Goose."

Ryan chuckled. "Bet that's a pretty sight. What'd the note say?"

"I'll let you read it."

"You know who it's from?"

"Yeah."

Dennis didn't plan to tell Ryan everything. This call was unofficial, and he would urge Ryan to approach the situation that way.

"Is it threatening?"

"Kind of," Dennis repeated. "Any chance you could swing by?"

"No problem. I can be there in the hour."

Dennis shut off the phone and went to pick up the note. He slid it out of the crimson-speckled envelope and read it again.

Dear Mr. Writer:

Or can I still call you that? Didn't you once say a writer is anyone who writes?

I hate Canada Geese. Do you know what it sounds like when you break their necks? The sound is delightful. Loud, wild, even with their head torn from their body. I wanted to leave this here to remind you that I'm not far.

We need to talk soon. But I will tell you where and when. In the meantime, watch your neck——I mean back!

Mr. Aspiring Writer (Who Writes)

Dennis put down the note, knowing this was just the start. The kid would soon be wanting more. Instead of simply harassing him, Cillian might start asking for money. Or things might get dangerous.

Even after doing Google searches linking Cillian Reed and writing, Dennis had found nothing on the young man. The young writer. The young fan he had ignored and then stolen from.

"Watch your neck—I mean back!"

That was a threat if he'd ever heard one.

Dennis looked around his house as though someone might be there. Then he cursed at himself, the note, the whole situation.

He knew it could be a very long winter if he kept this up, seeing things and being afraid of what was behind his back.

For a brief moment, Dennis thought of his safe in the garage, of the handgun locked there in a fireproof vault the size of a car engine.

The thought was a mild comfort.

4.

"There's not a lot I can do about this."

Ryan wore jeans and a sweatshirt. He was off today, but still thought enough of Dennis to come by. He was tall and lean with a crew cut and narrow eyes behind narrow glasses. He fit his role well: looking young and inexperienced, the kind of guy who wrote tickets but wasn't going to chase down any crazy murderers. He looked like he could be a teenager, even though Dennis knew Ryan was in his midtwenties.

"There's no name, nothing too threatening."

"What about the goose?"

"Well, yeah, that could be vandalism, but again, how do you know who it was?"

"I know."

"You have some interesting fans. It could be any one of them." Ryan smiled, but Dennis didn't return it.

"When should I officially report this?"

"Any time you'd like. You could make it official, start a report. Just in case."

"In case what?"

"In case anything else happens."

"I can't. I don't want any of this to be official. No reports filed, nothing like that."

"The police can't do anything if you don't report this."

Dennis nodded. "I just—maybe I just wanted you to know about it. So if something else happens, I can get your input."

"I say file a report. Nothing's going to happen from doing that."

"There are some questions I don't want to answer."

"Like what?"

"That's what I want to avoid. Questions."

"Are you sure you know who you're talking about?" Ryan asked. "It's not someone else?"

Dennis shook his head.

"Did you ever kill a goose in any of your books?" the deputy asked.

For a second Dennis wondered if Ryan was joking. He couldn't help laughing. "To be honest, I don't remember. I've killed a lot of people—animals too—in my books. Never killed a dog, I know that. That's the one thing my publisher once said. Never kill a dog. But as for a goose—you've got me there."

"I still think it might just be a fan's homage to you."

"Pretty sick homage, wouldn't you say?"

"You're the storyteller. Every author attracts certain readers, right? Imagine if you were writing those Fabio-covered romances."

"Yeah. I'd get women throwing their girdles at me."

"Now *that's* scary."

"I really don't think this was a random fan," Dennis said.

"Then look—just—if you reconsider, let me know. I can take down something official at the station. And if you see anything else that's—strange, I guess—just let me know."

5.

"Den."

He raised his eyebrows and mumbled something.

"Den, listen."

He groaned and shook his head.

"Den, I'm here. You have to listen to me."

"Okay, yeah, sure."

He tried to open his eyes, but they were heavy and the bedroom was dark.

"You have to be careful."

"Okay."

"Something bad is about to happen. To you. To Audrey."

He opened his eyes and reached out. His hand touched nothing but blanket and extra pillows.

The voice sounded—it sounded like many things. It was vibrant, full of so much love and life. But more than anything, it really truly sounded like Lucy.

It was her.

Dennis stared at the ceiling above, the silence of the bedroom suffocating, like an invisible gas covering him. The kind you breathe in a gas chamber.

He kept his eyes open, waiting to hear her voice again. But it wouldn't come.

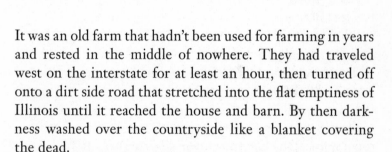

2005

It was an old farm that hadn't been used for farming in years and rested in the middle of nowhere. They had traveled west on the interstate for at least an hour, then turned off onto a dirt side road that stretched into the flat emptiness of Illinois until it reached the house and barn. By then darkness washed over the countryside like a blanket covering the dead.

The big guy's name was Bob. He led them to the house first, turning on a dim light in the kitchen. The bulb flickered like it was ready to take its last breath. Bob wasn't a man of many words. He liked to show things instead of talking about them.

And that was why they had come out here. Bob wanted to show Cillian something.

The wind screamed outside, the old house creaking and groaning in reply. The kitchen smelled of body odor and garlic, its white surfaces splattered in grime—the refrigerator now dark with rust, the sink coated in brown, the floor thick with mud and dirt. On the table sat a long hunter's knife next to a plate of dried-out fruit.

Bob opened the fridge, the squeaking door showing its age.

He didn't ask but handed Cillian a beer. Cillian took it and guzzled half of it down. He noticed his hand shaking.

"I'll be right back," Bob said.

Cillian finished the rest of the beer and looked around. His eyes took in everything, but they kept coming back to the large hunting knife on the table. For a second, as he heard the footsteps approaching, he thought of grabbing the knife. Just in case.

He had no idea what the big guy had done or what he might be planning.

All he had said was: "Want to see a corpse?"

And Cillian, fascinated, half drunk, and mostly skeptical, had told Bob sure.

The big guy lumbered back into the kitchen, stopped for a second and looked at Cillian.

The only thing Cillian knew about this guy was that his name was Bob and that he divided his time between living on this farm and living with his parents in the house in Geneva. Cillian still hadn't been inside the house, and the way Bob acted and spoke about it, he might never go there. Bob's parents sounded bizarre, their house closed off, their lives a mystery.

The way Bob looked at him made him think Bob could easily take the knife and cut him up and feed him to the pigs. If, indeed, there were pigs to feed him to.

"Come on," the big guy finally said.

It was a short walk to the barn through the fierce wind. Cillian could make out the bulky silhouette in front of him, the peculiar gait. Bob swung open a large door on the side of the barn, and they entered the silent, cold blackness.

It felt like a tomb.

Cillian stopped upon entering the barn, the smell unbearable. It wasn't a barnyard smell, the kind associated with livestock and manure.

This smelled like something gone bad.

Like something dead.

He paused for a minute, forcing himself to take a deep, stinging sniff. It wasn't something dead, but someone dead. This was what the dead smelled like, and it was worse than he'd imagined. His eyes watered, and his stomach lurched.

Bob's boots shuffled across the floor. Finally a small gas lamp flicked on, the unsteady flame illuminating the open space around them.

Cillian could see an old tractor rusting away in its last resting spot in the center of the barn. Stalls that once housed cattle or horses now sat unused, untouched. Hay still remained on the floor.

The big guy stared at him for a second. Thinking. Perhaps wondering whether to trust him, or perhaps wondering whether to kill him.

Cillian had doubted that Bob actually did what he claimed to do. But he didn't doubt it anymore.

It wasn't just the deep, undeniable stench. It was everything. This farm in the middle of nowhere and the way Bob looked at him with that blank stare. The feeling filled the barn the same way the smell did. It was thick, throbbing, and very real.

This was what Cillian had wanted to see, to taste, to touch: pure, unmitigated terror.

The big guy shuffled through the barn, leading Cillian past open stalls. Shadows scattered and shifted. At one point Cillian thought he saw something that looked like a hand. Something that looked like a skeleton.

Close to the last stall, the smell still putrid, Bob held up the gas lamp. He waved it, urging Cillian toward the enclosed space.

Cillian approached slowly, with hesitation and fear. The fear crawled all over him. It felt electric and fantastic.

The first thing he saw was a bruised, pink ankle sticking out of the dark muck.

Then he looked farther and saw who it belonged to.

And upon seeing the open mouth and ripped cheek, then taking in the motionless face that looked up at him with shrieking eyes, he knew one thing.

Nothing would ever be the same again.

Threats in the Dark

1.

—Do you believe in ghosts?

—No.

—But you write about them.

—I know. But I make things up.

—I believe in them.

—You do, huh? And why's that?

—Just because. Because I know they're real.

—You once believed in Santa Claus.

—But that's because you both told me he was real. I'm older now.

—You're twelve.

—So?

—I guess that's old enough to believe in ghosts.

—It's easy to believe. It's a lot easier than not believing.

2.

Dennis jerked up, twisting his neck and wincing in pain. He had been asleep in his office chair, the iMac in front of him sleeping as well, the lone lamp on his desk the only sign of life around. As he rubbed the back of his neck to get rid of some of the ache, he adjusted to the light. It was two thirty.

He hadn't been able to write or create in such a long time. Sitting in a chair and facing the computer didn't spark anything. It always just resulted in him playing a game or e-mailing or wandering around on the Web or falling asleep.

He looked at a picture of Audrey in grade school and remembered what he had been dreaming about. Sometimes he dreamed memories. It seemed like lately that had been happening a lot. And this one was from a memory of when Audrey wanted to read his books and he'd told her she was too young. She thought twelve was old enough to read her father's works, thus resulting in a conversation about things for children versus things for adults. And out of that came the conversation about ghosts.

Audrey believed in ghosts because her mother believed in them.

A lot changed after the miscarriage, especially for Lucy. And one of those things was her faith.

Dennis shut off the office light and headed toward his bedroom. The wood floor creaked as usual. But tonight the groans seemed louder, the darkness more foreboding. He was used to wandering the house in the darkness, by himself, without a care. But tonight he couldn't help thinking someone else was in the house.

The rustle of wind sounded outside. He entered his bedroom, greeted by silence, emptiness. He thought about the book he couldn't write, the bills he couldn't pay, the house in Colorado he couldn't sell. He had thought about selling this house, but Audrey wouldn't stand for it. Yet the place sometimes felt like a cold, dark tomb to him. A shrine to a dead woman.

An image of the girl jumping off the bridge filled his mind. He could see the embers beneath the bridge, glowing in the darkness of his imagination, just like they had years ago when he wrote that scene.

Then he thought about Cillian and about Samantha who warned him about all of this.

"*You've done something, and you need to be careful.*"

He could see her lifeless eyes and her bruised arms. He splashed water on his face, unable to get rid of the image.

"*This man wants to hurt you. And it's all because. . . . Plain and simple, the book cannot come out. It can't be released. Ever.*"

Dennis stared at himself in the large mirror.

Now what?

And why did Cillian assault a young woman simply to warn Dennis?

If he would do something like that just to make a point, what would he do to Dennis?

The thoughts made his head hurt. The guilt of taking the manuscript along with the threats and the hallucinations and the stress over his finances . . .

Perhaps this was what happened when pent-up sadness and loss finally got to you.

You start losing your mind.

But he knew his mind was fine. The creative juices weren't there, sure, but perhaps the upcoming meeting with his agent would help. Or maybe he'd take a vacation and get away.

Maybe you'll find another manuscript just sitting in the closet waiting for you to plagiarize, waiting for you to steal.

This voice was different, sounding a lot like Cillian Reed.

He shook his head and gave himself a look of disgust and disappointment before shutting off his thoughts along with the lights and climbing into bed.

Dennis had always been good at burying things. But the grave was overflowing, and he could no longer keep everything inside it.

Just as he was starting to relax into sleep the phone blared, and he jerked in the darkness to find it. The cordless was somewhere. . . . It was loud, louder than usual, but he couldn't find it.

It kept ringing.

Finally he found it in the armchair in the corner, a chair

that was more for decoration and for holding clothes than it was for sitting on.

The chair, another ghost of the past.

He clicked on the receiver.

It was Cillian.

3.

"Would you like to play a game?"

Dennis paused, standing up, gripping the phone. "What do you want?"

Laughter heckled him.

"It's a good day to die."

"Listen, you little creep," Dennis started, "your threats don't mean a thing to me. Why don't you try to come around here again?"

"No tears please. It's a waste of good suffering."

"What?"

The laughter continued.

"Don't watch many horror movies, do you, Dennis? You write about them, but you're not a fan of them. You don't believe in them. You don't *live* them. But that can all change. *I know*."

"What's going to change is you coming down here and getting the life beaten out of you."

"Whatever you do, don't fall asleep."

"Don't what?"

"Surely you know where that's from."

"Where what's from?"

"That quote. 'Whatever you do, don't fall asleep.'"

"This isn't a game, buddy."

"*Nightmare on Elm Street*. Now could *you* come up with something that good? I used to like your fiction, Dennis. I really did. But something happened."

"If you keep harassing me, I'm going to call the police."

"You got bored, Dennis. You got uninspired."

"I swear," Dennis yelled, "I'll call the cops."

"Didn't you already? Or is that young deputy just a good friend who gives you writing tips for nothing more than a handshake and a pat on the back?"

"Are you watching me?" Dennis said. "Are you actually watching me now?"

There was silence.

"'Cause if you are, you'd better run if I find you."

"Want to see something really scary?"

"This isn't a joke, kid."

"We all go a little mad sometimes. Haven't you?"

"I'm not kidding. You don't want to do this, buddy."

Cillian chuckled, then paused for a second. "Dennis, I have one question for you."

"I'm not scared of your threats. Nobody's going to believe that I stole anything from you."

"Dennis?"

He remained silent for a moment. Finally the voice spoke very clearly, very softly.

"'Have you checked the children?'"

He knew that movie line, and it wasn't funny.

Dennis started to rail on the cordless, but he was talking to dead air. Looking at the phone, he thought for a second. It was a threat, sure, but this time it was different.

This time the guy was talking about his daughter.

And he wasn't taking the chance that the guy was just joking around. Not with Audrey.

4.

"Audrey?"

The voice on the other end was muffled.

His heart raced.

"Audrey, are you okay?"

"Dad?"

"Yeah."

"Dad, what's wrong?"

"Nothing. I'm just checking on you. I'm sorry—look, I'll explain. Just tell me you're okay."

"I'm fine."

"I know I'm calling—"

"It's quarter after one. And that's here. It's like three in the morning where you are. What are you doing?"

"I don't want to alarm you—"

"Well, you are alarming me. Are you okay?" Audrey asked, now fully awake, her voice anxious.

"Yes. Just—you need to know. I've recently been having some problems with a crazed fan."

"Another one? Are you sure you're okay?"

"Yes, I'm fine. And tomorrow I'm going to talk to the police, okay? It just—this one—he's a first. He's not just kinda crazy. He's dangerous."

"Did he hurt you?"

"No, no—I'm fine. Everything's fine, honey. Just—you never know. Nowadays you have to be careful. You never know what someone's capable of. And I just want you to be careful, okay? Just be a little more careful than usual. Let your friends know. It's not like—I seriously doubt this guy is going to do anything more than call and e-mail, but you never know."

"Has he done anything else?"

Dennis thought of the dead goose. That little bit of information could be edited. Audrey, the animal lover, didn't need to hear about that. She might never step foot on their deck again.

"I just wanted to make sure you knew—to make sure that if you see or hear anything unusual you'll be careful. Okay? And let me know about it."

"Okay, sure. But are you being careful?"

"Yeah, I'm fine. Everything's fine. I'm just—you just watch out, okay? Just in case. Promise me you'll be careful."

"I will. You too."

Dennis shut off the phone and lay on the bed, expecting to hear the phone ring again. But it didn't.

He remained awake for a long time, staring into the darkness, waiting to hear something, wondering what would happen next.

2006

Cillian watched them through the bedroom window. The happy family with their happy smiles and their happy lives and their happy happiness. He wanted to cram their happiness down their throats and make them choke on it.

The bedroom smelled putrid. It was dimly lit, messy like the rest of the house, with boxes and bags and garbage and nastiness everywhere. The smell was so bad it had been difficult walking through the front door. The big guy's parents weren't around, or if they were he hadn't seen them. All he wanted when he walked in was to go upstairs and spy on the neighbors like he was doing now.

The bestselling author, his pretty wife, and hot daughter.

The invasion of privacy, the secrecy, the spying made Cillian feel a little better. Just a little.

How dare he be ignored?

Bob shuffled into the room holding a beer, offering him one.

"No," he said, staring out through binoculars.

It was midafternoon and the family had gone inside. For half an hour, Cillian hadn't seen anything.

"Want me to kill them?"

He stared at the big guy and realized he wasn't kidding.

"No. Look at me. Nothing happens to them. You don't do anything to them, got it?"

Bob just nodded.

He was sick, this guy. Interesting and fascinating in a sick, twisted sort of way. But utterly stupid. He didn't want Bob interfering.

He had big plans. He wanted to make Dennis Shore's life a little more . . . interesting.

Bob couldn't help. He didn't understand how to be subtle.

"You need a little taste," Bob said to him.

"A taste of what?"

The big guy rummaged in the corner of the room, pulling out a shirt and a pair of pants, then a few bags, a bed sheet.

"Look at this," Bob said, holding up what looked like a set of sharp prongs.

"What's that?"

"It's one of my—one of my toys."

"What's it for?"

"Hurting." Bob laughed in a way that a mentally disabled person might. "It's called the heretic's fork. Used in medieval times for torture. You put this part under someone's chin, then the other on his chest, tying this around his neck so he can't move. You don't penetrate any vital points, so it prolongs the pain."

Cillian examined the instrument, then the guy holding it.

This was why Bob intrigued him. And why it was good hanging out with him. This could go well in the newest book he was writing.

It was about a psychotic killer.

He looked at the big guy.

A psychotic killer who didn't have any feeling, any remorse, any gauge of good and evil.

The good—if there had been any—had left him a long time ago and had been replaced with grime and stink and filth, just like the house his parents lived in.

Just like his heart.

Great fodder.

Amazingly great fodder for a real author. Not for phonies like the guy next door.

Want to see real horror, Mr. Shore?

He watched Bob play with his fork apparatus.

I'm looking at it right now.

And I want you to get a glimpse too.

Malicious and Deliberate

1.

"I've got a problem."

Maureen nodded, but the expression on her face didn't change. The word Dennis often used to describe his agent was *unruffled*. She never seemed bothered, and her mood was always optimistic. Perhaps that's what it took to be an agent. To not let the insanity of publishing get you down, to see the possibilities instead of dwelling on failures.

As Dennis took a sip of wine, he realized he had probably had a little too much to drink. His head swirled around the muted light of the small dining room, the other tables quiet in conversation. They were at a quiet French restaurant, perfect for intimate conversation. After talking for most of the hour about Audrey and about Maureen's nephews and nieces, they were finally getting down to the wonderful world of business.

"I'm not really sure what to do about it."

"Well, maybe I can help you," Maureen said, taking another bite of her fish.

Maureen was probably in her late forties, even though she looked more like she was in her late thirties. Dennis always forgot how tall she was until he greeted her with an awkward hug. She was slender with dark hair kept short. She wasn't exactly attractive, at least not in Dennis's estimation. He preferred a little shorter, a little more round. Maureen had an edge about her, as though all of her interesting sexy parts had been whittled down to nothing.

He hadn't exactly planned to tell her what was going on with his writing. Or what *wasn't* going on with his writing. But he hadn't planned on ordering so much wine either. And if he was going to tell anybody, it might as well be her.

"I'm behind on my novel."

"Really? That's a first, isn't it?"

"No, not exactly."

"How far behind?"

"All I have is a title."

Maureen smiled with surprise. "That's all?"

"Yeah."

"And it's due at the end of October, right?"

Dennis nodded, raising his eyebrows, giving her a *what now* glance.

"You're a fast writer."

"Not *that* fast."

"Look what you did with *Empty Spaces*. Remember your anxiety before the benefit? Maybe nerves stimulate your writing."

He couldn't help but laugh.

"A lot of artists do their best work under immense pressure," Maureen said.

"Paying a second mortgage on a Colorado chalet isn't typical artist pressure."

"I'm talking about Lucy. I can't imagine how I'd go on if I lost my husband."

"Denial's a great thing. But it eventually catches up with you. Just like unpaid bills."

"You've had a tough couple of years, Dennis. We can always postpone the new book—"

"No."

"I'm just suggesting—"

"Maureen, things are—they're really tight. I never expected to be in a bind like this. Lucy's medical bills—I just wanted her to get better, you know? I didn't care about the costs. I hadn't been concerned about money since *Breathe* took off. And right now—I *need* that advance check. And the only way to get it is to hand in a good manuscript."

"I can ask James about getting the check to you early."

"I already asked. They can pay me when the manuscript is in hand, but legally they're not able to cut a check now. They're pretty strict on that, even with one of their top authors."

"I can talk to him again—"

"I just—you heard James talking up the new book when we saw him. How Random is ramping up its efforts—how they can't wait to see the new book. All this pressure—I never thought it would affect me. I never thought I'd let it get to me."

Maureen started to say something, then paused. "You still have time, Dennis. You can do it."

But even as he nodded, there was only one thing on his mind. He thought about the upcoming anniversary of Lucy's death, how it approached on the horizon like a blazing fire in the night sky. He didn't want to drive toward it, but he had to. There was no other direction he could go.

The wine tasted refreshing. He took a large sip and thought of Cillian Reed.

If the kid decided to tell someone and found a way to prove it, this conversation would be meaningless. It wouldn't matter whether Dennis handed his next book in. He wouldn't have that chance. All that would matter was what was left of his writing legacy.

"Dennis?"

"Yeah?"

"Are you okay?"

"Yeah. Just tired."

"I hope you don't mind me saying so, but you look tired. I saw that in New York."

"You know how you can fake it so well that you can almost convince yourself you're okay? Sometimes I think—no, I guess I know—that's what I've been doing. But I've had to. For Audrey. For everyone."

Maureen's eyes brimmed with sadness and sincerity. "You're allowed the chance to grieve too."

"Yeah, I guess so." He drained his glass as his eyes filled. He wasn't sure if it was the wine or traces of tears. "I guess I just don't do that very well."

"I don't think anybody does. And everybody goes about it their own way."

Dennis nodded. He glanced at Maureen, then at the paintings on the walls around them. He suddenly had déjà vu. He remembered being here with James and Maureen, with just one big change: Lucy had been here with them.

"I'm just—I'm afraid, Maureen."

She laughed. She always laughed when someone said that word around Dennis. "You're never afraid."

"I know. But I'm afraid now. I'm scared that I haven't grieved yet, but that I'm about ready to start. And where will it take me?"

2.

A writer has to be fearless.

His wife's words came to him on the ride home. Maureen was driving his SUV at his suggestion, the sleeping town of Geneva passing them by. He couldn't recall when Lucy had said it to him, but it had been just as his first horror novel was taking off and he found himself writing another.

He had made an offhanded remark to Lucy, telling her she needed to write a book too. And she had responded that she could never write.

—You need to be fearless to be a writer.

—No, you don't. You just make things up. Tell a good story.

—That's not all you do.

—Then what is it? It's not like I'm in the Marines risking my life. Or trying to find a cure for cancer.

—You're putting your heart and soul out there for others to see. For others to criticize and critique.

—Oh come on. Maybe with my first two novels. But we see how well those did.

—I'm not joking, Den. Breathe *isn't just a ghost story, and you and I both know it. You might be able to tell everybody it's just a spooky little story, but I know why you wrote it.*

—You told me to write it.

—It's about Abby, about losing her, about a family struggling with grief. But you did it in a remarkable way.

—I don't know about that.

—Everything you write is a part of you. That's what makes your writing special. But that's what also makes it hard. I couldn't do it. I couldn't go to those places.

—Please. I just have an overactive imagination.

—It's more than that. You're able to go to the dark places that we all have. Some people pretend they don't exist. But you dive into them and create a story out of them.

But as he and Maureen neared his house, Dennis realized it had been some time since he had done that.

3.

The whole night suddenly split open with white specters.

What at first looked like garbage blowing from his driveway onto Route 31 turned into pages drifting across the road.

"What's all over your lawn?" Maureen asked as she steered through the wall of shrubs and under tall trees toward the house.

They were everywhere. Hundreds, maybe thousands of sheets of paper.

Dennis couldn't control the expletive that escaped his mouth.

"What is this?" Maureen asked.

Dennis stepped out of the Volvo as it stopped halfway down the driveway toward the garage. Headlights cut through the darkness, illuminating the path under the trees along the lawn. The breeze blew a few sheets onto his windshield.

These weren't pages from a printer. These were pages from books.

And they had text on them.

Along with something else.

Dennis knelt down and picked up a piece of paper. He recognized it instantly.

He tried another one that had dark smudges on its edges.

Another had something written over the text.

"Dennis?" Maureen called. "What are they?"

"Keep the lights on," he said.

As he held up a page, he could make out the word that looked as though it had been finger-painted onto the paper. He quickly scanned the area and could see other pages had similar markings.

"What is it?"

He crinkled up the page, not wanting Maureen to see it. But as she climbed out of the car and grabbed a sheet from the windshield, she read for herself. "This is a page from one of your books."

"Yeah. They all are."

"What?"

She turned for a moment, then called out his name.

"Dennis—this has something written all over it. I think it says 'liar.'"

He picked up a handful of pages and saw stains, like smudged fingerprints. Others had other things written on them—curses, variations on thief and liar and hack.

"I'm calling the police," Maureen said, taking out her cell phone.

Dennis held page 285 from *Fearless*, his sixth horror novel that came out a few years ago. **FRAUD** marked the top in a smear.

He heard Maureen talking in the background. Dennis stepped into the SUV's headlights, seeing the driveway covered in pages, then seeing them stuck in the bushes around his house, in the large pine tree, in the maple tree, all over his lawn and even all over the front porch.

Thousands of pages.

Many looked ripped, as though they had been individually torn out of the books. Some were larger from his hardcovers, others looked like they were paperback size.

Dennis saw a cover from his book *Sorrow* ripped in half.

He saw the shell of a paperback.

Stepping onto the porch, he saw a hardcover edition of *Echoes* that looked like it had been mauled by a lawn mower. He picked it up—half of the book was missing, and the other half was shredded.

Half of his own face stared up at him from the mulch, the author shot used for one of his first few books.

"Someone's coming out," Maureen said. "I told them your place had been vandalized. I don't think you should even go inside until they come."

He stared at the scene in disbelief, his head still groggy from the wine.

"Who would do something like this?" his agent asked. "It's not funny. Not in the least. Look at this. I can't even repeat what it says."

Dennis was going to say something about one of his fans pulling a prank on him, or something to that effect, but he couldn't. He was speechless.

And it wasn't just because he knew who had done this and now realized the extent of what he was dealing with.

A cold, white fear smothered him.

All these pages had been written on with someone's blood.

2006

You can still get out of here if you want.

Streams of rain ran down the car windows. Cillian sat in the back of the car, tinted windows surrounding him, the outside dark except for passing cars and a few street lights. The big guy had told him to wait. To wait until they got in the car. He'd just watch tonight. Bob would show him how it's done.

Cillian's mouth felt dry. He could feel his heart pulsing. He breathed in and out steadily until it slowed down. He probably shouldn't be so excited and nervous and horrified. He was all of those, and he wanted to be all of those.

In a few moments, he would know what it was like. Not just to see someone dead, but to watch him die.

There is no turning back.

He knew that and didn't care.

He breathed in and out, slowly, deliberately.

Cillian didn't care. The hacks and the frauds and the phonies of the world, they could care. They could have their nice little sheltered lives, but he wanted to make it real, to make it deep. He wanted to know what it was like. That way, when he wrote, he could smell the terror, he could taste the dread.

And when I finally show Dennis my next novel, he'll be impressed. He'll finally be impressed and give me what I deserve.

Time.

It had been too long. He wondered if the big guy was having trouble luring someone to the car. If Cillian didn't know him, he wouldn't accompany the big guy to his car.

Then again, Cillian went to the farm with him.

Then again, Cillian hung out with him on a regular basis.

He didn't know how he was going to do it or when. All he knew was that tonight he would watch.

A set of voices caught his attention. They were close.

It was another man.

There was laughter, then the doors opened.

A man smelling like smoke and whiskey climbed into the front seat, then cursed when he saw Cillian sitting behind him.

"You've got a friend here, Bob," the stranger said with a laugh.

The guy introduced himself with a hard handshake. The stranger looked rough and young, probably midtwenties.

Bob climbed in and started the car.

"Told him about the party," Bob said to Cillian. "Gonna be a good time."

Cillian remained silent as the car began to move. The town passed by and soon faded away. He felt nauseous and unable to move or speak or breathe.

Bob tossed him a pint of alcohol. "Drink up. You'll need it."

The Tastes and Smells of Death

1.

It was midmorning by the time he cleaned up his lawn (as well as surrounding lawns) from the littering of book pages. The thing that surprised Dennis—surprise being a mild way of describing what he really felt—was the variety of book pages he kept finding. It wasn't just that there were so many, and there were thousands, but they came from all of his books. Not just hardcover and paperback, but he found Italian and German editions as well as a couple languages he didn't even recognize. And after double-checking his closet and other storage areas, Dennis knew the books hadn't come from his stash.

In fact it didn't look like anybody had been inside his house.

That didn't prevent the police from sticking around for at least an hour, asking questions, checking in and around the house, making sure everything was secure. Ryan had been there with them, acting more official than usual, an earnest look on his face. The deputy told Dennis he would drive by the house a few times that night just to be on the safe side.

When Maureen left, Dennis gave her a hug and apologized for the drama.

"Whoever did this certainly put a lot of time and effort into it," Maureen said. "Be careful, okay?"

He nodded and played it off, but he knew he needed to be careful.

The question now was whether to file an official complaint against Cillian. And what he would actually say. *The guy whose novel I stole is harassing me.*

Joseph Heller coined a term with his novel that summed up this situation: *Catch-22*.

As Dennis sat watching television that night, he couldn't help thinking this was what he deserved. *And it's just the start*, a voice kept telling him. *It's only going to get worse.*

Of course he assumed the pages scattered everywhere had been the work of Cillian Reed. But he had checked his answering machine, his cell phone, and his e-mail and had found no messages. No notes saying, "This is just a taste of things to come." Nothing to take credit for the mess.

It might have been a prank, but it was a vicious prank. Whoever had done it had taken the time to rip out individual pages of many of his books. It had taken time, and ripping a book—there was something not right about that. Not just one of his own books, but *any* book. A book always held value to someone. Whoever had planned and executed this stunt had something extremely personal against him.

Now, the morning after, finished with cleaning up this literary mess, Dennis decided to ask the neighbors if they'd seen anything.

The Thompsons were an affable family of five who had been living in the one-bedroom ranch south of Dennis's house for years. Dennis wished he shared a driveway with them instead of with the eccentric, elderly couple on the north side. Their property was worth a fortune, but they were unwilling to let someone buy it and tear down their house to build a gargantuan one. They often had family visiting and often traveled out of town. Dennis frequently saw the parents walking, but didn't know them besides the customary hellos. He went over to talk with them and spoke briefly with Ronald, who amicably told him he hadn't seen anything but thanked him for picking up the garbage so quickly.

Dennis debated going to the other neighbors, the messy, older couple on his north side, but decided to go anyway. It gave him a chance to be cordial and neighborly and to see if they had any idea who did this.

He stepped across the uncut lawn full of dry, dead patches. A big, rotting tire sat in the middle of the lawn, weeds growing over it. Leaves probably two or three years old lay in clumps everywhere. Several misshaped bushes stuck out near the entrance, blocking the modest door. He and Lucy had always wondered what the inside of the house looked like. Dennis stepped onto the cement entryway and rang the doorbell.

He waited for a couple minutes, then rang the doorbell again. He had seen their car parked in the driveway; it was never parked in the garage. Who knew what sorts of things were stored in that garage? He continued to wait, then knocked.

Finally he heard the door unlocking. It sounded like ten locks were unlocked and unbolted and slid open before the door cracked. At first he didn't see anybody, then he looked down to see the frizzy hair of the short, elderly woman.

He didn't know their names, so he couldn't even address her properly. "Hi there. How are you doing today?" Dennis said in an oddly formal fashion.

A stench leaked out of the slit in the doorway—a vile smell, like onions and garlic basting a dead animal. Dennis couldn't help scratching his nose.

The woman with big, buggy eyes just stared at him.

"I'm Dennis, your neighbor," he told her, feeling like an idiot. Of course she knew this, right? But the look in her eyes was blank, almost dead.

"I just wondered if you or your husband saw anything strange last night—anybody in your yard or in mine? Someone scattered a bunch of papers all over. I picked them all up but wondered if you saw anything."

"No."

Her answer came without a second to even think.

"Are you sure? Maybe you could ask your husband."

"He didn't see anything." Half of her face was still hidden behind the narrow opening in the door.

"Well, if you do think of anything, can you let me know? I'd appreciate it."

The door shut abruptly, and Dennis was left standing there, looking at the entryway in confusion.

Maybe they were the ones who did it, he thought. He imagined the older couple collecting hundreds of copies of his books amidst the other garbage in their house. He thought of the smell and couldn't believe it. It was putrid.

Dennis walked back toward his house. As he did, he nearly stepped in a large heap of feces. Something about it caught his attention. It wasn't the fact that the pile grossed him out. But this looked like it came from something huge—not a cat or a dog but a horse, or something bigger.

And it looked fresh.

He shook his head, wondering what the new day would bring.

Perhaps he would take Audrey's advice and get away. From the empty house and the strange neighbors and the crazed fan (if he could actually be called a fan) and the writer's block.

Maybe he'd do just that—get away.

But could he really get away from all this?

And if he did, what would he come back home to?

2.

I dreamed about Mom last night.

The first line in the e-mail from Audrey took his breath away. Dennis continued to read.

You know how I always say, "I wonder what Mom would say about that"? How I always wonder what she's thinking, what she might be wanting to tell me, to tell us?

Last night I dreamed I was in a flower garden, except instead of flowers all around me, they were cards. A thousand greeting cards, each filled with a message from Mom. They were hanging off the trees and in the bushes and everywhere. And each card said something important, the right words for the right occasion. I read a bunch of them, and I don't remember anything specific except this:

Mom loves us. And she wants me to look out for you.

I know it was just a dream, but still—it was kinda cool to think there were all these thoughts and feelings, and they were all written down in a special place to access whenever I needed to.

Wouldn't that be cool?

Just wanted to share that with you. Hope you're doing well. Talk soon.

Love ya.

Audrey

Dennis reread the e-mail, then read it again.

The cards hanging on the trees and in the bushes—that was a lot like his missing-pages episode last night, an episode he wasn't about to mention to his daughter. Not now, with her a thousand miles away.

It's just a coincidence, that's all.

But this was more than a coincidence, and he knew it.

Dennis shot Audrey a quick e-mail and forced himself not to think any more about it.

It was just a dream. Just imagined. Just like he imagined the girl jumping off the bridge. It was just grief and fatigue and change affecting Audrey, just like it was affecting him.

Nothing more than that.

After sending the e-mail, he looked outside. It was afternoon and one of those nagging, misty rains had been going on and off since morning. He wanted to take an afternoon walk to get away from his computer, but he couldn't. He was stuck here.

Stuck is an apt word.

He was about to get up when an e-mail arrived. He couldn't believe Audrey was getting back to him so quickly.

It was from Demonsaint4424@gmail.com.

Dear Mister Laughing-Himself-All-the-Way-to-the-Bank Writer:

I thought you needed some inspiration. In fact, I thought you needed some words. Writers need words, right? So I provided you with them. Hundreds of thousands of them. And those are your own words, not someone else's. They're yours. You can plagiarize all you want. Why steal from me when you can keep stealing from yourself? Your brain-dead readers won't even notice you're borrowing from your previous works. Writers do that all the time anyway. I mean—come on—when was the last time you read something *original* from any of those other laughing-it-all-the-way-to-the-bank writers?

I never told you this, but your last novel—the last one you actually wrote—entitled *The Thin Ice* was thin indeed. Thin plot, emaciated characters, and the only original thing *was* original when you did it first in *Breathe*.

Oh the mighty have fallen and the proud have been humbled and it will take a miracle to work your way back, Dennis Shore.

Do I have your attention?

Do I finally have your undivided attention?

CR

Dennis didn't think, didn't reread the e-mail, just ran his fingers over the keyboard.

You want words, I'll give you words.

He filled the screen with profanities and insults and threats. Finally he read the e-mail, knowing it would look pretty incriminating if it ever got out.

He deleted it and thought for a moment.

Cillian—
We need to sit down.
I'm willing to listen if you are.
Dennis

The instant-messaging box popped up in the corner of his computer. The reply came quickly. Almost too quickly for the number of words it contained.

Dear Random House Sweetheart:
Yes, we need to sit down, but you've done far too much sitting on that tail of yours and not enough living to know what real life is about. WHAT do you know about terror, *Dennis*? What do you know about horror? So many could really write about it. So many could actually describe the tastes and the smells of death, could actually detail what it's like to kill, to hurt, to destroy, to haunt. You—what do you know? What could you possibly know in that seemingly perfect little existence of yours, typing away for years, the inspiration and the passion slowly fading like the dew on the grass. Yes, we need to sit but when I say so.
I've listened for far too long and waited for even longer and now is my time and now YOU will listen and you will wait and you will sit and you will finally and forever KNOW.
There are things I want to show you, Dennis.
All I used to want—all I *ever* wanted from you was your time. Your input.

Now those are meaningless.

Something else burns inside. My ambitions and goals are far higher now.

CR

It was almost as though the instant message had already been written.

Dennis quickly replied, irritated and annoyed that he was being toyed with and jerked around.

You need serious help, buddy. I couldn't care less what "burns" inside of you. How about delusions of grandeur? And trust me—you need to leave me alone. Or this game you're playing is going to turn really dark. And really serious.

A minute later Cillian replied.

You don't frighten me, Dennis. But for the first time in your career, and maybe your life, you'll be scared. You'll be very scared, Dennis. You'll experience a fear that is missing from your books, no matter how terrifying a story you've ever concocted.

Nothing you've ever done or felt will touch the depths of fear and despair you're about to go through.

Nothing.

Part Two

The Lunatic Is in the Hall

Scarecrow

1.

He was close enough to smell her. Lucy always smelled good. Most of the time she claimed it was nothing, just some lotion she had put on, the shampoo she had used. But even while the scents were different, they were really the same. They were Lucy. Intoxicating, light, alive.

The last word lingered in his mind, even as he looked across the table at her.

He knew where he was. The coffee shop on Third Street. She got her usual. He tried something different every time. They sat by a fireplace, amidst a crowd of people and loud music.

Alive . . .

She laughed. And he felt something deep, scraping at his insides, peeling away at him.

That sound. The way her cheeks glowed, her lips circled, the lines under her eyes wrinkled.

It took his breath away.

It took his breath away because this wasn't real, she wasn't real, her laugh wasn't real.

She wasn't alive.

Rather than wake up from this dream, he stayed here. Gazing at her.

She's not real, and this isn't real. Nothing is real, not like that anymore.

He pictured her so vividly.

God did he miss her.

So much time had passed; yet he could still see her clearly, could still hear her perfectly, could still be with her like this.

Dreams like this had been few since Lucy's death.

But not anymore.

2.

So far Dennis had not heard from Cillian. It had been eight days and nothing. No e-mails or phone calls, no dead animals or pages from his books strewn across his lawn. Nothing.

The same could apply to his writing. Every day he heard more accolades about *Empty Spaces*. Sales were excellent and reviews were excellent and everything about it was excellent. Meanwhile its author spent the day searching the Internet, watching CNN and ESPN, reorganizing his office—doing everything he could except write. And it wasn't like he hadn't tried. The words just did not want to come. And they certainly weren't there to find.

He drove downtown through the crisp early October air to get his mail. *To waste time instead of writing*, a voice whispered. It was true. Sometimes morning drives did wonders for his creativity. But he was beyond help at this point. The writer's block had turned into a fortress.

The sign on the church that morning provided no levity. "If you're headed in the wrong direction, God allows U-turns."

Dennis shook his head. Part of him wanted to ram his SUV into the church sign. *How about that for a freaking U-turn?* The sign wasn't amusing. It was ignorant.

At the post office, he picked up a stack of mail and thumbed through it. Some reader mail, some junk mail, a few random things from his publisher.

Nothing from Cillian.

The absence only heightened Dennis's tension. He knew the young man wasn't going to leave him alone. What was he doing? Finishing his Great American Novel for Dennis to read? Perfecting the opening chapter of his magnum opus?

For what?

He turned onto State Street and headed toward Randall. He needed to get a few supplies at Home Depot. Traffic this morning seemed heavier than usual. He eventually pulled into the parking lot with a dozen or more vehicles scattered across it. As he walked toward the large entrance to the hardware store, he glanced at the midmorning sky. It was coated with soft clouds, not puffs but clouds that filled the entire sky, like a blanket. It made the sky and everything a little darker, not in an ominous way but in a subdued, gentle manner.

He walked through the sliding glass doors, past the carts. Dennis thought about getting one, then realized he was only here to purchase some lightbulbs and take a look at snowblowers. His acted up last winter, and he had procrastinated till now to buy a new one. With a long driveway, there was no way he could go through another winter without it.

Dennis passed multiple signs and the returns desk. He didn't see anybody behind the counter even though the light for the section was on. The aisle opened up, and he found himself surrounded by lawn mowers. To his right was the garden center with doors leading outside, to his left lay most of the rest of the store. He didn't see anyone as he found the lightbulbs, picking up a couple four-packs.

The overhead music amused him. The speakers piped out old Genesis when Peter Gabriel sang lead, before he walked out of the group and made Phil Collins an international pop star. The music seemed unusually loud. He couldn't hear anything else.

He looked around and still didn't see any other customers—or helpful employees.

That was unusual. And the number of cars in the parking lot meant there should be a good number of shoppers here.

He turned down one aisle. Nothing. Another. Still nothing. The music continued to rail on, the guitars and drums pounding and piercing.

Suddenly it broke, and a prerecorded message started. "We here at Home Depot would like to ensure that—"

It broke up, crackled for a minute, then came back on. "—your children are safely secured to the—"

Another screech and whirring. Dennis stopped, looking around for someone to laugh with, but there wasn't anybody else.

Then the music changed.

It started playing an old song with a harmonica.

"You gotta be kidding," Dennis said.

Again he turned, but nothing.

The song was "Moon River," the original recording with Henry Mancini. He knew it well. It was the song Lucy and he danced to at their wedding. Not unusual for Muzak, but still.

Just as the singer was about to start, the speakers creaked again. The crackling continued for a minute, then silence.

Deathly silence.

Dennis strained to hear feet moving, carts shuffling, voices talking.

There was nobody around.

He walked down a plumbing aisle, paying no attention to the sinks and the faucet settings. Everything was still. The music hadn't come back on. He seemed to be the only person in the whole store. And yet, for some crazy reason, Dennis felt like he was being watched.

He could never remember a Home Depot this empty.

The aisles towered over him, the echoes of the massive ceiling bringing nothing but the tapping of his shoes against the concrete floor.

"Hello?" His voice withered away.

He shook his head, feeling stupid for calling out, knowing he'd eventually find someone.

A song began playing. "Sweet Dreams (Are Made of This)" by Eurythmics. At least the eighties synth-pop song pepped up the mood in this tomb of a building.

Dennis walked toward the security mirrors, and as he passed underneath one, he looked up at it, seeing the long aisle behind him.

A figure bolted past, far down the aisle. He turned, but couldn't see anything.

"Hello?" he called out again, but the music quickly covered his voice. He kept walking, passing a display mirror with a gaudy gold frame. The reflection showed a figure behind him. Approaching. It was a woman wearing jeans, a white sweatshirt, something smeared all over her clothes and face.

Something red.

Her face was covered in blood, especially around her open mouth.

And for a brief, wrenching second, Dennis had a crazy thought. *I've been here before, and I know what happens.*

The figure started running toward him, and as he turned she ran into him, over him, the collision knocking both of them to the hard ground.

As the song disappeared, crackling off, he heard her sickly cough, then a scream. It was unholy and unearthly. It sounded like something shrieking from the bottom of a well, her mouth clogged but her rage fierce. As the woman's mouth and eyes widened, droplets of blood splattered over him.

Dennis shoved the woman off him and jumped up, landing

on one of the boxes of lightbulbs. He sprinted down the aisle past the doors and windows section, through the lumber, and past the tools.

The wailing woman followed.

I've got her blood all over me.

Just as he started toward the front of the store to get help, a burly stranger stepped in front of him, blocking his path. The man's hands were wet with blood. The stranger looked like he had just come from an all-you-can-eat rib buffet where they served human ribs. He had not worn a bib, nor had he used his nice and handy moist towelette.

The man screamed and lunged at Dennis.

This is not real. I've seen this before, and this is not happening.

But the tower of toolboxes he knocked over felt real. The gash against his chin felt real. And the piercing screams of two zombie-like figures felt real.

So why am I wondering whether I need to cry out in horror or laugh?

Dennis took off back to where he came from, rushing down a long aisle that cut through the store. He turned over displays as he ran, trying to fend off his attackers. Down the plumbing aisle, he saw two more figures dart their heads in his direction, then start running toward him.

He made it to the lawn equipment where he picked up a rake. The woman got to him first, and he waved the rake at her, suddenly realizing it wouldn't do a bit of good. He saw the racks of shovels and picked one up, hurling it at her. He missed. He tried again, this time landing the edge of the shovel against the woman's head. She howled and went down to one knee.

Get out of here, Dennis. Now.

The hulking figure in the jean jacket bolted toward him. Dennis grabbed an ax, quickly prying off the plastic piece attached to the blade. It was a lightweight ax with a sharp, wide blade. The man charged him, so Dennis swung, hitting the man once, then twice, then again, and again.

When the figure finally collapsed to the ground, Dennis took two more axes off the rack and bolted toward the entrance.

Get out and you'll be fine. Just get out.

Someone grabbed him, and he used the handle of the ax to crack the man's face. Another figure started running down an aisle at him, so Dennis chucked one of the axes toward him to scare him off. It didn't do any good.

He made it to the entrance, but the sliding glass doors wouldn't open. He cracked open the glass with the last ax, kicking out a hole big enough to pass through. Just as he kicked for a final time, warm and sticky hands wrapped around his neck, the figure's mouth opening wide.

He's trying to bite me.

Dennis grabbed the ax by the center of the handle and hammered the blade into the top of the man's head. He didn't watch the rest. He heard the young man hit the floor as he scrambled out of the building.

"Thanks for shopping with us!" a sign said in the parking lot.

Dennis ran toward his car, clicking the unlock button on the remote. His shaking hand dropped his keys, scrambled to pick them up. Finally he lurched inside the car, locking the doors and revving the engine. For a minute he just sat there, his hands bloody, his body shaking.

For a long time, he just stared at the front doors to Home Depot. Waiting. Waiting for the zombies to come out. Waiting for them to attack.

The knocking on his window jolted him, making him jerk and try to get the car into drive. Then he saw the woman's face, her quizzical smile.

"Are you okay?" she asked through the glass.

Dennis shook his head, nodded, then looked toward the front of Home Depot.

"Are you sure?"

"Yeah," he said, surprised to hear his own voice talking so naturally. "What's wrong?"

The woman looked baffled. "You tossed a rake in my direction, then ran off. I just—it seemed like you were running away from somebody."

Dennis stared at the front of the store. The glass doors opened and closed. Couples and families walked in and out. The glass hadn't been broken. Zombies weren't piling out. This woman didn't have blood around her mouth.

Dennis held up a hand. "No," he said. "Just, uh, just didn't find what I was looking for. Sorry about that." He nodded and watched the curious woman walk away. Then he noticed his hand.

It was bloody.

His pants and shirt were speckled with blood.

He couldn't breathe. His mind spun. He didn't want to know if the blood was his own.

He was too scared to know.

Dennis jammed the Volvo into drive. Even with the heat on and the doors locked, he couldn't stop his body from shaking. And even though he gripped the steering wheel as hard as he could, his hands still quivered.

3.

The first time had been the girl by the bridge. But he could blame the long day of watching football and drinking too much before driving Hank home that rainy night.

This was different.

This was crazy.

Dennis had taken some Tylenol for his headache, but it wasn't working. He drank a glass of water and sat in his kitchen, his hands still shaking, his mind still reeling.

What is happening to me?

The experience in Home Depot was another scene that came directly from one of his novels. The book was *Scarecrow*, his zombie novel. Yet he couldn't remember the story being as terrifying and as real as his experience today.

He needed to talk to someone, to make sure he wasn't losing his mind.

He'd never talked to a shrink, not even after everything with Lucy. People who went to shrinks needed someone else to control them, to guide them along, and Dennis wasn't one of those people.

Why that book? Why now?

He hadn't picked up *Scarecrow* since it came out three years ago. He had forgotten about that scene early in the book. Why had it come back to mind now?

Dennis sucked in a breath, then drained the water and stood up.

He refused to go batty. Whatever happened in Home Depot—whatever his mind had experienced—could be held at bay.

All he needed was to get his writing motor running again, and then everything would be back in its right place.

4.

The doorbell tore him out of his sleep.

Dennis jumped up, looking around the family room, the clock saying it was close to midnight. This wasn't unusual, falling asleep on the plush love seat as he watched a game on ESPN or read a book. He had been reading Ken Follett's latest and feeling envious of how the author made it seem so easy when he had drifted off. The beer and the day had worn him out.

For a second, he thought about grabbing something—a baseball bat, a knife, the pistol he stored in the garage.

But instead he rushed to the door, the doorbell continuing to ring.

Maybe one of those bloodsucking zombies from Home Depot would greet him with "Trick or treat!"

But there was nobody.

A brown cardboard box tied with string sat on the welcome mat on his doorstep.

Dennis scanned the area, walking outside and down the walk toward the driveway to see who might have done this. He knew, of course. He didn't need to see Cillian's face to know this was from him.

The guy was too scared to face Dennis like a man. He was too scared of what Dennis might do to him.

"Why don't you come out of the shadows?" he shouted.

But nobody stepped out.

Dennis stared at the box for a moment, then picked it up.

He already knew what was inside without opening it. He could tell because of its weight, because of the bulky way it shifted in his hand.

Inside he locked the front door, double-checking to make sure. He brought the box into the kitchen and found scissors to snap the string.

For a second Dennis wondered if he should continue. Cillian was playing a game with him. Why, he wasn't sure. To get under his skin perhaps. To make his life a nightmare before the real reason came out: extortion, blackmail.

Opening this would just continue the game.

But Dennis needed to, even though he already knew what the contents were.

The first thing he saw was the orange paper. A thick stack of orange pages bound by a rubber band.

What was with Cillian and orange paper?

Then he saw the typed words on the cover page of the manuscript.

Brain Damage

A Novel By . . .

Dennis glanced over his shoulder before touching the manuscript. He wondered if somewhere outside in the darkness Cillian watched him.

"A novel by . . ." Very cute. Very smug.

This was an entire manuscript.

He checked the back.

There was even a finish with the words *The End*.

An entire book, right here.

Just like a year and a half ago when he found the manuscript from Cillian in his closet.

He's toying with me. Playing. Enticing.

But why?

For a long time Dennis stood there, staring at the manuscript, wondering what secrets lay inside.

And every second that passed, a low deep murmur in his soul whispered back at him.

You'll never be able to write again.

5.

The constant rattling of the wind outside was the only sound. He swallowed, his mouth dry. The bottle of scotch was on the table in the family room, and he found himself pouring another glass, then draining it. His eyes watered from the shot, his skin warm, his nerves blazing.

The pages he had read lay in front of him, resting on the table like a pulsing heart.

All twenty of them.

Chapter One.

Dennis wanted to go back to an hour ago and throw those pages in the garbage along with the rest of the novel. Or better yet, find a match and burn them. He wished he had not read them and wished no one else would ever read them.

The chapter made him feel dirty.

His legs felt locked in ice, his breathing unsteady. He was about to have another glass of whiskey when he noticed his hand trembling and decided he needed to get up and go to bed.

"But it's not going to be that easy, is it, Dennis?"

He could hear Cillian's voice, the way he emphasized his name as though it were a curse word.

Why is he getting to me?

But Dennis knew why. He closed his eyes, and his mind wandered. That was the beauty and the horror of the creative conscience. It wasn't always about what a writer showed. Often it was what he didn't show that terrified the reader.

And in this case Dennis could only imagine what would follow the twenty pages he'd read.

The manuscript was close to four hundred pages long.

He couldn't understand where Cillian was coming from—how he could create something so—so ugly.

I've written some harrowing stuff, but nothing ever remotely like this.

An image crossed his mind. Bloody feet, bare and slender, running over a gravel road.

It made him sick, the image, what was happening, what would happen.

It's vile and something's seriously wrong with this young man.

The rape that opened the story was not just graphic. It was disturbing in its frankness and depravity.

Dennis got up to turn off the lights, but froze when he heard something.

This is crazy, Den. You're just spooked.

He turned off the final light and headed upstairs to his bedroom. The wind shook against the house. The steps creaked in their familiar way. The small hallway light illuminated his way as he went. And all Dennis could think about was a bloody hand grabbing his ankle and yanking him back into the darkness.

He stared at the steps. Just steps. Just feet walking up them.

How could someone imagine such horror and spell out such inhumanity?

He shook his head as if the action might erase his thoughts.

But even in his bedroom, even standing in the bathroom washing his face and brushing his teeth, even looking at his dark closet as he took off his jeans and shirt, even climbing into bed wondering what might be hiding at the bottom of his comforter by his feet waiting to take a bite out of them, Dennis could not get rid of the images.

They were vivid and real.

The printed word had power.

Stop this. It's crazy, man.

But the thoughts wouldn't go away.

And he pictured the scene he had read once again.

And he wondered what would happen next.

And he felt sick imagining something like that happening in real life.

Knowing that it could.

Afraid that Cillian Reed might be writing from personal experience.

2006

The trees fly past and the windshield bounces and the sky tumbles and the seat belt tears into his shoulder and his chest as the world swirls and a branch crashes through the glass next to him.

"Get him."

Cillian still feels spinning, still feels turning.

"Do you hear me? Go open the door and get him."

He shakes his head. "Why can't you?"

But then he sees the big guy's slashed face, the glass on his forehead and cheek, a nice chunk of his jaw ripped open, the blood oozing out.

"Okay," Cillian says, not needing to ask.

And he releases his seat belt and falls onto the ceiling of the overturned truck. He cuts his hands on the glass as he crawls out the window.

The last thing he remembers is driving down the remote street in the woods, Bob tossing a lukewarm Budweiser back at him, listening to the two men talk in the front of the car. Bob met the drunk twenty-something guy at the run-down bar in Elgin and told him about a party. A party that doesn't exist. At a place that isn't there.

This isn't the first time they've done this. But it will be the first time that it's all left up to Cillian.

Until now he's only watched and taken notes.

This time his hands will be used for something else.

Cillian stands next to the car that has flipped and slammed against a tree.

He remembers the drunk guy asking questions and not liking the answers Bob gave. The guy abruptly jerked the wheel and forced them off the road.

Up ahead the man staggers down the road.

Cillian starts to run after him.

What are you going to do when you get to him?

But he just keeps running, his hands and arms bloodied. He feels dizzy, maybe from a concussion.

"*Get him.*"

He can hear Bob's words.

"*Get him.*"

The stranger turns around, then stops. His eyes say everything. He stumbles and bolts over the ditch and heads into the woods.

They're still barren since it's mid-March. The man trips over a log and gets back up, locking eyes with Cillian.

This time I'm the monster. This time he's running from me.

And for a few minutes they run through the labyrinth of trees and limbs and bushes until the man looks back and nicks his right foot on a root and falls face-first into the leafy, muddy ground.

Don't stop. Whatever you do, don't stop. You know what waits back there at the car if you do.

Cillian finds himself acting quickly. Bob has taught him well. His knees force the man down. His hands find the man's neck and squeeze. And as the man jerks away, clawing, flailing, he remains on top of him.

He puts the palm of his hand on the man's forehead, driving him in the soft ground, his other hand deep into the guy's taut neck.

Then his palm goes over the man's mouth, and he shoves the air out of the man until his tossing and turning and flapping body finally stops convulsing.

But he doesn't let go. And as Cillian keeps one hand clenched over the man's neck and the other jammed over the man's mouth, he can feel his own tears dripping down his cheeks and his hands and body shaking.

But that doesn't mean there isn't a smile on his face.

Because it's the most glorious moment of his life.

Echoes

1.

Dennis walked along the river on a small path that led to a forest preserve. It was late in the day, and it was nice to be able to walk uninterrupted while most people were stuck in their cars in traffic trying to get home. There were many things he enjoyed about being a full-time writer, and this was one of them.

A strange knocking sound got louder as the path fed into a parking lot. There was one car in the lot, a beast of a blue Chevy. It sounded like someone was inside, banging to get out.

Dennis looked around as he discerned a muffled cry.

Someone was screaming from the car, but screaming with their mouth closed.

He dashed to the car and peered into the front seat. As he did, he heard the pounding from the back. Somebody banged against the trunk, their yells stifled.

Dennis examined the trunk but couldn't find a way to open it.

"I hear you—I'm going to get you out," he called, tapping on the trunk.

Whoever was inside wailed away as if they didn't believe him.

"Okay, hold on," he yelled.

He tried to open all doors, but they were all locked. The screaming and bashing continued. Dennis sprinted over to the woods nearby and found a rock. He used it against the driver's window, bashing the glass and finally opening the door.

The keys were still in the ignition.

But the driver is nowhere to be found. Right?

He grabbed the keys and opened the trunk, assuring whoever was inside that everything was going to be fine.

But when he opened the trunk and saw what was shrieking and kicking and fighting inside, he knew things weren't going to be fine.

The young woman—what was left of her—would never be fine, no matter how long she lived.

Bleeding eyes bore into him, the tape around her mouth almost chewed off. Similar tape was wrapped around her wrists and ankles.

She screamed and jerked and as he tried to pull off the tape. She fought and convulsed violently.

She was terrified of him.

Whoever had done this to her—and he could imagine what had happened—wanted her to be found.

But she was already dead.

As Dennis reached to pull her out of the trunk, he woke up. Not with a jerk, but rather opening his eyes and seeing the darkness around him.

He wasn't in a forest preserve.

It was his bedroom.

He reached over but didn't find anybody.

He breathed in deeply and looked toward the ceiling. His hand brushed the sweat off his face.

He didn't need to wonder why he had dreamed that.

It was from the second chapter in Cillian's novel *Brain Damage*.

2.

Grief was sometimes like listening to an approaching war in the distance. The tanks and the armies and the destruction had not yet arrived at Dennis's doorstep, but he had heard the rumblings for eleven months now. And every now and then they sounded closer.

As he drove toward downtown Geneva, the October day bright and still, Dennis reflected on these rumblings. Perhaps he had been able to squelch the winds of war simply by running away from them. The eleven months had been so busy, with Audrey's final year of high school and then sending her off to college. He hadn't had enough time to really, truly write. And he certainly had not been able to grieve effectively, however that was supposed to be done.

Dennis knew he'd been so focused on helping Audrey grieve that he hadn't allowed himself any time to do so.

Perhaps writer's block is part of my grieving process.

Sometimes he wondered if it would hit him like a tsunami you could see approaching on the horizon. He remembered the stories of the tsunami that hit Thailand back in 2004, and how people initially thought it was just a nice, fun wave coming at them. But once it hit they realized it was deadly and they were in dire trouble.

Dennis felt Lucy's absence every day, yet it didn't prevent him from moving on without her. He stuffed the emotion aside, confined it in a box, and left that box to drift with the rushing tide while he went the other way.

But the wound was still there. And sometimes like this morning when he awoke from a terrifying nightmare only to find another one—a lonely house and himself aimlessly attempting to work on a story day after day after unproductive day—he found himself missing her. Just her sweet spirit and her smile, there to cheer him up, there to make him feel alive.

In some ways he felt as dead as Lucy.

3.

That afternoon, walking through the crowds at Geneva Commons, deliberately surrounding himself with life and activity, a terrifying thought struck him.

How will I know if I'm going insane?

He used to have Lucy and Audrey as sounding boards and voices of reason. Now it was just him.

And he was cracking up, losing it. Having nightmarish visions from the books he had written. Terrifying dreams from the book he was reading.

What if I've already lost it and don't know it?

The fear didn't leave, no matter how many strangers surrounded him, no matter how busy life was around him.

4.

He opened his eyes. For a second he could see nothing but black. But then, little by little, he was able to discern shadows and shapes, outlines and overtones in the suburban night.

Dennis sat up, and instead of finding himself in bed, he was on the freshly cut lawn staring up at the midnight sky. The grass beneath him was wet and cold. He could hear cars in the distance, the steady rush of the river, a train passing on the nearby tracks.

I'm not dreaming. Not this time.

He patted his face to make sure. The last thing he could remember was reading that unholy tale Cillian had left by his door. The one he kept reading even though he swore he wouldn't continue. He must have drifted off in the armchair.

And then what? How'd I get out here?

He stood, his back aching, his mind foggy. The dampness on his backside was real. The chill in the air was real. And the light in the third-floor room of his house was real.

I didn't turn that on.

Long hair draped over pale skin and bruised arms came to mind. So did Cillian's glaring face.

I'm losing it.

He closed his eyes hard and opened them again as if that might help, but saw once more that the light was on. It was the second room on the third floor used for storage. He and Lucy had always intended to turn it into a memory room or a room for Lucy's crafts. Now it just contained echoes of the past.

Echoes.

Dennis hadn't been in that room since Lucy passed away. The door was always shut, the blinds closed. But those blinds were now open.

And a figure stood at the window, looking down.

Dennis almost choked on his breath as he backed away before forgetting everything and sprinting back toward the house.

Whoever was in there was going to get hurt. Whoever was in his house messing with his mind was going to be messed with.

Dennis was tired of this. Tired of being afraid.

He hated feeling helpless.

He bolted onto the deck and tried the back door but found it locked.

He turned and ran around the side of the house to the front door, but it was locked as well.

I didn't lock myself out of my own house.

There was a spare key under the deck. He used it on the back door, his hands shaking, then searching out the light switch since it was pitch-black inside.

Just as he turned on the light, a black creature sprang at him from the kitchen island.

It was a creature of the night, a creature from hell, with bright red dead eyes. . . .

But as the fur brushed him and he noticed the missing claws, he realized it was just Buffy. The cat Audrey had gotten after Lucy passed away, the cat he couldn't say no to, the cat that came and went as it pleased.

He was lucky he didn't snap the cat's furry neck.

"All right, Buffy. You need to learn not to jump on people." He put the cat down and thought about getting the gun.

You keep thinking about it, don't you? When are you just going to go get the thing?

But he refused. If Cillian was upstairs trying to scare him, he'd deal with it his own way. A gun would complicate things. And could make things messy.

As he started to go upstairs, a noise stopped him.

It was laughter.

And it made his already chilled body break out in bumps.

It was the laughter of an old woman. Hoarse, ragged, haunting—the laughter smothered him.

I didn't just hear that.

But it came again, a scratching cackle that sounded ancient.

Someone's just trying to spook me out. That's all. That's all it is.

He went up the steps slowly, barely breathing, his body quivering from the cold, his eyes wide.

The laughter came again.

The step underneath him creaked.

So did the house.

This house doesn't creak like that.

On the second floor he began ascending the twisting narrow stairs to the third level. His bad knees, thanks to years of baseball and softball, prevented him from making the climb very often. But now someone was playing with him. Someone was trying to scare the guy who made a living scaring others.

Someone was playing with his fears even though Dennis had few of them.

I'm not scared.

So he tried to tell himself. But the creaks and the laughter and the wind outside continued. And the light upstairs glowed, the sliver of illumination visible beneath the closed door.

As he reached the top of the stairs, everything suddenly went dark. He held onto the railing, afraid he would go tumbling if someone suddenly jumped out at him.

Or if someone decided to push me.

He waited, straining to hear anything. But there was sudden silence. No wind outside, no groaning in the floor or the walls, no children laughing.

He stepped up to the door.

He opened it slowly, carefully.

I know where you are.

His finger found the switch and flipped it on.

And nothing.

There was nothing.

Nobody was in this room. There wasn't anywhere to hide either. No closet up here. No bed to hide under. Just boxes and a couple of bookshelves and an overhead light.

Even the blinds were closed.

Dennis scanned the room, listening, waiting, watching, but nothing happened. He opened the blinds and looked outside, but could barely make out anything in the darkness.

The darkness he had just awoken in.

I'm losing my mind.

As he started to head back downstairs, déjà vu struck him.

He remembered his haunted house story.

And the scene that happened almost just like this one. With the man awaking outside, going into the house to the empty room on the third floor only to find nothing.

That was the start of the haunting, the start of the story, the start of everything.

But I made that story up. I wrote that almost a decade ago.

Climbing down the stairs, Dennis knew he needed to see someone, talk to somebody. To make sure he wasn't going insane, like the character he had written about so many years ago.

2006

Cillian had never felt so cheated. So infuriated.

You might as well have come to my house and stolen twenty-five bucks from me and slapped me in the face and peed on my carpet while you're at it.

He didn't bother to toss the book across the room. No. He was going to do something else with it. But he needed to decide what first.

His man had lost it. Officially lost it.

Book seven—actually, book nine but the first two didn't count—jumped the shark. It was a sellout. It was autopilot land. It was clichéd. It was beyond horrific—it was *boring*.

It was about as scary as a Girl Scout. Scratch that—even those could be scary. This was dull city.

Maybe he would cut the book into pieces and mail it back to Dennis Shore. No, that would be far too obvious.

He needed to do something different.

He needed to make an impression on a man who had obviously stopped trying to make impressions.

Cillian had a few ideas. And they made his mind and his mood feel much better.

The Gift

1.

He was parking his SUV on Third Street when he saw her.

The curly brown hair, the slender frame, the bouncy walk.

It was only from behind, but Dennis knew it was Lucy walking down the sidewalk.

She was right there, across the street. In person. There to touch.

He wanted to run after her, but instead he stayed in the car, backing up the Volvo and driving down the street, racing to see her face, already knowing the truth but hopeful anyway.

When he finally passed the woman, he instantly saw that she very much *wasn't* Lucy. She was younger, and her features were completely different.

Dennis shook his head as he looped back around onto Third Street. Once out of the car, the sun shining on his face, he felt ridiculous.

He had deliberately gotten out of the house. Every moment he spent there he feared someone ringing the doorbell to tell him the truth was out. He had stolen something, and the world finally knew. He was everything those pages strewn across his lawn had said: a liar, a fraud, a hack.

And the only thing left for him to write would be his obituary.

Away from the house he could worry less. A deli on Third served an amazing egg salad sandwich that Lucy turned him on to years ago. Today he enjoyed the sandwich even though he was still shaken from thinking he'd seen her earlier.

His mind was getting away from him.

He just didn't know who to talk to or where to go.

Everything else going on in his life paled in comparison to the feeling of being alone.

2.

The phone rang as he drove to the bookstore.

"How was the sandwich, Dennis?"

He was being watched. Somewhere Cillian was spying on him.

"Don't you have a life?"

"As much as you do."

"Where are you?"

"Answer me something, Dennis. Where do you get your inspiration?"

It wasn't just a simple question. It was a taunt, a jab.

"Where do you get yours?"

A low, seething laugh answered him.

"What's so funny?"

"You answer me first, Dennis. Where do you get your inspiration?"

"Lots of places."

"Lots of places? Like the loving arms of a beautiful wife? Or the angelic eyes of an adorable daughter? Places like that?"

"Don't go there," Dennis threatened.

"I know what inspired *Breathe*. But what about your next few books? The ones that were still written with passion?"

Dennis shook his head. "They all have passion."

"Really, Dennis? Do you really believe that? Come on. Hard work does not necessarily mean the book has a soul. Words on the page does not necessarily mean they have a heart."

"Your story is as soulless as they come."

"Maybe. But you're still reading it, aren't you? Did you have some sweet little dreams last night?"

"I swear on my life—"

"Why did you write *Echoes*?"

The question surprised Dennis.

It surprised him because he knew exactly why he wrote that book.

How can this guy know? How can he keep pushing the right buttons?

"What are you trying to do?"

"Something you can't. To bring something you can no longer bring."

"You're insane."

"And you're sane? Really, Dennis? Isn't it awful trying to create something out of nothing?"

Dennis didn't answer.

"You have to live life in order to write about it. You can't just turn everything off and expect to be able to create."

He remained silent.

"You lost it several books ago, didn't you? But you didn't tell anybody and you still have the name, and those poor schleps still buy your books, but you lost it some time ago, didn't you?"

"Leave me alone."

"You brought this on yourself, Dennis Shore. *You* brought this on your house and your family. *You* invited me into your life without asking if I even wanted to be there anymore. *You* had a chance, but that chance died and so will everything else in your precious, deliberate life. I am never going to leave you alone."

3.

It was 1995 and since the owners wanted the house sold quickly, they were willing to sell it far below the listed price. It needed some work, sure, but Dennis was willing to put in the time. To buy something like this in the upscale town of Glen Ellyn for this price was amazing. But this was back when the housing market was booming. Dennis was still working at the advertising firm in Chicago, taking the train back and forth to the city. This house was a short walk from the train station.

Everything was ideal. The only thing the owners neglected to tell them was that the house was haunted.

He hadn't thought about it for some time. Lucy once told him if there was a contest for being able to box up and misplace memories, Dennis would win it. And even to this day, after everything that went on in that place, Dennis wouldn't admit the house was haunted.

Why did you write Echoes?

Cillian's question still resonated in his head that evening even after running into an old colleague at the coffee shop in Geneva. He hadn't seen Kevin Ward since Lucy passed away. Everyone simply called him Ward. They used to work at the ad firm together, and while Dennis ended up leaving to try to make it as a writer, Ward started his own design firm and was still going strong.

Seeing Ward reminded Dennis of the house and all the strange occurrences that happened in it.

He didn't write *Echoes* to document that period. Just to try to make sense of it. But that didn't happen, even after the book became a national bestseller, avoiding the sophomore slump some predicted after the blockbuster success of *Breathe*.

Not once during all the interviews did he ever tell anybody that *Echoes* was about the house he lived in. But even though Lucy didn't read all of it, she skimmed enough of the novel to know it was about the two of them.

"So you did believe me," she once told him.

"I never said I didn't believe you."

"You said there's no such thing as spirits and things that go bump in the night."

"Lots of things go bump in the night," he said. "But those things can be explained."

"You can't explain what happened."

"I tried."

"So what's the verdict?"

"You're really not going to read it?"

"I have enough memories from living twelve months in that house to last a lifetime, thank you very much. I don't need anything else to give me nightmares."

"There is no verdict."

"But you admit that those things happened?"

"Yeah, I saw what you saw."

"The handwriting on the walls. Audrey's room rearranged. All the stuff that went missing."

"All of those could be explained."

"By whom?"

"Someone could have done all that."

"See—you still don't believe what happened."

"It's the other stuff," Dennis said.

"What?"

"The—the smells. The sounds. The other things you said you saw."

"The things I saw? And you didn't?"

"I don't—I don't know."

"Or you just chose to forget because you couldn't make sense of them, because you couldn't control them."

"Lucy—"

"When will you ever learn that life is not about control? That you never have any?"

"I have control in the pages of my books."

"But that's not *real*, Den. What we experienced and lived through—that's real."

"Sometimes I don't know," he told her. "Sometimes real life makes less sense than fantasy and science fiction."

He waited for her to say truth is stranger than fiction, but she didn't.

"I just wrote it as a way to try to understand."

"And do you understand?"

Dennis shook his head. "No. The guy in *Echoes* ends up in a mental institution. I guess I should be thankful I'm not in one."

"We were in one for a year. Thank God we're out."

4.

He pulled into the driveway and got out of his car, scanning the house to see if any lights were on.

He's getting to me. That psychotic kid is finally getting to me.

It took him a long time to go to sleep that night.

5.

The next morning the music was so loud in his office that he almost missed the phone call.

"Is there a rock concert going on in the house?"

"Yep. I've turned the house into a club. You need to come around sometime."

"Hey, Dad."

"This is an early call for you. It's only eight o'clock your time."

"I have a class at nine," Audrey said. "And some of us do have to get up on time."

"Are you saying I don't?"

"You could sleep until eleven and still get your work done."

He chuckled. "What's up?"

"I wanted your advice."

"No."

"No? I haven't even asked you anything."

"If it has anything to do with a guy, the answer is no."

Audrey laughed. "You act like I'm going to get engaged to the first idiot I see."

"No. But maybe the second. Or the third."

"Don't worry. It's about my Literature class. The professor in there."

And for the next twenty minutes, Audrey detailed her experiences with a know-it-all female professor. After telling Dennis all about her first few classes and about the attitude and tension between her and the teacher, Audrey asked him what she should do.

"She's jealous," he told her. "I bet that's it."

"Jealous? What do you mean?"

"Because you're smart and you actually questioned a few of her theories and some of the ways she does things. I bet she feels a little threatened."

"What? No. It's not like I'm being disrespectful."

As Dennis offered ideas and suggestions on handling the teacher—one of them to dial it down and be more laid-back, responses he knew would be difficult for Audrey—he found himself thinking this was a conversation she should be having with her mother. This was the sort of thing mothers were for—when their daughters were having issues with other women. Guys could be competitive pricks, but women could be far more cruel and conniving. Lucy would have been good at navigating these waters with Audrey.

"What is it?" Audrey asked him.

"I was just thinking—about your mother."

"Yeah. I've thought a lot about her lately."

What was there to say now? Something trite like, *At least she's looking down at us from heaven*? He wasn't going to feed his daughter any of that bull. He didn't say anything since there wasn't anything to say. She missed her mom, he missed his wife, life sometimes sucked, the end.

Now there's a story for the publishers. Package that sucker up and send it off.

"How's the writing coming along?"

She just *had* to ask.

It was a normal question that everybody asked. And he'd never once said it was going badly or that it wasn't going at all. Perhaps all his joking during the years about having writer's block was coming back to bite him in the butt.

"Can I get your advice?"

"Yeah, sure." It was the most animated Audrey had sounded yet.

"It seems like your father has a bad case of writer's block."

"That's funny."

"I'm serious."

"What?" She sounded genuinely surprised.

"Yeah. Can you believe it?"

"Has that ever happened?"

"Nope."

"Do you know why it's happening now?"

"No."

"I don't know how to help. You know me—I have trouble writing anything."

"You're a great writer when you apply yourself."

"But I'd rather be outside, be in the ocean, hang out with friends."

"Like most people," Dennis said.

"Is it the story you're writing?"

"Maybe, though I don't have any other stories waiting to be told."

"How far are you on the book?"

"Not far at all."

Audrey laughed. "Get somebody to help you write it."

That's not funny. Not in the least.

He sat for a moment, looking out the window, wondering what she would say if she knew. Wondering what she would say *when* she found out.

"Dad?"

"Yeah."

"What is it? What'd I say?"

"Nothing."

"Do you remember when I'd get stuck on a term paper or on my homework? Do you remember what you and Mom would do?"

"We used to do a lot."

"Take some of your own advice. You've got the house to yourself. Turn up the music. Get outside."

"You heard how loud the music was."

"So go outside. Get out. Live life."

He thought of running into Ward, of the dinner invitation he still had to reply to, of how isolated he felt being all alone in the house.

Audrey continued. "Do some of those exercises. 'This is what writers do, Audrey.' Come on. You're Dennis Shore!"

He laughed. *Sometimes that's a name that's hard to live up to.*

Audrey said she had to go. She thanked him for his advice and told him she loved him. The words never got old, however many times he heard Audrey say them.

6.

Ever since the Home Depot "episode" Dennis avoided running errands. But he was coming back from the grocery store when an unknown caller ID lit up his phone.

"Yeah," he said into the phone.

"I just read your list. And I have to say, it's quite surprising."

"What now?"

"Let me read it to you. 'The Scariest Movies I've Ever Seen' by Dennis Shore. *GQ*, huh? When did you write this?"

"A while ago."

"It's quite an interesting list."

Dennis thought back to the list he had created six months ago. He couldn't even remember every movie he'd included.

"Of course, it's nothing too surprising. *The Thing. Alien.*

Silence of the Lambs. Nothing too original. Did you simply Google the top ten scary movies and average out everybody's lists?"

"Sorry I didn't add anything twisted enough to make your top ten."

"Oh, but you did. I like this list. In fact, in many ways this could be the list of stories from which Dennis Shore stole in order to build his writing career. Let's see. *The Sixth Sense* would be your first novel. *The Shining* would be *Echoes*. *Alien* is very much like *Marooned*. Need I continue?"

"And you think you're original? Your story is just a twisted version of *Silence of the Lambs*."

"Oh, I was hoping you'd say your number one scary movie. *Se7en*."

"You couldn't even get close to writing something that brilliant."

"Look who's talking."

"What do you want?"

"I just thought I'd share that I left another small present at your door, celebrating the fact that you had *something* published. Something that was yours, unless, of course, you stole this top ten list from someone else."

Dennis cursed into the phone.

"Now now now. That's not very nice."

But as Dennis was about to say more, Cillian hung up.

He discovered the gift Cillian had left for him in a cardboard box on his doorstep. And after Dennis opened it, dropping it in surprise and horror, the first thing he did was call Deputy Cummings.

He was going to do something about his young, demented, and seriously stupid harasser.

Enough was enough. This time he had gone way too far.

She looked pretty. And untouched.

A photo out of an Abercrombie catalog, a face out of an MTV show. Long, curly, highlighted brown hair, long legs, a long-lasting smile, and a long life ahead for her.

Cillan had seen her yesterday and today, making sure she didn't see him, making sure he knew who she was with.

And finally, on this stifling and bloated summer day, with the crowd in Grant Park swarming the stages during this ridiculous way to suck people's money, he had found her alone.

And that's when he went up to her.

"You look hot," he told her.

"Excuse me?"

"Warm. Sweaty. Thirsty."

"I'm fine."

"I have an extra." Cillian offered the beer to her.

"No thanks."

"Really, it's okay."

The girl wiped her forehead and looked around. She laughed and took the beer. "I could be arrested for this, you know," she said, taking a sip.

"You'd have to do a lot more than that to get arrested. En-joying the show?"

She stared at him for a minute, suspicious and amused. "Sure."

"What was your favorite performance?"

"What was yours?"

"It's somewhat boring to me, these festivals. There are lots of other ways to have fun."

"Look, buddy, I'm with a group of friends, okay? So just— don't get any ideas."

He smiled. She was feisty.

He liked that.

"How old are you?" Cillian asked her.

"How old do you think I am?"

"Old enough."

She sipped the beer and looked around. "My friends are coming back any minute now."

"Good."

"Yes, that's good." But her face showed that it wasn't really, that she wasn't sure when her friends were coming back, that she wasn't sure whether she should be sipping this beer and talking to this stranger.

"You from around here?" he asked, knowing the answer.

"Sure. You?"

"You're not very specific, are you?"

"You don't take hints, do you?"

I don't need hints, not where I'm going, not where I can take you.

"Oh, there they are. They're coming."

"Good."

A voice hollered over the crowd, calling her name.

"Audrey! We got you a T-shirt."

Cillian smiled and raised his eyebrows. "A T-shirt. You'll remember Lollapalooza for the rest of your life."

Audrey Shore just looked at him with eyes that mocked, that patronized.

I can wipe that silly little snotty look off your face.

"Enjoy the shows, Audrey," he said as he walked away, losing himself in the crowd. But Cillian never lost track of the teenager surrounded by friends.

She wouldn't always have them around.

Marooned

1.

"I can't do anything about it."

"What do you mean you can't?"

"There's no address on the box, no letter or note or anything inside."

Dennis cursed and slapped the picture on the dining room table. "That's not enough?"

The deputy had arrived half an hour ago, and Dennis had told him everything—everything except the fact that he had stolen a novel from Cillian. But he had shared Cillian's arrival at the book signing in New York and his threatening comments, calls, and e-mails. The dead goose, the desecrated books with blood on their pages (which Ryan already knew about).

You forgot to share with Ryan that you're starting to see things. That you're starting to lose it.

Whatever had happened before, this was now a step too far.

"And you said he called you right before you got this?" Ryan asked.

"Yeah. Almost as if he was right outside my front door when he called."

Ryan picked up the picture. "Do you know when this was taken?"

"It's got to be recent. At least since she went away to Biola. Her hair is long now, just like there."

"So how'd he get this, then?"

The freckle-faced deputy wrinkled his nose as he examined the photo.

"I don't know. It just showed up at my doorstep in a box. A photo of Audrey."

"And there was nothing else inside?"

"I already told you that."

"And did you ask your daughter if she sent it?"

"Do I really need to?"

"Maybe she did. You never know."

"She didn't send it. I know who sent it. And I don't care if he's just playing head games with me, this is over. This stops right now."

"Yeah, okay. Just—calm down a minute. Let me think."

"Can't you run some background checks, just look into him?"

"Yeah, I can do that. But Dennis, I need to see some proof."

"I want to scare this kid away."

"What's his name again?"

"Cillian Reed. I've looked online, but nothing's come up. Not even a MySpace page."

The deputy wore regular clothes since he was off for the day. Dennis had immediately called him after he'd spoken with Audrey, who was on her way to class. He had just wanted to hear her voice to see if she was okay. A part of him doubted Cillian would actually do anything to hurt anybody, but the photo crossed the line. Plus there was the matter of Cillian's vivid imagination. Dennis just wanted to be safe and sure.

Ryan wrote the name down on a business card he found in his pocket.

"I can see if he has a record, do a background check. But, Dennis—"

"Don't even say it."

"What do you think I'm going to say?"

"You're going to say I've got a lot of eccentric fans."

"Well, I wasn't going to use the word *eccentric*. I'd say more like bizarre. Twisted."

"It's one thing for him to threaten me, but this—this is too much."

"Yeah. I understand. Look—there's a situation that's been going on—our department is searching for a missing girl. Her name is Josie Davis. She disappeared from NIU about a week ago, but her family is from this area."

"What do they think?"

"They're not optimistic. But nobody's saying that of course. Not yet. It's too soon. But that's got everybody's attention. A twisted fan—you've had these before, you know."

"And that's why I don't want—why I don't need you to say anything, okay? Just check up on it when you can. I'll owe you."

"No problem."

"Yeah," Dennis answered. "Hopefully."

2.

Only ten minutes after Ryan left, the phone rang. The caller ID read, "Unavailable." Dennis let it go, waiting for a message. But none came. Instead the phone rang again. This time Dennis picked it up.

"Yeah?" he growled.

"You shouldn't have done that." The voice was flat, lifeless, without emotion.

"Where are you?" Dennis shouted.

"That was foolish."

"No, putting the box on my doorstep was foolish. This isn't a game."

"I never said it was."

"Are you watching my house?" Dennis asked, taking the cordless phone and looking out the windows to his front lawn.

"Are you scared, Dennis?"

"This is over. No more e-mails and no more calls and no more threats, you got that?"

"Then you'll force my hand, Dennis."

"Go ahead—tell the whole world, I don't care. I really don't. Nobody will believe you. And nobody will care."

"They will care. Just like you do."

"Go ahead and try me. I just want you to leave me the hell alone."

"What does hell have to do with it?" Cillian's voice was hushed, unemotional.

"You stay away from me and my daughter."

"Answer my question, *Dennis*. What does hell have to do with it?"

"Stay away from me."

"You don't believe in hell, do you? Which is such irony, especially for you who makes a living writing about the darker side of life."

"You don't frighten me."

"*I'm* not trying to frighten you, Dennis. There are other things to be frightened of. I'm the least of your worries. Of your daughter's worries."

Dennis gritted his teeth. "You listen to me—stay away from her, do you hear? I swear to God—"

"Ah, there you go again. What does God have to do with it? You say these things, but you really don't mean them, just like your popcorn prose, just like your clichéd stories."

Dennis opened the door and stepped outside. "Where are you? Huh?"

"Have you already forgotten our discussion of your top ten scary movies, Dennis? Did you not see the movie *Se7en*?"

"What are you babbling about?"

"Remember what Brad Pitt finds at the end of the movie? In the little box? Do you, Dennis?"

And then Dennis connected the list with the box. And he recalled why *Se7en* disturbed him so much the first time he saw it. Gwyneth Paltrow reminded him in many ways of Audrey, of what Audrey might become when she grew up. And the end of that movie shocked him and made him want to guard his wife and daughter with his life.

Dennis cursed into the phone.

"That's right, go ahead—say your profanities, Dennis."

Dennis clicked off the phone and cursed as he found Ryan's cell phone. He called quickly.

"Yeah?"

"He just called me."

"Who did?" Ryan asked.

"Cillian. He's watching me. He knew you came over."

There was a pause.

"He threatened Audrey."

"Are you sure?"

Dennis cursed again. "Yes, I'm sure!"

"Okay, okay, okay. Just—just hold on. If he's here, then he's far away from your daughter, right?"

"This has to stop."

"And it will. There are a lot of laws about harassment. Just give me a minute. Call Audrey and make sure she's safe. Tell her to be careful. We're going to want to get this guy on tape. Or get an e-mail from him. Anything. Just—look, I'm almost at the station. I'll call you back in a few minutes. Just take it easy and don't do anything, okay?"

Dennis pounded the phone back in its cradle, then found himself staring at the box that had arrived that morning. He picked it up and flung it across the room.

He felt watched.

And paralyzed.

3.

The phone jolted him awake. It was late afternoon, but he had been dozing at his desk after drinking a couple beers to loosen up. All they had done was make him more tired. He rubbed his eyes and looked at the phone on his desk, alive and wailing, screaming to be answered.

It's him again.

He had already spoken to Audrey twice today. He had told her to be careful—not alluding to anything, not saying anything like, *Hey, by the way, there's an aspiring writer who's been watching and stalking and harassing me who left a photo in a box and referred to the climax of Se7en so hey, have a great day.*

Audrey had to persuade him not to get on a plane and come out to see her.

If he didn't think his stalker might follow him, Dennis would be on a plane now.

The phone continued to ring. He finally picked it up, clicking it on without saying anything.

"Hello?" The voice allowed him to breathe. It was Maureen. "Dennis? Is that you?"

"Yes. Hi, Maureen. Sorry, I'm just up here in my office."

"Figured I'd check in with you. Can you talk?"

"Sure."

"I was going to write you an e-mail but thought I'd just give you a call and let you know my thoughts about the chapters you sent."

"About what?" Dennis asked, having no idea what she was talking about.

"The first few chapters—the ones you e-mailed me a couple days ago. For *One of These Days*?"

He paused. Didn't breathe. Just listened, wondering what she was talking about.

"I didn't realize you had changed the title."

He sat up.

"Changed the title?"

"Yes. *Brain Damage*, huh? Interesting title. It works."

"It does?"

"Sure. And I have to say—it was quite . . . well, it was quite dark."

"Dark?" he repeated, not knowing what else to say, too numb to speak.

"It seems very different from anything you've written."

"Really?" He knew what she was talking about. But . . .

Did I send her those chapters? Did I somehow do it when I was dreaming? When I was in a fog?

"Different, but in a good way. It's extremely disturbing."

"Disturbing—in a good way?"

"More disturbing than anything you've done before," Maureen said. "But—it's also quite remarkable. It has a visceral edge to it. And it even has more of a literary feel."

He forced a halfhearted chuckle. "Yeah."

"Dennis, are you okay?"

"Sure," he said.

You just received several chapters of another book I didn't write, in an e-mail I didn't send.

"You don't sound very excited. This is good, Dennis. You're making tremendous progress. I'm sure this sort of story isn't particularly easy to write, especially the violence—"

He didn't hear anything else she said.

Dennis could make out words on the other line, could hear himself answering them, but nothing connected.

Nothing except that somehow Cillian had gotten to her.

But then he heard her final thoughts.

"Dennis—I don't think you understand me. This might be the most important book you've ever written. It's disturbing, but it's also—well, frankly, I think it's profound."

He swallowed, fighting the feeling that he was falling off a skyscraper. Because he was. Free-falling.

And sooner or later he'd land.

4.

Dennis couldn't remember the last time he'd been this drunk. But several pitchers of beer with wooden-leg Hank could do that to the best of them.

He'd met his friend in a small bar tucked away off Batavia's main street, a middle point between both of their houses. Hank liked cheap beer and jukeboxes. He had chosen the sound track for the night: a selection of Pink Floyd's greatest hits.

Dennis didn't have the heart to tell his good-natured friend he would rather not hear any Floyd. He wasn't in the mood. It reminded him of his writing, and Dennis wanted to think of anything except his writing.

Hank had spent a lot of the night talking about his job at the Firestone auto shop close to his house. He hated the manager but could do his job in his sleep. Dennis liked the fact that Hank rarely asked about his writing. Hank got it—his friend was a bestselling author, blah, blah, blah. That actually didn't earn Dennis any respect in Hank's blue-collar world. Dennis was just glad they'd made movies out of some of his books so Hank knew what he'd written about.

After enough beer, Hank started talking about his ex, Julie. It would take a lot to get past that conversation.

"She called me the other night."

"What for?"

Hank cursed. "To tell me she loved me."

"Are you serious?"

"As a heart attack."

"She just called out of the blue?"

"Nah, I'd tried calling her. A few thousand times. So she called me the other night and I was wasted and she got crying and all this, and then she ended up telling me she missed me but this was the way things had to be, you know? And I told her something about how it doesn't have to be that way, that things are only absolutely done when you die, like for Lucy and you, that's the only time when final is final, you know, man?"

Dennis nodded. Hank was jabbering a little too much.

"And she said she loved me but it had to be this way and I had to stop calling her and then—yeah, just a whole big pile of nothing."

"Maybe it would be good to stop calling her."

"Yeah. And it would be good to stop breathing too, you know? It ain't gonna happen. I wish I could eject my heart, but that's not going to happen either."

It was time to change the subject. Dennis stood up to go to the restroom.

The combination of the loud music from the small, suffering speakers surrounding him and the dim light in the bar and the dank smell in what used to be a smoking establishment before they banned smoking everywhere all made Dennis dizzy. For a second he wobbled on his legs. Hank laughed at him.

"Look at you. Lightweight."

"Shut up," Dennis said. He passed the jukebox playing a familiar song and felt a headache coming on.

Is it possible to feel hungover before the morning comes?

He didn't know. He felt hungover by a lot of things in his life, first and foremost by the young writer who kept taunting him.

Next time I see that guy I'm going to scare him away. He's going to know that I'm not playing games and no one, and I mean no one, threatens my daughter.

Before getting to the dingy bathroom, Dennis checked his cell phone. And sure enough there was a text message waiting for him.

You remember *Marooned*, don't you?

It was his third horror novel and the first to take a critical beating. He had tried doing a sci-fi horror thing, a homage to the movies *Alien* and *The Thing*.

He tried to text back but couldn't. There was no phone number to reply to.

I'm losing my mind.

He shoved the phone back in his pocket and vowed to drink enough beer tonight to forget Cillian's name and face and anything else about the creepy kid.

Hopefully the nightmares would stay away too.

5.

"They're coming."

Dennis had briefly shut his eyes. He knew it was time to go when he was dozing off at the table with half a pitcher of beer staring back at him.

Dennis couldn't understand the words coming out of Hank's mouth. The Pink Floyd celebration had stopped, and now random songs blared out of the jukebox.

The song playing now sure didn't seem random, however.

It was The Cure's "A Forest." He loved the early Cure, the strange, simple songs from an English band breaking out of the punk movement and helping start what would later be known as goth.

The music seemed louder.

Hank mumbled something.

"What?"

Hank's face was grim, haunted. The red-haired guy was almost physically unable to look menacing, yet there he was, a shadow over him, his eyes heavy and his lips tight.

"They're coming," Hank said.

"What are you talking about?"

"Don't lie to me."

"What'd you say?"

"I said don't you lie to me."

"You're drunk."

"You know they're coming. Don't lie to me."

"Hank, what're you talking about?"

Hank reached over and grabbed Dennis's forearm. Hank was a big guy, one you wouldn't want to get into a fight with. Somebody who worked on car engines all day had a little more strength in his hands than somebody who spent all day at a keyboard.

Dennis winced and jerked his arm away. He cursed. "What's your problem?"

"Tell me," Hank said.

"Tell you what?"

"Are you one of them?"

Dennis stood up. "Hank, man, come on. I think it's time to go."

"You can't go."

"Yeah, I can go, and you're going to go too."

"You can't go," the deadpan voice repeated.

Dennis had seen Hank do a lot of things while he was drunk—he'd seen the guy throw up, topple down a flight of stairs, get in a fight with four guys—everything except this.

He'd never seen this dark side of Hank.

Dennis walked over to grab Hank's arm, but instead his friend took the half-full pitcher of beer and slammed it against Dennis's face. Dennis went sprawling across the wooden floor of the bar. Thankfully the pitcher was plastic, but it still carried a wallop.

For a second he lay on his back, out of breath. He could see the figure standing over him, and for a brief moment he looked into Hank's eyes—but they weren't Hank's eyes.

They belonged to someone else.

It's him. It's Cillian.

But that was just for a second as the pain in his jaw and cheek throbbed.

"Hank, what the—"

"You guys get on out of here," the bartender said, obviously annoyed.

Hank grabbed a bar stool and chucked it toward the bar. It

hit the edge and snapped in pieces. The bartender didn't hesitate. He took the palm of his hand and slapped it over Hank's head.

"Get outta here now or I call the cops, Hank."

Hank was still muttering something as Dennis stood up.

"You're both part of them! You're with them! I can see through you!" Hank bolted out the door.

Dennis felt even more dizzy than before.

"What a head case," the bartender said.

Dennis gave him an extra twenty. "Sorry about that."

"Yeah, sure. You might want to see where he took off to."

Outside on the street, the misty drizzle felt refreshing. Dennis walked down the block and saw a figure next to the truck.

He's so drunk he can't even get into his own car.

Dennis called out, but as he jogged toward his friend, he could see the terror on Hank's face.

"No no no no no no!" Hank shouted over and over again.

The big guy was in tears. As Dennis reached the opposite side of the truck, he could see Hank sobbing, blabbering, trying desperately to get inside.

"Don't hurt me! Please, don't hurt me! Don't take me away! Don't!"

"Hank—man! What? What's wrong?"

Dennis lurched around the vehicle, and Hank suddenly fell to the street, his hands covering his head and his face, his voice like a small child's, his wailing continuing.

"Don't hurt me! Don't touch me! Not again! Not anymore!"

Dennis went to offer a hand to Hank, but the shrieking only grew louder. He backed up.

"Please just leave me be! Please go away! Go away! Take your evil somewhere else!"

Dennis had no idea what he was seeing, what he was experiencing. Hank looked terrified, like a ten-year-old boy screaming at a talking skeleton.

Dennis could feel himself shaking, the light rain falling on his forehead and his cheeks.

"Just go!" Hank shouted as if his very life depended on it. "Please go. Go and leave me be!"

So Dennis left him.

And as he walked back to his vehicle, he couldn't stop shaking.

When will they learn? When will they ever get it in their heads that it's not about the work, it's not about the pages or the word count—it's about feeling the words, about living them. And you can't know until you've lived them and tasted them.

Rain dripped off the window ledges, the fading sun hidden behind afternoon clouds, the soggy night descending.

Cillian knew that's when the demons would come, when the visions would resume, when he would be able to write.

For some time now he would start to get a headache about midday. He worked odd hours serving tables, which didn't help the headaches. Sometimes the sun would make his mind hurt, as though he were a vampire. He dreaded the days because they lasted so long.

But night would come, just like the approaching evening right now, and that's when things would change.

Nobody would believe him, but he didn't have to make anybody believe. People were fools, and fools were only interested in themselves. They didn't take the time to notice. But he noticed. He watched. He smelled and listened and touched. He waited. He enjoyed.

And the darkness would cover him like a blanket, smothering him, burning him.

Sometimes he would find himself hunched over at the small desk typing away, his fingers cut and bleeding.

Sometimes he would wake up naked with a notebook in hand and scribbles and drawings and a pen that thankfully wasn't stuck in his side like one time years ago.

Sometimes he would try to combat the darkness with alcohol, but that didn't help. Bob had given him some drugs to try, but they didn't help.

Life was full of spirits, full of voices, full of brokenness, and he opened the window at night and swallowed it in and let it cover and corrode until he woke up somewhere not remembering the last six or eight hours of his life.

The rain fell. Sometimes he would go outside and sit in the street and wait for oncoming cars to approach and nearly hit him and swerve and honk their horns. That was amusing.

They don't understand, and they can't see what the words are really for, what they really mean, what the story really is.

Somebody turned down the light, like a dimmer slowly turning off.

He thought of the hypocrite author who had lost it, the poser who still pawned off used goods and useless stories.

You don't even believe in God, and that's sad because I know better. I know I believe in God, so what does that make you?

He turned to the chair in his small bedroom and saw the eyes looking back at him, the animal perched, the sickly wet fur and the fangs, this creature that watched, that smelled, that wouldn't go away.

Bob can't see him, but that's okay because Bob's got his own set, his own ways, his own thinking.

Sometimes he would read what he had written the night before—thousands of words, dozens of pages—and he would be scared. They weren't his words. They belonged to someone else.

But he liked this because something was working.

This is true inspiration. This is how you really do it, Dennis

Shore, and one day, one day, if I'm lucky, I'm going to show you how.

He found a sweatshirt and crumpled it and put it against his mouth and nose and inhaled.

It still smelled like her.

And soon he would be with her again.

Tasting Blood

1.

"Can I come in?"

Dennis looked at the half-opened door to his office, the light from the morning sun streaking across his carpet. "Of course."

Lucy was already dressed for the day, having worked out at a health club not far from the house before having breakfast and then getting ready. She wore jeans and button-down shirt. His wife looked ten years younger than her age.

"It's always so cold in your office."

"That's because there are lots of windows. But the higher the sun gets, the more my office and my fingers warm up."

"Productive morning?" she asked.

"Yeah. I think so."

"Which one is this again?"

"I'm calling it *Empty Spaces*. It's about a serial killer."

Lucy raised her eyebrows and gave a humored look. She didn't ask the question she always used to ask him when his career in writing macabre tales began: *When are you going to write a love story?* He eventually got testy with the question one day and told her he'd do it when someone gave him a million dollars to write it, something that wasn't going to happen any-

time soon, not while his name was Dennis Shore, not while his
books scared the snot out of readers looking to be scared.

She sat on the blanket draped across the leather armchair
that was supposed to be for reading and mostly served as a
bed for their cat, Buffy. For a moment she stared around the
office.

"What's up?" Dennis asked her.

"Nothing. Just came in here to be with you."

He looked at her, the light brown hair still long, her eyes
so deep and earnest, her mind going a hundred miles an hour.
She was always thinking and acting and living and doing.

"Bored?"

"No," she said with a smile.

Something was up and both of them knew it.

"Okay, wait a minute. Did I miss something? Someone's
birthday or anniversary?"

She laughed. It was like a drug, that laugh. So confident, so
joyous, so right.

"I want to tell you something," Lucy said.

Dennis leaned back in his chair and watched her, waiting.

"Let me guess—something about the cancer."

"Uh, no," she said. "I doubt I'd look this happy if it was."

"Then what is it?"

"It's about Audrey."

"Something good?"

She nodded, still smiling, the morning sun's glow accenting
her strong jawline and those ocean-deep eyes. Dennis couldn't
help smiling back. He waited.

And waited.

And waited.

And suddenly, he found her gone.

The chair was still there, as was the blanket, but Lucy wasn't
sitting in it.

He found himself in his office, his iMac still asleep, the
light from the windows leaking in. Dennis moved and his back

snapped in pain. It took him a moment to realize how he'd gotten here, to realize the time, to realize he'd been sleeping in his chair for hours.

The room was quiet. Too quiet.

He hadn't wanted to wake up. He wanted to stay sleeping, to live out that morning and that day and that life. He wanted to see her again and to hear her voice and see her smile and feel her life.

Dennis glared at the chair and could almost smell her.

It was real and it happened and that's why you dreamed. You can relive moments from the past.

But the dreams always, always turned into nightmares.

He still remembered what Lucy had told him.

He still remembered his promise to her.

But you never told Audrey, did you? You couldn't, and you rationalized that it was because she was buried and gone. But you promised, Dennis, and you never fulfilled it.

It was a slap across his face by a cold, rigid hand.

The glow and warmth of the morning in his dreams was long gone.

Just like Lucy.

2.

"Hank."

"Hey, man."

"You sound awful."

"I feel worse than I sound."

Dennis had tried twice that morning to get a hold of Hank. If he hadn't answered on this third attempt, Dennis was going to head over to his house. He wasn't sure if Hank had made it into his truck last night, much less make it back home. Part of him wouldn't have been surprised if they had found his body in the Fox River somewhere.

"What day is it?" Hank asked.

"Thursday."

"Good thing I don't work Thursdays."

"What happened to you last night?"

"Huh?"

It sounded like Hank was struggling to get out of his bed, or wherever it was he had fallen asleep.

"Last night at the bar. What happened? You sorta flipped out on me."

"Really? I don't remember. Last thing I recall is sitting at the table with you, downing beers."

"Did you have much before I got there?"

"No, not that I can remember," Hank said.

"I've seen you gone, but never like that."

"Like what?"

"You just—you batted me on the side of my head with a beer pitcher, then threw a bar stool at Jimmy. I've got a nice bruise across my cheek to prove it."

"Oh man. I'd better go by there today."

"And that wasn't the worst. You just—I don't know, Hank. You were pretty messed up."

"What'd I do?"

Dennis didn't want to tell him that he'd turned into a blubbering mess. Hank couldn't fully appreciate it even if Dennis described it to him in full detail. The sight of his friend weeping uncontrollably and crawling away from him in terror—it was probably one of the most unsettling scenes Dennis could remember seeing.

"That bad, huh?" Hank asked after Dennis's silence.

"Hank, you just—you really sorta buckled under the pressure."

Hank just laughed. He was back to good ole Hank. "Yeah, well, you were the one who wanted to go out."

"Is everything okay?"

"What do you mean? With what?"

"With you."

Again Hank laughed. It was a laid-back, gruff but tender

laugh, the kind even the grumpiest of individuals would have to smile back at. And Dennis, as always, obliged.

"I'm up to my neck in debt, and my ex keeps in touch enough to continue breakin' my heart, and you and I both know I drink way too much. But other than that, yeah, everything's okay."

"I'd lay low for a while, you know. Just—take it easy."

"*You* take it easy."

"How about we both take it easy?" Dennis replied.

"Okay then. We still watching college ball this Saturday?"

"Of course."

Dennis got off the phone and could still hear echoes of Hank's desperate cries. He couldn't understand why Hank had just snapped, why he was suddenly paranoid and deranged, and why he had been scared of Dennis.

Then he recalled the text from Cillian.

"You remember *Marooned*, don't you?"

Suddenly it washed over him.

The story and the characters and the images and the scenes.

And it made sense.

And for the first time, he realized what he was dealing with.

3.

He huddled in the walk-in closet next to his bedroom.

He couldn't stop shaking.

Even though it was bright and sunny outside, he remained in the shadows of the partially closed closet, the racks of clothes hovering above him.

"No," he said out loud, quiet but still audible. "No."

Thoughts buzzed in his head like a swarm of bees, and no matter how he might run and how he might swat his arms to get rid of them, they were still there and not going anywhere.

It wasn't just that he was losing his mind.

He could deal with that.

But this . . . this made no sense, none whatsoever.

How could he know?

But another voice inside him told him the truth, the truth he didn't want to face.

He didn't dare articulate it.

Dennis didn't even want to think about it.

How could Cillian know?

First it was the girl on the bridge, a pivotal scene from *Breathe.*

Next came the nightmarish romp through Home Depot, a pivotal scene from *Scarecrow.*

Then the terrifying voices filling his house just like they had in his novel *Echoes.*

And now this.

The scene where the buddy in the story confronts the protagonist. Written in *Marooned* and somehow bizarrely played out last night between Hank and Dennis.

But these occurrences didn't scare him as much as the text message.

And the fact that Cillian somehow knew.

But there's no way he could know unless I'm making him up, unless I'm making the text up.

But Dennis saw the message again this morning. It was still there in his phone.

And it made everything in his world tremble.

"No," Dennis said, still rejecting it, still not believing, still not able to go there.

But he was already there.

He was in the middle of it.

And quickly sinking.

4.

This time Dennis e-mailed Cillian.

The e-mail was short and sweet.

I want to meet with you, face-to-face. Today.

He wanted answers. For his own sake and sanity.
He could accept what they were. But he needed to know.
He waited for a response but none came.

5.

Every time he called her now, Dennis expected to hear the worst. He'd never been an overly worried father, but now worry coated everything he said and did.

The line rang, and he knew she wasn't going to pick up. He'd been calling her too often, driving her crazy with worry, making sure she was okay, making her friends think her dad was a quack. Thankfully that didn't stop Audrey from answering her cell phone.

"Helloooooo?" she asked in a high-pitched voice.

"How's Southern California?" he asked, trying to feign nonchalance.

"A lot better than Geneva, Illinois."

"Maybe I need to find out."

"Dad—"

"I know, I'm calling again. But really, I had a crazy thought."

"You make a living having crazy thoughts."

"This one involves you."

"This can't be good."

"I was thinking about coming to visit you."

"Weren't you just here?"

"What if I came back out?"

"Dad."

"What?"

There was silence.

"Audrey?"

"Are you being serious?"

"Of course I am."

There was a sigh, then another pause.

Dennis knew what that meant.

"We talked about this," she finally said.

"Yeah, I know."

"And what'd you say?"

"I promised."

"So what are you doing?"

Dennis knew where she was going, what she was referring to, but this was different. When he promised to give her space and promised he would be okay being on his own for the first time, he hadn't known that some twisted, sick freak would be harassing him and making threats against her. How could he tell her that? She simply thought he was caving in, that he was missing her and missing having family around.

And the truth was, he was missing her and Lucy.

Or maybe the truth is I've flown over the cuckoo's nest and gotten my wings clipped.

"I'm coming home at the end of the month."

"I could come out there."

"It's been one year. We agreed, didn't we?"

"Maybe I could just—"

"Dad."

"Yeah?" He thought for a moment, then said, "Okay, fine, fine. I'll stop. But listen—just be careful."

"Dad?"

"Yes?"

"I'm fine. You be careful. Watch the Disney channel. Listen to some country music. Go to a tanning salon."

He smiled. Leave it to Audrey to give him a good laugh.

He loved her and reminded her again that he did.

But love couldn't prevent something horrible from happening.

Dennis knew this bitter truth and knew it well.

6.

"How precious."

The voice lodged itself deep inside him, rattling, shaking, tearing. Was it just his imagination or was Cillian's voice changing the more time passed, distorting itself into a voice with many layers and textures?

"What's precious?"

"Being a father."

A rage continued boiling inside him. "Are you—are you listening to my conversations?"

The laugh unsettled him. "However could I do that, Dennis?"

The phone call had come only minutes after he spoke with Audrey. How could Cillian know he was talking with her unless he was spying or listening in?

"You never answered my e-mail," Dennis said.

"I'm answering now."

"And?"

"Where would you like to meet?"

Dennis stared through the blinds of the kitchen at the back of his yard. He wouldn't have been surprised to see the guy talking from back there, waving at him as he spoke into a cell.

He named a pub in downtown Geneva. "Nine o'clock."

"I was rather hoping you were going to invite me over for dinner."

"This isn't funny anymore."

"Do you hear me laughing?" Cillian asked.

"I hear that smart-aleck tone in your voice, so yeah, I hear you laughing."

"There's a time and a place to laugh, Dennis."

"Yeah, sure. I'll give you something to laugh at."

"That sounds like a threat."

"It sounds however you want it to sound. Meet me at O'Malley's at nine."

"Can't wait."

"Me neither."

7.

Dennis watched him arrive ten minutes after nine. He had been sitting in the darkness of his car waiting since eight thirty, just in case Cillian was early. But the guy swaggered into the pub late. Dennis remained resting behind the steering wheel, parked facing the sidewalk and the building front. It was another twenty minutes before Cillian stepped out of the pub.

He could see the lean figure standing outside, as if waiting. Then he lit up a cigarette, smoking casually as if he had no cares in the world.

Dennis wished he could see Cillian's face. He wished he could see the expression behind the taunts and threats and games.

The figure began to walk away from Dennis, down the sidewalk.

Dennis quickly climbed out of the car and began striding toward him.

In the shadows he walked.

Down the street he walked.

Turning the corner he walked.

All the while following Cillian, who ambled without a destination.

Where'd he park?

In the lawn lining Third Street in front of a sleeping store, Cillian stood. He faced Dennis as if he knew he was coming. That didn't stop Dennis. The trees gave them enough darkness. The street didn't have much traffic.

He walked toward Cillian.

"You get an F for spying," the voice called out to him.

Dennis approached him and didn't bother looking around to see if someone else was standing there in the shadows. He didn't worry about another car passing by and seeing them. He didn't wonder if an elderly woman was walking her aged poodle.

He didn't think of anything except the box with Audrey's photo inside.

And he thought of this as he launched his fist against Cillian's creepy, leering face. His knuckles connected with the guy's temple, slamming him backward, sending him spiraling to the ground.

For a second Dennis stood his ground, watching the figure sprawled on the grass. Cillian reached for his forehead.

"Heck of a punch for a writer."

"Get up," Dennis said.

Cillian laughed as he stood to his feet. "So you didn't want a beer, huh?"

Dennis punched the guy in whatever tiny gut he had. Cillian keeled over, out of breath. Without thinking, rage and hate filling him, Dennis grabbed the guy's oily hair.

"You ever threaten my child again and I'll kill you. You hear that? I'll kill you, you sick little freak." And his hand, now aching, slammed against Cillian's nose. He heard something crack.

Cillian fell to his knees, coughing. For a moment he leaned back, making a sound.

What is that?

Dennis didn't recognize the noise. But then, as Cillian sat back up, his hands covering a nose that gushed blood, Dennis knew exactly what the noise was.

It was laughter.

"How does it feel, Dennis?"

"Get up."

"Get up for what, Dennis? For another punch?"

"Get up now."

Cillian wiped a hand across his face, smearing blood. Even in the muted light Dennis could see it clearly. Pearly white teeth grinned, the whites of his eyes sticking out like glowing orbs in the night.

This time Dennis slapped him across the face. It seemed far more insulting than a punch. "Get up."

"Hit me again, writer."

"Stand up."

"You hit like a girl."

Dennis grabbed the collar of Cillian's T-shirt and jerked it, ripping half of it away.

"Such aggression. How does it feel?"

"Shut your face."

"How does it feel to taste blood, huh? Feels good, huh? You probably haven't felt this alive since the day of your wife's death, have you?"

Another fist landed against Cillian's face, sending him crumpling in the wet grass. But this just made the laughter intensify.

"Go ahead, hit me again, Dennis. Go ahead, pummel me. Make me pay. Make me hurt."

Dennis felt dizzy as tears filled his eyes. His hand throbbed, and his gut raced. He backed away.

You gotta stop this. Gotta stop, Den.

Cillian looked at his bloody hand, then wiped his bleeding nose. "How does it feel?"

"You stay away from me and my family. I mean it," Dennis said, pointing a finger at the eyes that never strayed away.

"Or what?"

"I mean it," Dennis said, backing away now.

"Or what? Or *what*? What are you going to do? What could you possibly do to me?"

The way Cillian said it frightened Dennis. This wasn't some young fan toying with him.

This was some sick mess of a young man challenging him.

"You can't do anything anymore, Dennis. You're weak. Look at you. Look at your face. You're scared to death, aren't you? You're scared of what you've done, but more than that you're scared because of what you *can't* or won't do, right? I got it right, didn't I? I know you, Dennis. I'm a fan and I've been a fan for a long time and I can see through your words. You expose your flaws through your writing, even as lame as your writing has become. I know. I see. I understand."

Dennis turned and ran down the sidewalk, away from Cillian, from his words, from his smile. Back in his car, Dennis noticed the bloody gashes on his knuckles. He leaned his head on the steering wheel and closed his eyes.

He just wanted this nightmare to be over.

2008

Everything was set and ready. But he couldn't go through with it.

Rhonda lay on the couch, waiting for him. He had slipped away from her, masking his shivers and shakes as he walked into the kitchen, ready to grab the knife. It would be easy, and it would all be over in just a few minutes.

But in the kitchen his hesitations seized him.

He couldn't even hold the knife straight. It was a butcher knife, a large one that Bob had given him.

For several harrowing moments he stood in the kitchen, listening to the music in the background, then hearing her voice.

"You comin' back? I'm getting cold."

And he told her just a minute.

This was his moment. His big moment. It had all been planned out perfectly. He'd spotted her and talked to her and lured her and convinced her. And now all he had to do was one more little thing.

But he couldn't.

Instead he ran to the bathroom and found himself throwing up.

He wasn't sure how long he was in there. He must have blacked out.

When he came back to consciousness, he stood up.

As he stepped into the hallway, he noticed markings on the carpet. The bedroom door was open. He looked back toward the living room and saw a shadow approaching.

And then Bob filled his sight.

He was going to ask what he was doing, but he knew. Cillian knew that Bob had been waiting for him in the bedroom, waiting with plastic sheets protecting the bed and the floor, waiting with gloves, waiting with tools.

What happened to me?

But as Bob approached him, he could tell that Bob had done what he couldn't do.

The plastic gloves were dark and wet, his face splattered, his neck torn with something resembling a bite. Bob stared at him like a disappointed father, not saying a word. He didn't have to say anything.

"Where is she?" Cillian asked.

Bob didn't answer. He had that distant look he always carried—a look that seemed void of something vital to the human spirit. Cillian was afraid for a moment, not sure what the big guy was going to do.

"There's a little of her remaining in the family room. You can clean up the rest."

Bob went back into the bedroom and shut the door.

The Truth

The Saturday sunset was rich with oranges and reds, the sky burning like a pumpkin aglow on a fall night. Dennis drove toward Ward's house. He'd be seeing Kendra for the first time since the funeral.

He stopped by a winery to purchase a couple of bottles for the evening. As he drove down Third Street, he saw the spot where he had beaten Cillian. No police tape surrounded the area, no visible markings in the ground could be seen. Yet Dennis still felt like he was being watched, like he was in trouble, like someone was going to grab him any minute now.

Ward had e-mailed him several times about coming over and hanging out. They'd finally set a date for this Saturday evening, almost a week before Halloween. Ward said the kids would be out this evening, so it would just be the three of them.

The three of them.

As soft rock played in the background, the window cracked to let a little air in, the light of the day fading in the west, Dennis thought of that phrase. *The three of them.* Threesomes weren't any good. Someone was always left out. You needed a pair. Two or four or more, but never three.

I wish she was by my side, dressed up, holding my hand, holding one of the bottles of wine, carrying a smile on that beautiful face.

It struck Dennis as he drove past familiar places that maybe he ought to move. Every corner and building and shadow reminded him of her. The smells and the sounds and sights all acted as a compass pointing due north toward the memory of Lucy. He had assumed he was strong enough to live in those memories, to breathe and thrive and move through them. But maybe not.

She should've remained behind, not me.

He could see The Little Traveler, where she used to go with her mother and Audrey. There was Grahams, where they'd get ice cream or chocolate pecan scalies or chocolate covered pretzels. There were a hundred other places that held a hundred other memories—simple, ordinary memories that now seemed legendary and mythic because Lucy was part of them.

God, I miss her.

Sometimes the ache seemed physical, like some gaping hole in his stomach. It felt like a literal missing part, like someone had scooped away his vital organs and left all the fat and flab behind.

He found himself approaching the church and wondered if he even wanted to read the sign.

But of course, he did.

And of course, it had to say something that nicked him, that cut just a little.

Ripples don't come back. Actions have consequences, good and bad.

And then, out of the blue, he thought of Cillian's laughter as he punched him in the face.

He thought of the beating and wondered what ripples it had created.

2.

He could hear them in the kitchen, and it made him smile.

It was good to be surrounded by signs of life: the sounds of dishes being rinsed and put in the dishwasher, a married couple laughing about old times, the timer going off and the dog barking; the smells of wine and lasagna and some fantastic berry dish cooking in the oven; the large open family room with the plush couches and the country French design, the pictures of family adorning the walls, the glow of candlelight mixed with canned lighting.

It was good to be in the Wards' house again after all this time.

Ward came in with one of Dennis's bottles of red.

"Here—finish this up."

"I'm good."

"Then be better," Ward said, a grin on his face.

His friend looked relaxed, his eyes a bit squinty after several glasses of wine himself. Ward wasn't much of a drinker, and when he did partake, Dennis could always tell.

"You doing okay?"

"Yeah. I might just fall asleep on this couch though."

"We have a guest bedroom."

"That's in case we start doing tequila shots later."

"Kendra might bring that out," Ward said with a laugh. "One never knows."

"Something smells delicious."

"When company comes over, she brings out the big guns. Otherwise it's mac and cheese and Ho Hos."

"I'll gladly help you out anytime."

"Hey—we have something for you. Kendra found it earlier. Hold on."

Ward disappeared for a minute, asking his wife where "it" was. Dennis savored a sip of his wine, feeling relaxed and warm and comfortable. The stereo played a selection of soft songs. A song by Sting that Dennis didn't recognize. It fit the mood of the evening. Relaxed, classy, calm.

His eyes felt heavy. That's how relaxed he was. He could doze off right here on this couch. The shuffling of feet made him stretch and stop drifting.

"Look at this," Ward told him, handing him a photo.

It was a shot of the two of them back at Databank, where they met. The advertising company had been bought in the late nineties after they were long gone. Very few people they knew still worked there.

"Look at us. So young."

"Look at me," Ward said. "So much hair."

Dennis laughed. "When was this taken?"

"I don't know. We had just gotten to know each other."

"That seems like another lifetime ago."

"Several lifetimes ago."

Dennis looked at the men in the picture, two guys in their thirties (though Dennis liked to razz Ward about being older) with the whole future ahead of them.

"We look like trouble," Dennis commented.

"We were lucky to get out of there. Some of the guys got canned when the merger took over."

"Isn't it nice not to have to worry about mergers?"

"What do you mean?" Ward asked, trying to hide a smile but unable to. "I'm being bought out."

"Really? McDonald's finally called, huh?"

"Taco Bell."

Ward's wife was cute and petite and a perfect hostess. During dessert, a delicious multiberry pie-like concoction that Dennis enjoyed so much he asked for seconds, Ward and Kendra talked about their daughter's recent engagement. She had graduated from college that May and was now working in downtown Chicago.

"Those days seem like a long time ago, don't they?" Ward asked shaking his head.

"Yeah."

Perhaps it was the way Dennis said it, but Ward and Kendra both looked sad and speechless. Dennis realized he had put a little too much emotion in his response.

"Sorry," he said.

"No, I'm sorry for bringing it up."

"For bringing up your daughter's engagement? Come on—that's great."

"No—I mean—just the reminiscing."

Dennis smiled. "You know, Lucy's name is not forbidden. It's not like I'm going to turn into some sobbing mess if we talk about her."

Both of them nodded with sympathetic, sad eyes.

It was okay. He was used to this. He wasn't sure how people were supposed to react.

"I still remember the day I proposed to her. That was—let's see, how many years ago? Man. It was a long time ago."

"You were married when I met you."

"Twenty-five. That's how old I was when I asked Lucy to marry me. That was twenty-six years ago. Can you believe it?"

"No," Kendra said in a tone that said *I can't believe she's gone. None of us can believe she's gone.*

"Where'd you propose to her?" Ward asked.

"You guys ever been to the Fabyan Forest Preserve? Just south of our house off Route 31?"

"The one with the windmill?"

"Yeah—that's across the river. They've redone a lot of the preserve in the last few years. I proposed to her on a summer day alongside the river. Lucy loved the water and for some reason loved the Fox River. I told her—I promised her—one day we'd live in a place right by it."

"You got your wish."

Dennis nodded at Kendra. "Yeah. Yeah, we did."

"Do you go back much?"

Dennis shook his head. "No. Actually I haven't been back in some time."

He knew how long it had been. The last time he went there was with Lucy. He didn't want to go back now. Nothing existed there except ghosts of the past waiting to haunt him.

A buzz disturbed Dennis's thoughts. He reached into his pocket and took out his cell phone, blaring a tune his daughter had programmed. "I can't get this thing to play anything else," Dennis said. "Sorry. I should've turned that off." He looked at the number and saw it was Ryan. He decided to let it go to voice mail, but during the next hour all he could think about was the message waiting for him.

3.

On the drive home, feeling upbeat after a refreshing evening with friends, Dennis listened to the voice mail from Ryan.

"Hey, Dennis. This is Ryan. I did some investigating on that guy who's been harassing you. I think you've got someone giving you the wrong info. This guy that you told me to look up—name of Cillian Reed. About nine months ago a man by the name of Daniel Cillian Reed was found dead in a garbage dump. Actually, *he* wasn't found but parts of him were, I guess. It was pretty grisly. They had a funeral and everything. I've got the file on him and can show it to you.

"I guess the guy had started going by Cillian, but everyone—including his family—knew him as Daniel. That's probably why you weren't able to find anything on him. But it made the news—I remember them talking about it not long ago.

"So whoever's telling you this—someone's screwing with your head, Dennis. But then again, sounds like something one of your fans might think is funny, you know? Taking the name of a dead man and posing as him for a laugh.

"I left a package at your door—everything I could make

copies of from what I found. Give me a call once you've looked it over. And let me know if this guy keeps bothering you. Like I said, I bet it's just some crazed fan trying to make a point."

4.

He can feel his heart beating as he opens the package simply marked *Dennis*.

His hands shake.

The light overhead seems too cold and too dim in this cold, dim house.

He slides open the folder.

And then he reads the note.

Hey Dennis.

Someone's really messing with your mind. Here are several pictures. The first is a shot of an arrest photo for Daniel Cillian Reed taken in 2003. Another is for disorderly conduct taken in 2005. There are a few copies of some newspaper articles in the <u>Tribune</u> and the <u>Daily Herald</u> detailing Daniel's death. Pretty grisly stuff. But as I said, this can't be your guy unless he's a ghost. ☺

Call me.

Ryan

Dennis starts to look at the photo, but he already knows.

He already believes what's happening.

He knew it the moment it clicked, when he thought about the text Cillian sent about *Marooned*, about how Cillian seemed to be lurking in his thoughts.

Grinning with that delirious smile is Cillian in a mug shot, then Cillian in another mug shot looking drunk and obnoxious. And then the papers showing photos of Daniel Cillian Reed from high school.

It's the same guy who showed up at his book signing, the same guy who's been stalking and harassing and threatening him, the same guy he beat to a pulp.

The same guy who was murdered a year ago.

He waited in the veiled covering of the atrium tucked under the ghostlike trees in the forest preserve. Wind blew around him and through him and he shivered, zipping up his coat. He wasn't sure why Bob had wanted to meet here, but since the debacle the other night, he would do whatever Bob wanted him to do.

And Bob wanted to meet him here at midnight.

The moon reflected off the slow moving river. He had walked here, leaving his car parked a couple miles away. The forest preserve closed at dusk, but that didn't mean it wasn't easy to get into. He had simply walked through the woods and down past the oriental garden to reach this metal-encased dwelling.

The sound of shuffling feet gave Bob away. He wasn't trying to slip up on Cillian. Maybe tonight Bob would show him something new, something else that horrified and shocked and fascinated. With the big guy, Cillian was constantly surprised.

"You made it," he said.

"Yeah," the reply came, along with a sigh.

"So what's going on?"

For a moment Bob just lingered in the gloom of the enclosed building. Cillian could barely make out the big guy's face, but he could see the outline of his shoulder and towering head.

Bob looked out toward the river. "Why do you always talk about fear?"

"What?" The question seemed out of the ordinary—and out of the blue—for the big guy. "What do you mean fear?"

"You're always talking about finding ways to scare yourself. What do you mean by that?"

Cillian's laugh felt hollow and forced. "Not a lot frightens me."

"No?"

"Very little."

Cillian squinted, trying to make out Bob's face, to see if he had anything in his hand, to see what this was about.

"What's the scariest thing you've ever seen?" the big guy asked.

"You mean the scariest movie?"

"No, I mean in real life. Ever."

Cillian slowly shifted toward the edge of the atrium, a three foot concrete wall behind him. If he wanted to—if he needed to—he could get out of here.

You frighten me like no one else has because there is no fear on your face and no sensation in your soul. There is just black like this night, like this place, darker than anything I could ever paint or imagine. Blackness.

Cillian lit up a cigarette, a habit he had picked up since being around Bob. "I have to think about that question."

"What happened with the girl?"

"I just—I froze. It won't happen again."

"It's one thing to hurt someone, but can you understand what it's like?"

Cillian inhaled his cigarette and kept his eyes focused on Bob. "What what's like?"

"To kill. You've hurt. The man you chased in the woods. You hurt him and maimed him, but you didn't finish him off."

"I know. I tried. I couldn't."

"Does death scare you?"

"Killing does."

Bob's face was expressionless, emotionless.

"It just—I don't know. I thought—"

"It's permanent," Bob said. "And that's what scares you, isn't it? There's no going back. And it's not a movie or a book. It's a real life and it's suddenly gone and there's nothing else to do except dispose of the parts."

"Yeah."

This was a bad idea coming here, being with him. This was a bad idea.

Cillian had a crazy thought. Even as Bob continued to talk.

"You said you wanted to see something scary, didn't you?"

"I've seen some pretty freaky stuff, man," Cillian said.

He thought of the switchblade in his pocket. He thought of using that.

He thought of finally killing, this time not out of curiosity but out of self defense.

"Do you know that when people die, there's no magical thing they say, no special way they die. The one thing is always this."

Do it, do it now, man. Do it.

Cillian started to put a hand in his pocket. "What's that?"

And then something ripped in his side. And he looked down to see Bob's hand plunged against his gut.

"It's surprise," Bob said, pressing the blade so far into his gut that Cillian wondered if it was sticking out his back.

He couldn't say anything, couldn't breathe.

"Surprise at how stupid they are. Surprise at knowing they only have seconds to live."

Cillian coughed and choked and spit up blood. The blade started to slowly cut up his chest. He could smell Bob's breath and feel his warm skin.

"Hey—Bob—what—"

He couldn't talk, was too surprised, too horrified.

Stupid. You're stupid to have ever gotten involved with this guy. He's the real deal, and you're just an amateur. You're just a poser and now . . .

"It doesn't hurt as much as it shocks, does it?"

"Bob, man, what are you doing?"

"I'm doing something you couldn't do and would never be able to do. I'm showing you. This . . . is . . . how . . . you . . . do . . . it."

At each word, the blade worked itself up and around Cillian's open cavity of a chest.

But Cillian still watched and listened and comprehended.

And Bob started to twitch and laugh and grin.

All while he kept thrusting the knife in, deep, deep, deeper.

"What's the scariest thing you've ever seen?" he asked Cillian again, all while Cillian tried to pull the knife out and push Bob away, even as he knew he was about to die, that he only had a few seconds left.

His voice came out shaky, distorted, gargled. "You . . ."

Bob didn't respond to his answer. He just looked at him with a blank stare.

I can see his face. Even in the darkness I can see it. What's happening? What is this? No, this can't. No, dear God. No, please. No, it can't, I can't, it cannot be.

Just as Cillian started to scream, the big guy put a hand over his mouth.

"There is no fear left. Not anymore."

The hand clamped over his mouth and another hand worked the blade around. Cillian finally saw blackness cover him and realized the horror was not over and everything he had imagined and believed in and hoped for was just the start of the horror that awaited him.

Pain and Suffering

1.

The house's heartbeat awakens him. Steady, pulsing, tapping against his eardrums, against his mind. Dennis sits up in a large bed with pillows and blankets intertwined over him. He turns on the lamp and wipes a forehead full of sweat. Either he has a raging fever or something he ate at Ward's didn't agree with him or he finally realizes what's going on and it's terrifying him.

But he stands and opens a window and forbids it to be the latter.

He looks at the small bookshelf with special printings of some of his books. There they are: there's his little ghost story that could, *Breathe*, in its original hardcover printing, before the movie and the madness and the second better-looking hardcover came out. There's the last book he actually wrote, *The Thin Ice*, that caused *Publishers Weekly* to write, "Dennis Shore, even while on autopilot, can still scare with the best of them." What did they know? There's *Sorrow*, a serial-killer story that gave him an ulcer.

They're just made up, Dennis, stories in your head, and this is one of them. This is a made-up story. This isn't really happening. You're

*going to wake up and find that Cillian isn't there and everything was
just a big dream.*

He hears cries from outside.

Dennis looks through the window but sees only thick
darkness.

"Dad!"

He recognizes the voice.

"Dad, help me!"

And without thinking or hesitating Dennis sprints down
the stairs and tears through the kitchen to the back deck and
the back lawn, which is wet and cool against his bare feet.

The voice is louder.

"Dad, over here! Daddy!"

She hasn't called him daddy in a long time.

His feet take him down to the edge of the water. And then
he sees her in the smoky, shadowy waters of the Fox River. Her
curls, her long pigtails.

"Daddy, help me!"

Audrey is desperately trying to swim toward him but is
being pulled away.

A flashlight beams over the water, and Dennis sees where
it's coming from. It's a small boat, the figure inside leering at
him with white teeth and dead eyes and long stringy hair.

It's Samantha.

"She's dead just like I am, just like Lucy, just like we all will
be, so join us, Dennis. Join us. Take a step and don't come
back. It's better down here with the dead, with the disbeliev-
ing. Join us, won't you?"

Dennis.

Suddenly the light and the loud chanting voice and the
figure in the water all dissolve.

Dennis, wake up.

And he does and finds himself in his bed in the darkness,
the comforter and blankets on his side messy, the other side
neat.

He sits on the edge of the bed, wiping his forehead.

He opens the window, hearing nothing but the slight spill of rain.

He remembers the voice that urged him awake, and he wants to hear it again.

It was Lucy's voice, and it felt like it came from right next to him.

He would do anything to hear that voice talk to him again. Just once. That's all.

2.

In the morning Dennis felt like someone had grabbed him feet first out of bed and swung him around a dozen or more times before leaving him resting on a cold hard rock.

All morning long he examined the pictures from Ryan. He debated calling the deputy, unsure what he would tell him. He'd lie, of course. Ryan would think he'd lost his mind if he told him the truth.

And what exactly is the truth, Den?

He couldn't shrug this off, couldn't bury this in that stone psyche of his. He couldn't outrun this or outwork this or out-think this.

Something nagged at him, and he found himself sorting through his office, something he usually avoided. He wanted to find something, anything, that might have the name Cillian Reed attached to it.

When they had first moved into this house, Dennis had ar-ranged the office exactly the way he always wanted an office to look. There were framed record covers hanging on the wall, a closet full of his books, a wall of shelves with his CD collec-tion organized in ways only he could fully understand. There were pictures of Lucy and Audrey and reminders of his career achievements scattered throughout the office. Over time, even though they had been stored in his closet and out of mind, the piles of clutter had grown, and since Lucy's death, they had become immovable fixtures in his life. The three boxes of fan letters and e-mails, the stack of marketing information, the folders filled with contracts and royalty reports. Audrey had been on him for some time to hire an assistant, but Dennis kept avoiding it.

Lucy was always my helper. Nobody can ever replace her.

Perhaps it was stupid to refuse clerical help. He needed assistance with the small things, things that usually didn't get done. Answering reader mail, for instance. He had long since neglected it, especially after Lucy passed.

Now he found himself on the floor with the closet doors open, going through the boxes, ruffling through letters and printed pages, trying to find anything with Cillian's name on it.

And after two hours, much of it spent reading author mail for the first time, he spotted an envelope with crisp black writing on it. It was open, the letter inside folded neatly. The return address was from Mr. Cillian Reed.

Mr.

It was just like him to call himself a mister.

Dennis quickly took out the one-page letter and read it. He couldn't remember reading this before.

Dear Mr. Shore:
I've been a big fan of yours since I came across a copy of *Breathe* years ago. I've read all your books and written to you several times. I even sent you a copy of my novel *Reptile* in hopes you'd read at least some of it and give me your honest input. Having not heard from you, and having been let down by your last few novels, I felt I needed to write you one last time to share some of my frustrations. Whether or not you answer this letter—whether or not you even *read* this letter—is something I can't think about.

All I can do is share my thoughts and feelings and let the rest go.

I believe that something happened to you somewhere along the great yellow brick road of writing stories. I can't say which book it started with, but I have an idea. I'm thinking *Marooned* was where it began, and *Fearless* was where it finally blossomed and remained. Your first two novels were exceptional, but since then . . . well . . . the well went dry, the inspiration evaporated, the storytelling went on autopilot.

You let us down, Mr. Shore.

I wish you could know what it's like to be a fan of someone, to have high hopes, to await the next book with anticipation, and to finish that work and be so disappointed. It's not one book. No. It's a career. A wasted career. A wasted talent. A waste of time. *My* time.

Furthermore, it's been disappointing to write and never hear back. Time and time again.

I will continue reading, not because I think your inspiration might come back. No. I need to read things that make me laugh out loud, even if that's not the author's intention.

Keep cashing those checks.

Keep selling out.

Sincerely,

Cillian Reed

The letter felt heavy in his hands. The postmark said November 2005, six months after the publication of *Fearless*. Could he really have overlooked this?

There were other things going on in my life back then.

He tore the letter up.

For a moment Dennis looked around the office. Surrounding him on the carpeted floor were hundreds of handwritten letters and printed pages. A wealth of praises and thank-yous. But somehow he had found the needle in the haystack.

Maybe if he continued looking he would find more.

But he was tired.

He hadn't felt this tired in a long time.

He needed to get out of the house and breathe and sort this out.

Stepping outside to a chilly day, a statement sounded over and over in his head.

"You let us down, Mr. Shore."

But if Cillian had been so utterly disappointed, then why bother Dennis now?

Especially if he was dead?

3.

He drove in silence. A thousand thoughts filled his mind.

This can't be happening. Somehow all of this is my imagination. The dead don't speak. The dead don't bleed.

I spoke with Cillian. I saw him. I still have scabs on my knuckles from beating him.

What if this is someone else posing as Cillian?

I saw the photos—it's him—the same guy who wrote to me, the same guy I angered by ignoring, the same guy I somehow let down, the same guy I stole from, the same guy haunting me.

But you don't believe in ghosts, do you? So now what?

"I'll see you on the dark side of the moon . . ."

The skies were cloudy. As he drove home, the stereo in his car turned on.

His hands were on the steering wheel.

Pink Floyd blared through the speakers, hurting his ears.

The song was "Empty Spaces" from *The Wall*.

Then he heard static, then voices. He heard the last conversation between Cillian and himself, as though it had been recorded in a tunnel, with strange, eerie echoes following their voices. Floyd continued playing in the background, softer, so Dennis could hear Cillian's taunt.

"Look at you. Look at your face. You're scared to death, aren't you? You're scared of what you've done, but more than that you're scared because of what you can't or won't do, right?

"You're scared to death.

"Scared to death.

"Scared.

"Death."

It sounded like there were a dozen Cillians, all talking while Floyd grew louder and louder.

And then the phone rang. And the voices and the music stopped.

Dennis didn't want to answer it. But if he was losing his mind, the phone would be talking to him soon enough. He opened it and didn't say a word. He could hear the laughter on the other end.

"So now you know."

"What do you want?"

"What do I want, Dennis? What do I want? How dare you ask that question?"

"I'm finished with you."

"No you're not," Cillian said.

"Yeah I am. I don't care who or what you are—I'm done with you."

More laughter. "You know *exactly* who and what this is so don't give me that. This is your worst nightmare coming true."

"My worst nightmare already happened. You don't scare me."

"I've barely even tried scaring you, Dennis. Just because your wife died and you convinced yourself you let her go and got through that doesn't mean a damned thing to me because you don't know the meaning of pain and suffering. But—and hear me out, Dennis—*you will*."

"You're just a sad little nerdy boy who lost his comics somewhere."

"You don't know me. You don't get me. You can't even *begin* to understand me. You've read some of my work and obviously think it's good enough to steal, but DO YOU UNDERSTAND WHERE THAT COMES FROM? DO YOU?"

The voice howled on the line, and Dennis didn't answer. He couldn't.

"You don't know fear, and you don't know pain. But that's all gonna change."

"I'm done. I'm done with your calls and your e-mails and your threats."

"You stole something from me, so I'm stealing something right back. And it's far more valuable than some story from a twenty-year-old who thought he knew it all."

"And what would that be?"

"Hope."

Just as Dennis attempted to answer Cillian's threat, a truck slammed into his passenger side door and catapulted his SUV sideways.

The world went black.

Part Three

The Lunatic Is in My Head

There was something in the barn. Something alive, making noise among the dead.

Robert Holzknecht never slept soundly, and on this night he kept hearing things. The squeaking door of the barn opening, the sound of equipment dropping to the ground, a clanging.

Robert, or Bob as he was known by the few who happened to use his name at all, found a meat cleaver to take to the barn. It was late, the night still and cool, the farm deathly silent except for the haphazard sounds from the barn across from the house.

There wasn't a light that he could see.

He strode over the worn dirt path to find the barn door open.

He didn't slow down. He walked in and quickly found a light.

Cold, dim light bled onto the stained floor.

Bob looked around, opening the stalls, checking out the loft. There was nothing.

After fifteen minutes of checking, he turned off the light.

Bob.

The voice sounded like it came from behind him. But he

turned and saw nothing. He flipped on the light again and found nothing.

Bob.

The voice came from the loft. But no one was up there.

It's time, Bob.

He recognized the voice. He knew it well.

It's finally time, Bob.

"Where are you?" he asked, looking around the deserted barn. He'd long grown used to the stench in here, to the sacrilege.

I'm here.

The cleaver rested in his hand. Bob knew he wouldn't need it. Not now.

"What do you want?"

I want many things.

"What do you want from me?" Bob asked, staring at the high ceiling.

I want you to do what you do.

Bob just waited, listening.

He wasn't frightened.

He wasn't surprised.

I want you to finish what we started.

Bob knew the voice too well. The young guy never shut up, and even after shutting him up once and for all, the guy had occasionally come back.

With whispers in the night. Taunts in the darkness. Messages on mirrors. Voices in the silence.

The young guy named Cillian Reed still spoke to him. But never like this, never this deliberate, never this focused.

"What do you want me to do?"

He waited. Bob was patient. He could wait all night if he had to.

Finally Cillian's voice sounded all around him.

I want you to spy on our author friend. This is a very big week for him.

Bob didn't respond.

He remembered the man Cillian was talking about.

I want you to do something I cannot do. Something I'm forbidden to do. Do you understand?

"Kill him?"

Yes. But only him. Not the girl.

Bob nodded.

And then he will understand. He will see. He will see the only hope he has left in the world completely alone, her two parents gone. And he will know the meaning of hopelessness. He will know the meaning of suffering. He will know that hell does exist, and he will join me there.

The light went off and Bob found himself in darkness, the smell of death all around him, the silence soaking in.

He headed back to his house, back to his bed.

Bob knew Cillian would be back soon.

It wasn't the first voice that had come to him.

He was smart enough to do what the voices told him.

Hiding

1.

The phone woke him. Dennis jumped, dizzy, as if he were on the deck of a ship in a violent storm. The ringing rattled inside his head.

He felt worse this morning than when the truck collided with his vehicle and sent an air bag slamming into his face. He'd blacked out, only to awake and find both vehicles damaged. After a mouthful from a driver claiming Dennis had run a stop sign, Dennis boarded an ambulance and was treated for minor cuts and a concussion.

Hank had taken him home last night and was the first to call this morning.

"You okay, man?"

"No," Dennis admitted. "I feel awful."

"I saw your Volvo. You should feel awful."

"Thanks for taking me home last night."

"You were saying a lot of crazy stuff, you know."

"Really? I don't remember."

"Yeah. About ghosts and devils and spirits and such. I'm telling you—you need to get out more."

"I was out when this happened."

"I mean out with other people. With the living. Too much time spent with ghosts."

The throbbing in Dennis's head continued. It hurt to talk to Hank.

"I'm going to take some of those pills I got last night."

"How 'bout I come by and bring you some lunch?"

"You don't need to."

"Who's going to take care of you then, huh?"

"Yeah."

"You got a car to ride around in?"

"Yeah, I'm fine. Though I doubt I'll be driving anytime soon."

He hung up the phone and thought about the car in the garage. It was Lucy's car, one that hadn't been driven since she passed. Dennis had tried to get Audrey to take it, but she said she didn't need one at college. He knew she felt like he did—that it was somehow wrong to take Lucy's car out, to use it flippantly, to act like it was just a car.

The image of Lucy driving the convertible was still cemented in his mind. He'd surprised her with the yellow Porsche Boxster the summer before she passed away. It was ridiculously expensive and flashy, but he said it didn't matter. Nothing mattered in those days except trying to make every single day count.

The only regret was that she left too quickly.

Driving the car felt wrong, but so did getting rid of it. Even when his bills were draining his accounts, the thought of selling the bright, sporty car seemed wrong.

Dennis wondered where the keys were. But he knew. Even in his groggy state, he knew exactly where they were.

2.

—Den?

—Yeah.

—Come here.

—What is it?

—Just come over here for a second. Turn off the TV.

—Is Audrey okay?

—She's fine.

—Okay, what then?

—I didn't say mute it; I said turn it off.

—Okay. There.

—Do you know that I love you?

—Uh-oh. You met some young Italian guy, and you're running off with him.

—If that was the case, I'd already be gone.

—What's up?

—Den . . .

—Hey—what is it? Why are you crying?

—I just—I can't—I don't know how to tell you.

—Lucy, what?

—I didn't tell you because I didn't want you to worry. Because I was thinking—I thought it was no big deal.

—Didn't tell me what? Hey—what is it?

—I got some bad news today.

3.

In the silence of the sunroom, he sat in the chair.

Dennis hadn't been in this room since Lucy passed away.

Almost one whole year.

It was easy to close the door and forget about the colors and the light and the warmth of this room. He sat in the armchair and looked at the sunlight streaking through the trees onto the yard. She used to come in here to get away, to read, to do her puzzles, to arrange their photo albums, to take naps. Dennis had his office, she had the sunroom.

Dennis found the keys exactly where he expected. On the desk. On her desk.

Touching them was like touching her skin again. He found himself thinking of that afternoon when she told him she had seen the doctor, that she had cancer. He couldn't believe it. Nor that she hadn't told him she'd been going for tests. He was angry and hurt, but did anything and everything he could to get her help.

On the written page he could make miracles happen. He could awaken the dead, perform the supernatural, be a god to his characters. But Lucy wasn't a character, and he was no god. All he'd been able to do was watch from the sidelines as she grew more and more ill.

And so many good things in his life, in his family's life, died when she died.

He held the keys and cursed. It wasn't surprising, the anger still inside him, the rawness. He had avoided this room and these keys and the photos and the videos because they just hurt too much. He hated sitting here, hurting, pining away, grieving.

It's been a year and what's changed?

Breathing hurt. Was that because of the car accident last night or because of being in this room?

He had refused to believe that she watched him from above or beyond. But there was a part of him now that wondered, questioned.

Don't.

Words she had spoken to him still resonated. But he fought remembering them, hearing them.

Don't come back. Don't come back and hurt me.

He had listened to her and had said he understood and had said he would consider what she said, but after she was gone those words were like these keys. Put in a drawer and forgotten.

Why now, after all this time?

But Dennis knew why. Audrey was gone.

It was just him and this large coffin of a house.

Just him and his stupid characters in his stupid books.

He had done everything he could possibly do to get Audrey

through the death of her mother. But that meant he'd done very little for himself.

Is this how I'm coping, how I'm paying for not taking care of myself? By losing my mind and making up ghosts?

But another voice told him there was nothing imaginary about what was going on. The only thing imaginary was his denial, his shelving reality.

Just because you hide a car and throw away the keys doesn't mean it doesn't exist.

His eyes caught the waters of the Fox River.

Just because you don't always see it doesn't mean it's not there.

He spotted the picture of Lucy. So sweet, so strong, so secure.

A thought filled him, one that had filled him whenever she spoke of taking her last breath.

If your God exists, then I want to see him. I want to ask him some questions, starting with why?

But even now he knew that no God existed. A real God couldn't be that cruel, that unusual, that mean.

He wouldn't take someone like Lucy and leave someone like Cillian.

Lucy had died believing, and Dennis was glad she had. But he didn't believe and never would believe because that was life, real life, not life on the pages of a book where characters needed to see and feel some kind of hope.

Hope is waking up and seeing the sun and knowing you're still alive. It's breathing. That's all we have.

But Lucy's picture argued with him and said he was full of it and always had been.

You can no longer hide behind your pages, Den.

4.

"I've got a bike. You can ride it if you like."

The sound jolted him, coming from the kitchen, blaring through speakers, the unmistakable sound of Syd Barrett before he'd lost his mind, singing about a bike and other crazy things.

Dennis darted into the kitchen and looked around. He found the base for Audrey's iPod, but there was no iPod in it. Instead it was playing on its own.

He tried to find the volume to turn it down. As he approached it only got louder.

The music grew zanier until its end when it culminated in bells and whistles and eerie turntables, then the echoey duck-like calls.

The music stopped.

"I just—I don't know how to tell you . . ."

He froze, turning around.

"Lucy?"

It had been her voice.

"I just—I just—I just—I just—I just—"

It was like a recording, skipping, replaying over and over.

He spun around in the kitchen, but when he stopped the kitchen kept spinning, turning, moving.

"I've got a bike. You can ride it if you like."

Syd was now standing over him as he lay on the tiled floor, staring at the ceiling.

He remembered seeing this picture on the back of an album, the sun and the sky in the background behind the young singer with the wild hair.

And then he smiled and laughed.

"There is no dark side of the moon, Dennis. Matter of fact, it's all dark."

5.

He looked up at another face he recognized.

"Dennis? What are you doing? You okay, man?"

He waited to hear the bell of a bike rattling by, but it didn't come.

Dennis sat up on the kitchen floor, no loud music playing,

no deceased former English rocker hovering over him. Hank stood there in jeans and a Bears sweatshirt, having placed some bags on the counter.

"I got some sandwiches. How long you been like that?"

"I'm not sure," Dennis said, standing on wobbly feet.

"Whoa, buddy. Come on. Let's get a seat for you."

Dennis eyed the Bose base for the iPod, but there was nothing.

On the counter lay the car keys to the Porsche Boxster.

I've already crashed one car. I don't want to go for two.

Hank stared at Dennis for a long time, then finally said, "I think maybe we need to go out. Get some fresh air."

"Sounds good to me," Dennis said. "You mind driving?"

Hank just laughed.

6.

A couple hamburgers had led to a couple beers, which had blossomed to more. They sat in the pub listening to songs from the '80s and watching ESPN. Throughout the conversation Dennis kept wondering whether to tell his friend what was really happening.

He wasn't even sure where to start.

"Do you believe in ghosts?"

Hank's eyes stayed on the television in the corner, his shoulders hunched. Finally he looked at Dennis and shrugged, nodding. "Sure."

"You say that very calmly."

"Yeah, so? I haven't been haunted by one, so I can't say I feel as strongly about them as I feel about, say, Julie, you know."

"What if I told you I was being stalked by a ghost?"

Hank took a sip of his beer but didn't seemed fazed. "I'd probably believe you."

"I expected a little more skepticism."

"No, here's the thing. It makes sense. You write all those

stories about ghosts and demons and evil. You're opening yourself up for them to come after you if they really exist. And who knows? I believe they do. In some form at least. But why would they come after me? You know?"

"Why would they come after me?"

"Have you asked this ghost?" Hank asked as if this were just a game.

"You're mocking me."

"No, I'm not. I'm playing along. I know you well enough that you don't believe in any of that."

"But do you believe? Seriously?"

"Sure," Hank said casually. "Why not?" He paused. "You're a skeptic. Put yourself in one of your books. You'd be the main character of course—the guy who doesn't believe but writes the stories anyway. What's the fancy word to describe that?"

"Irony?" Dennis asked.

"Yeah, that's ironic. Now me, I'm the sort of guy in your stories that always gets killed. The loyal dumb friend."

"Who says you're dumb?"

"Come on," Hank said, staring at Dennis. "I didn't say I'm a complete moron, but I'm not going to be the president of anything anytime soon. I'm happy just hanging around here, drinking my beer. And I've seen enough movies and read enough books to know guys like me get killed in those stories."

"But what if—Hank—what if all that—those stories and movies—what if it really was real?"

Hank stared at him for a minute. "Is this something new you're working on for a book? A scene you're trying to play out with me?"

Dennis didn't know how to convince his friend to take this seriously.

He still needed to convince himself.

7.

On the way home they passed the church as they drove toward Dennis's house. It was late afternoon—both of them were tired, and Hank had to work the next morning. No late night for him. As the church sign approached, Dennis read its message.

HE WILL HELP YOU IF YOU LET HIM.

Dennis wondered who the "he" on the sign referred to. Surely God. God will help you if you let him.

Come on, he thought. *I'm looking for something a little more clever.*

Hank was oblivious to the sign. He looked over and grinned. "That concussion feeling any better?"

"Yeah, thanks."

He will help you if you let him.

But Dennis wondered how "he," how anybody, could help him now.

He stands in the kitchen, the hatchet in his hand.

Bob is ready.

Nobody will know. It will be like it has always been.

Shock followed by quick action.

He wears rubber gloves over leather gloves. His boots are wrapped in plastic bags. Things can get quite messy, especially with a hatchet.

He shuffles across the floor, past the island, toward the stairs.

No.

He looks toward the dining room masked in darkness. The glow of eyes stare at him.

Not yet. Not now.

Bob waits, listening, wondering what the voice wants.

He will hurt you. It can't be here.

Bob nods.

Suddenly a black mass darts across the floor.

Bob watches the cat as it finds a resting place on the couch nearby.

He waits to hear the voice.

Go ahead.
He approaches the unsuspecting cat.
Animals have always loved Bob.
But he's never loved them back.

The Picture

1.

The line on the screen blinked. He stared at it, at the white, at the single sentence.

How long had he been in his office simply staring at the screen? An hour? Longer?

The line thumped. On, off, on, off. Waiting. For something. Anything.

Wind rattled the screen. It was cold in his office. He'd left the window cracked.

Dennis went to close the window. The clock told him it was after midnight. He'd spent a good portion of the day with Hank, hanging out and wasting time. He'd spend another good portion trying to write, but doing no writing at all.

As he surveyed his backyard, he instantly noticed the figure.

It stood upright, facing him, staring blankly into the window.

It was Cillian. He smiled and waved.

Dennis didn't wait to see if he was imagining this. He sprinted down the stairs and tore out the back, past the deck and onto the grass.

But outside in the dark, nobody was around. Dennis stood

there, looking all around, sucking in breaths. He kept turning to make sure Cillian didn't grab him from behind. He hated when they did that in the movies. It was so obvious and so stupid. But there was no one.

He heard a train in the background, the tracks rattling, a horn blaring. As Dennis started back toward the house, he saw a silhouette in the window of his second-floor office.

Once again it was Cillian, waving, grinning, taunting.

Dennis closed his eyes for a long time, then reopened them. Cillian was still there.

He can do that because he's a ghost, Dennis.

But Dennis had hurt him, had knocked him down, had felt his blood against his knuckles. How could Cillian be a ghost?

If he is a ghost, that means he can't hurt you.

Dennis ran back into the house. He knew where to go.

Enough's enough.

Dennis went into the garage and found it. It was on the bottom shelf inside a locked toolbox. Only he knew the combination to the lock. The metal toolbox had a few tools in it but also something else.

The gun felt strange in his hand.

He had bought it after the first crazed fan had been found in his house. After that Dennis knew anything was possible. Some kid could come dressed in black with mayonnaise smeared in his hair and a lollipop in his mouth and Dennis wouldn't be surprised. He'd bought the .38 just in case.

In case of something like this.

But you didn't think of something like this, did you, Dennis? How about a cross and some garlic and a wooden stake?

But he wasn't dealing with a vampire. He wasn't sure *what* he was dealing with, besides someone who was clearly crazy. He ignored his thought as he checked to make sure the gun was loaded. It was.

He climbed the stairs, expecting to find Cillian in his bedroom.

Is it possible to kill someone twice?

All he wanted to do was scare him away. And scare him for good.

Or maybe find out what he wants with me. What he really wants.

But inside his office there was nothing. For a few moments Dennis played cop as he walked through the house holding the gun. He probably looked as ridiculous as he felt.

Lucy would have a field day if she saw you now.

After twenty minutes of looking and listening, Dennis went back into his office. He sat in his armchair and leaned back, the pistol resting in front of his keyboard.

He stared at the dark metal of the gun. It hypnotized him. The silence bothered him. He was about to try writing when an instant message crossed his screen, startling him.

What's it like to wait? To wait hour after hour, day after day?

Dennis quickly typed back. **Wait for what?**

Wait for inspiration. Wait to see what's next. Wait to hear from your daughter. Waiting for Godot.

He shook his head.

What do you want from me?

The long reply came quickly.

I've told you time and time again what this is about, but you never listen, you never learn. Why does it have to be about *anything*? Why does there have to be a point, Dennis? Is there a point in human suffering and sadness and death? What's the point in that? Nothing. Nothing but emptiness. How full are you feeling?

It's after midnight, and do you know where you are? Where
is your daughter? Where is your wife? Where is your mind?
Why do you have a gun in front of you? Are you going to use
it? Do you ever think of using it on yourself to join your wife?
Don't tell me you haven't thought of that, even ever so briefly.

Dennis quickly typed back a hate-filled curse.

My, my, Dennis, such profanity. What a fraud. You can curse at
me, yet you don't dare put such juicy adjectives in your books.
Don't want to offend people, now, do we?

What do you want? Dennis asked him again.

This—this—all *this*—it's exactly what I want.

What? You want me to lose my mind? Good. Great. Done.

Can you hear me laughing, Dennis? Because I am. I couldn't
care less about you losing your mind. I lost far more. And I
want you to understand that.

Dennis typed heavily, his fingers beating the keys. **Understand what? What is there to understand?**

Dennis waited.

Well???? he typed.

Finally the screen in front of him turned black, as though
he had slipped in a DVD.

He saw himself, standing in the walk-in closet, then staring
at the rows of clothes. His knees buckled, and he found himself cowering on the carpet beneath those very clothes. His

cries were silent, ragged, ripping. His hands balled into fists as he fought with himself, weeping and shivering.

Dennis watched this, his hands shaking, then reaching out and slamming the iMac away from him.

But even on the floor, it continued to play the scene.

And then he heard the arrival of another message. He went over to read it. Even though the computer had shut off, Dennis could still see the text on screen.

It's one thing to curse at the critics or blow off your fans, Dennis. But you cursed God. And don't think he didn't hear you either.

Do you want to know something?

God abandoned you.

He took your wife and then left you both.

Now *there's* something terrifying to write about . . .

And with that, the computer went dead.

2.

A hatchet lay on his bed.

It was bloody.

Dennis looked around the room, approaching the walk-in closet and turning on the lights, careful to make sure nobody was going to jump out at him. But nobody was there. At least nobody in flesh and blood. He went to the bed and picked up the short, heavy instrument.

He stared at the edge of the blade. There was blood and wet clumps, as if it were—

Don't even go there.

But he couldn't help it. It looked like small chunks of flesh and even dark hair were caked on the edge of the hatchet.

He held it out as if it might have a virus attached to it.

This isn't imagined. This is real. This weapon I'm holding is real.

The wooden handle had a black marking that looked like a roughly drawn H. *I've seen that before.*

But even as he was thinking about it, almost ready to place it, he heard a door open and shut downstairs. He cursed and ran downstairs.

At least now he held a weapon.

You just were holding a gun and look what good it did you.

At the bottom of the stairs, Dennis could see the front door still open. He noticed a shadowy mass in the doorway.

Looking closer he knew what the dark ball was.

It was his cat, Buffy.

And the fur matched the hair that was on the hatchet.

Whoever did this had decapitated the fluffy, black animal.

And I know exactly who did this.

Dennis winced and stepped over the dead cat, heading toward the driveway.

What if you did this? a voice asked him. *What if everything that is happening is happening in your mind and really you're the one, you're the killer?*

But this wasn't a movie-of-the-week. There wasn't going to be a double twist ending: he writes horror novels because he lives them out (cue the menacing laughter). He didn't kill the cat, and he wasn't a killer.

The question wasn't whether he was losing his mind.

He was losing his patience. And on the driveway, in the middle of the night, having just stepped over the cat his daughter had given him that now missed its head, holding a bloody hatchet in his hand, Dennis started to scream.

"Where are you? Show your face if you're brave enough! Show yourself. You coward! You weakling! Why don't you try to do that to me? Huh? You pitiful little ant! Come show your face! Step up and face me."

But Dennis found himself screaming at the air, at the enveloping night, at the shadows on the driveway, at nobody. His voice was hoarse and his head spun and he knelt down on the driveway and bent over.

He didn't know what to do.

He didn't know what the ghost wanted.

And he was afraid that time was going to run out before he found out.

3.

—Go ahead, open it.

—I'm afraid.

—Why?

—Ever since you got me the car, I'm afraid of what you'll get me next.

—Just go ahead, Lucy. Open it.

—Okay, fine.

—Be careful.

—What is it?

—Keep opening.

—Oh. Wow.

—That's what heaven is to me. That picture. I found it and I just—I wanted to give it to you.

—It's beautiful. Look at them. They look like they're just passing the time away.

—They're in Venice. I bet they're both ninety years old.

—Thank you.

—Look at the back. Turn it around. I gave the piece a name.

—"Us and Them."

—Yep. Us and the rest of the godforsaken world. That's heaven. That's my wish.

—Thank you, Dennis. It means . . . I can't tell you . . .

—You don't have to. You never have to because I know. I'll always know.

4.

Dennis woke up.

His forehead and cheeks and neck and chest were coated with sweat.

He reached over, hoping he would find her there, that this whole dreaded, horrible thing would be just a dream. But there was nothing but space and emptiness next to him.

He swallowed, and his throat felt dry.

The memories won't go away, and they never will.

He remembered giving her the color photograph a few months before she passed. It had been a special gift and a special moment.

Why couldn't I have more of those?

He had blocked out the picture and that memory just like he had blocked out so many other memories. He was good at blocking things out, at compartmentalizing. But when your life was falling apart, things got messy.

He could see her smile so vividly even in the darkness. He could hear her voice so clearly.

God, I miss you so much.

He thought of the picture and remembered what happened to it. The memory stung as he tried to let it go. But it had nowhere to go, so it stayed at his side.

And sleep wouldn't come for a long time.

Bob sees the yellow sports car parked with the top down. He can't see the driver's face but notices that he hasn't moved for some time. The trees hide him as he moves toward the lone car in the dark parking lot, the river bleeding out in front of them, the moon peeking through clumps of clouds.

The metal pipe in his hands is all he found in his truck. It will do the trick. It can dent the hood of a semitruck, and he knows because he has done it. A soft, fleshy head and a pliable skull will be no match.

Bob steps onto the pavement, his feet silent, his form barely noticeable in the murky shadows.

He will have to dispose of the sports car as well.

The river ahead provides a possibility, but he doubts that will work.

His hand tightens around the pipe as he approaches.

It will be quick, probably only four or five blows.

A gust of wind slides by.

And then suddenly he hears footsteps.

Numerous footsteps.

They're not ordinary steps. The clicking sound is different, the pace hurried and frantic.

They're approaching him.

He turns and sees only glowing eyes.

The beasts slam against him and he falls, dropping the pipe, his cheek and jaw pounding off the pavement. Something tramples over his back, his hand, his head, something heavy and wild. He looks up as some beast pounds against him, sending him falling back again.

In darkness with his eyes closed, he grasps for the pipe and finds it, lashing out. But it doesn't hit anything.

Bob gets to his knees and looks toward the outline of the sports car. Several long-legged animals stand between him and the vehicle.

As if they're protecting it.

He licks his lip and tastes his own blood. For a moment he considers attacking them, breaking their pretty heads, filling the car with their limbs.

Then he stands and sees the pack, knows it's too much. He turns around and walks back into the woods.

Shadows in the Darkness

1.

Dennis hadn't done something like this in years.

It didn't matter that it was October and not, say, May. The temperature was in the seventies. It would probably be in the fifties and stormy by the time Halloween rolled around—it always was. He sat in Lucy's yellow Porsche Boxster with the top down, his fourth beer in his hand, looking out at the river sliding by, the music turned up loud.

He could remember the spring of '77, a sophomore in college hanging out with his friends at University of Illinois in Champaign at some forest preserve, drinking beer and smoking weed and listening to this album. He hadn't listened to *Animals* all the way through for years, and he found himself appreciating it even more now than he had back then.

Back then when I didn't realize how sacred and special and swift life could be.

He'd experimented with his share of drugs in the old days. He could remember taking acid the first time he went to see the Floyd, how it changed his life. He didn't really remember *that* much of the show, but he could still remember how alive he felt. How the music seemed to be playing inside of him, how the lights and the sounds all vibrated and bubbled over and made him feel like an astronaut and an explorer and a conqueror even though he was still a pimply faced, long-haired college student.

Now Dennis listened to music and drank and tried to wash away the burn of the memories.

This was where he proposed to Lucy.

This tranquil location set off next to the river, surrounded by large trees and now a park and a garden and even a small atrium. Back then it had been more simple. You could park and walk through the forest and look at the river. He hadn't wanted something grand or ornate. He wanted a peaceful place where Lucy could be herself and he could surprise her with the ring.

And it had worked perfectly.

Twenty-five years ago.

He needed a lot more beer to drink to that. To drink the memories away.

He shouldn't be here, separated, isolated. She should be here with him. Or she should be here instead of him.

It's always the same. Always the same.

He hated reminiscing because the same old thoughts always filled him. *She should be here* and *he should've been the first to go* and cliché after cliché.

The reality was that life happened and life sometimes sucked and life couldn't be avoided.

He drained the rest of his beer and turned up the music, but it didn't help.

Do you see me, Lucy? What would you say? Get on up. Get going. Stop sludging around.

But Dennis knew he had done the best he could during the last year, getting up and getting going. He'd done it so well that it had brought him here.

I've tried and I've done everything but I can't erase the memory of us.

Nor did he want to. She would be with him forever, and he

wanted it that way. Take away any other memories of childhood or college craziness, but don't take away the family memories. Not Lucy and Audrey.

The music pulsing through his car sounded eerie, otherworldly.

What would his life be like if it had a Beatles sound track? A little more peaceful and sweet? How about The Rolling Stones? A little more demonic? The Doors? A little more psychotic?

I don't know if I could get any more psychotic, thank you very much.

He pictured the look in Lucy's eyes when he proposed, when he opened his hand and showed her the ring. She didn't care that it wasn't big. She cared that he was asking, that he was on one knee asking, that he said he loved her and always would, that he was inviting her to be a part of his journey.

She didn't hesitate but said yes yes yes yes over and over again.

Dennis shut his eyes and listened to the music and drank his beer and remembered.

He remembered her smell, her touch, her skin, her hair, her voice, her walk, her every little thing.

And with a smile on his face, he drifted off into his own happily ever after.

2.

The knocking sounded from miles away. Gentle, but persistent.

Dennis wiped his eyes and could barely make out the river through the trees, the glow of the moon reflecting off the steadily moving water.

The empty beer in his hand had dropped on the floor. The CD had stopped playing. And no one was around.

But then he heard a shuffling. He turned and jumped, seeing the big shadow in the darkness.

Then another.

He turned toward his left and saw another.

Deer. A bunch of deer are hanging out just watching me in the darkness.

Dennis turned slowly, quietly. The deer were full-sized, the kind that could do major damage to a car. He had never seen deer this close up.

They stood almost as if . . .

That's crazy, Dennis.

But he had seen far crazier things. They just stood there in the darkness like guards standing over a castle, their long, lean bodies serving as a wall.

One of the deer looked straight at him, and he squinted to see its beautiful strong face in the shadows.

I heard knocking. Pounding. What was that?

Dennis put a hand on the side of the car. The deer slowly moved away, not frightened like he thought they might be. One by one—there were four of them—they headed back into the woods.

All except the one that had stared into Dennis's eyes.

It was a surreal experience, being here in the dark, feeling spooked, but also feeling completely at ease because of this remarkable creature.

Can I see its eyes, or am I just imagining it?

But he thought he could. And he thought . . .

I'm thinking a lot of things and most of them are crazy.

The deer turned and walked back into the woods to join its companions.

And with that Dennis started up the car and drove off.

October 27, 2009

The voices won't go away. Not just Cillian's, but all of them. They confuse and contradict and make him want to go out and cut.

Bob knows he shouldn't be here. He shouldn't do this. There are certain ways of doing it, certain rules he always goes by.

But there are no more rules. Not anymore. Not when the dead show up to haunt him.

He scans the area and doesn't see anyone. It's empty. Grocery stores usually are around midnight. But that doesn't mean guys who would rather be smoking pot and listening to rock and watching television aren't working, doing the cleanup shift.

He passes the display of apples and the barrel full of pumpkins to go through the swinging doors. There is a small hallway lined with bags of potatoes and boxes of bananas. The floor looks freshly swept. He turns a corner and sees the back area where several sinks and tables are used to cut fruit. The knife on the counter is large enough to slice a cow. He takes it and continues walking through another set of doors into a freezer.

Bob doesn't hear any voices now. Cillian's voice is gone,

but he knows it's just temporary. He wishes he could kill him again, that he could make him shut up permanently.

He wants all the voices to go away.

The spiky-haired kid is loading a box of oranges onto a cart. He glances up and doesn't appear surprised.

"What's up?"

Bob approaches him, the knife at his side. The guy doesn't see it.

"Lookin' for someone?" the guy asks casually, hauling another box onto the cart.

Before he can say something else, the knife makes sure he won't be talking anymore, or at least makes sure he won't be saying anything decipherable. The gash in his cheeks and lips is deep.

The young man grabs his mouth a second before he starts to howl, and the knife finds its way to his apron, then works its way upward. Bob grabs the kid's mouth and presses down hard and feels the blood and hears the screams.

It's over in moments. He stands there, surveying the mess.

His skin tingles as his body shudders, his eyes rolling back for a moment. Everything in him tightens, then he lets out a long, shaky breath and opens his eyes.

He stares at the boxes. He knows he doesn't have much time.

He'll need to clean this up.

Nobody will suspect anything happened. Not to this kid. They'll think he simply took off.

Nobody will check this dirty cooler he will mop. Or the boxes he will take to his truck.

Nobody will know.

And for now, the voices remain silent.

Fearless & Run Like Hell

1.

He was awakened by the sound of digging.

Dennis had gone to sleep with the bedroom window open. At first he thought he was dreaming the rhythmic noise. But as it continued and the sound of metal striking rock sent echoes into the quiet night, Dennis knew he wasn't dreaming.

It was 2:24 a.m.

He threw on some clothes and didn't bother bringing anything outside with him. It probably wouldn't matter anyway.

On the deck the wood beneath him groaned as he approached the noise. It came from down by the river, past the oak and the river birch trees.

Dennis slowed as he approached the source of the sound.

He could make out a shadow behind the tree. A man wearing no shirt, his chest and neck streaked with what Dennis imagined to be dirt.

Or blood.

The figure looked at him, leering at him with white teeth. "Care to join me, Dennis?"

Dennis was torn between continuing forward and bolting out of there.

Cillian shook his head, his face distinguishable now that Dennis's eyes had adjusted to the moonlight. "Such a pity."

"What's a pity?"

"You. You're pitiful, Dennis. You let me down. You are constantly—constantly—letting me down."

"Then maybe you should go bother someone else."

"Maybe if you didn't disappoint me I would."

"What can I do for you then?"

"See—look. Look at this. You don't get it, do you?"

"Did you decide to bury my cat?"

Cillian laughed. "That's a good one. You never cared for that thing anyway, did you?"

"You didn't have to tear its head off."

"Oh, I'm sorry. Would you like it back?"

"No," Dennis said flatly.

"This is much too big of a hole for Buffy."

"Deciding to bury yourself?"

"You're so full of wit tonight. Is it because you visited the little park in the forest and saw some of God's creatures?"

"What are you doing?" Dennis asked.

He looks and sounds and even smells real. How can this be a ghost? It can't be.

But Dennis had seen the pictures. They were real. And this guy was dead.

Cillian looked up, sweat beading on his forehead. "Yes, even the sweat is real."

"Can you read my mind?"

"Sometimes. But not in the way you might think."

"How might I think?"

"You don't understand, and you refuse to understand, Dennis. You're too stubborn, too confident. Even after all this time. After everything that's happened."

Dennis walked over to the hole.

"What is this?"

"I'd say it's big enough for a man your size, wouldn't you?"

"Are you gonna kill me?"

"You know I can't do that, Dennis. And you call yourself a horror writer."

"I like to think that I write more than just horror," Dennis said.

"You write garbage that's not worth filling this hole!"

Dennis stared. He wanted to grab the shovel and hurt Cillian with it, to knock him out and throw him in this hole and bury him.

Can you bury the dead? Will they stay down there?

"You know what's going to fill this hole? Right in your backyard? Your buddy. Perhaps he will give you inspiration."

Dennis thought of Hank.

What have you done?

"What buddy?"

"Oh, no, not the stupid one. No, he'll get something else. The friend you call Ward."

"What have you done?"

Cillian started laughing.

As Dennis went after him, he vanished.

The shovel dropped, and Dennis picked it up. It was real. The dirt was real, as was the hole.

He ran the dirt through his fingers.

Dennis sprinted back toward his house, not caring about the time or Cillian's disappearing act or anything else.

Ward has a wife and a family and he can't be involved in this. It would be my fault. I can't allow that to happen.

His hands shook as he dialed the number.

2.

"Hello?" The voice whispered. It was Ward's wife, Kendra.

"Kendra, I need to speak to Ward."

"Wha—Dennis?"

"Yeah, it's Dennis. Something—I just—is he there?"

There was a pause.

She's looking for him but he won't be there because he's downstairs lying in a pool of blood.

"Dennis, what's wrong?" Kendra asked.

"I can't tell you now—I just need to speak to Ward."

"Okay."

There was movement in the background, muffled voices, the shuffling of the phone.

"Hello."

It was Ward. Groggy and subdued but still Ward.

"Are you okay?"

There was a pause. "Hey, Dennis."

"Are you okay?" he repeated, demanding an answer.

"Yeah. Are you?"

"I just—something happened tonight."

"What?"

"I can't—I was worried about you."

"Dennis, man—it's almost three in the morning."

"I know. And I'm sorry."

"Are you sure you're okay?"

"Yeah, yeah. Just, uh, just be careful, okay?"

There was another pause.

"Ward, look, I'll explain everything. Just—give me a call sometime tomorrow. Apologize to Kendra for me."

"Yeah, sure."

"And Ward. Don't . . ."

"Don't what?"

What are you going to tell him? Don't lose your mind? Don't anger any dead people? Don't go close to any holes in the ground?

"Look, I'll talk to you tomorrow."

Dennis lay the phone on the counter. Suddenly he heard the dial tone, as if the speaker on the phone was on. And through the speaker he heard laughter.

Taunting, menacing, hilarious laughter.

"Just keep diggin', Dennis! Keep diggin'! I'll finish up for you tomorrow. Just you wait. I'll finish up for all of you. Just you wait!"

3.

He awoke in the third-floor bedroom, the unused guest room across from the storage room. The morning sun striped over the bed, revealing his muddy clothes and clumped shoes. He felt hungover though there was no reason he should.

Had he dreamed the whole thing about Cillian digging the hole? He decided to go downstairs and see if there was anything in the backyard.

Who says you didn't do it yourself in a nightmarish fit of energy?

His lower back ached. His mouth felt dry, pasty. As he went to the stairs, wondering how he had ended up here, something in Lucy's old room caught his eye.

For a moment he just stood there, staring.

On the wood floor rested the photo album.

Not *a* photo album but *the* photo album.

I know I haven't looked at that since she passed, and I know I wasn't looking at it last night.

It was perhaps the ugliest album ever made, with a bright yellow and blue cloth covering that said words in bold like **LOVE** and **LAUGHTER** and, in case you wondered what the album was for: **PHOTOS**. He had picked it out for Lucy on their first anniversary, giving it to her filled with funny photos. He had given her something else too, though he couldn't remember what—a necklace or a gift certificate. But he remembered this gift. As the years passed, the album filled with more funny and memorable moments from their life together.

It still had a couple blank pages, pages she had added not long before she passed.

Dennis had thought of taking it out after she died, maybe about every five or ten minutes of every day of every week after she died. But he knew it would be too much. The best way—maybe the only way—to deal with someone dying was to go out and live as hard as you could. Sitting upstairs on the third floor looking through memories wouldn't do anybody any good.

Did Cillian do this to hurt me? Is this one of the many ways he's wanting to peel open the scab?

The room chilled him. He looked down at his arms covered in goose bumps.

Get out of this room.

He picked up the photo album.

As he walked down the narrow stairs to the second floor and his office, it felt like he was carrying a box of dynamite. As he entered his office, he heard something fall to the carpet.

It was a photo.

He picked it up and looked at it.

There she was, smiling, laughing, saying something. It was a snapshot taken in the last month of her life. She still looked like she had twenty or thirty years left. Who could have known?

He quickly slipped it back into the album.

I don't remember ever seeing that picture before.

Dennis put the album in his closet. He couldn't look through it. Not now. Maybe in another year. Or another decade.

The photo lingered in his mind. He couldn't place it. Had he even been there when it was taken?

It's easy to forget when you want to. To stuff it away in some dark place that can only be found through the mossy swamps of pain.

Dennis looked out his window and saw the hole in the back-yard, the shovel next to it.

It was real, just like the stains on his clothes and the grime on his hands.

4.

Dennis spent the day in denial.

He avoided the growing pile of bills. He avoided the messages left by Ward on his answering machine. He avoided the e-mails and calls from Maureen asking how the manuscript was coming along. He avoided reading any more of Cillian's horrific story. He avoided the thought of slapping a cover letter on it and sending it to Maureen.

He avoided the reality of Cillian and what that really, truly meant.

Dennis was a pro at avoidance.

And despite everything he had seen and gone through, he still couldn't force himself to get help.

5.

When the doorbell rang at 5:45 that afternoon, Dennis found something to greet the guest with.

The .38 in his office.

He swung open the door, raising the gun and expecting to see the familiar sneering face.

Instead it was Hank with a case of beer and a bewildered expression.

"Okay, I give up," Hank said, holding out the beer. "Take it. It's all yours."

Dennis stepped outside to see if anyone else was around.

"Don't worry. The neighbors didn't see you."

"It's not Sunday," Dennis said as if to remind Hank.

"*Really*? Is that the only day I can come over?"

In the kitchen, as Hank loaded the Coors Light Draft into the fridge, he glanced at Dennis. "Here I am thinking you might need someone to swing by and visit. Looks like I'm right. You okay?"

Dennis shook his head.

"So what's the deal?"

"Remember what I told you the other day?"

Hank stared suspiciously at Dennis, still skeptical.

"The thing about the ghost?"

"Yeah," Hank said.

"That's why I'm holding this thing."

"So you're for real? It's really happening to you?"

Dennis sighed. "Something is happening. I don't know what. I don't know if I'm losing my mind or what."

"If that's the case, you think carrying around a gun is a good idea?"

"I don't know."

"Is that thing loaded?"

"Yeah."

Hank handed him a beer. "If it's a real ghost, it can't hurt you. Not really."

"How do you know?"

"I looked it up online the other night. They say most ghosts are stuck in holding patterns, as if they're confused and don't have anywhere to go. They need something to change before they can pass on to the next place."

"Which would be what?"

"I don't know," Hank said. "Heaven. Hell. The great Dairy Queen of the beyond."

"You believe in an afterlife?"

"I want to. I want to believe there's more than just this. There has to be."

"No there doesn't."

"Tell me something, Den. Why is it that Lucy *and* Audrey both believe in God and heaven and all that, and it's so hard for you?"

"Wanna know why I write scary stories? Because they're real. People like horror because it mirrors real life. Turn on the news and what do you find—one horror story after another. Those tales of happily ever after—now those are fiction. There is no such thing as happily ever after."

"Den—tell me. Are you okay? Like, seriously?"

"I'm scared, man."

"Scared of what?"

"What's worse? Going crazy or seeing the dead?"

"I got some medication my doctor gave me when I was going through the depression and stuff. It messes with your head, but you could try it."

"I don't think that's a solution."

Dennis didn't feel like sitting. He got up and stared out the back window at the yard. The shovel still rested on the grass. He told Hank that he was going outside for a moment. He set the gun on the kitchen counter, feeling a bit foolish now for carrying the weapon around.

It felt cooler outside than he expected it to be. The warm weather had gone. He shivered as he walked toward the hole.

It was big enough for a man. For him.

Dennis examined the shovel. On the handle was a familiar tag. A black *H* cut into the grain. He had no idea what the *H* stood for.

Dennis brought the shovel to the front of the garage, resting it on the side of the house.

He wondered what sort of tool would show up next.

A riding lawn mower with a big fat H *scrawled on the side.*

Dennis looked through the trees at the leaf-covered yard belonging to the neighbors. They never seemed to rake their leaves, even after getting fined.

Maybe the H *stands for Hank. Or Hysteria. Or Hell.*

6.

After finding little to eat at Dennis's house, they decided to head to downtown Geneva, parking on Main Street and walking a block to the hole-in-the-wall lit by a sign that said Pa cho. It was missing the *n* and the *'s*. Part of the allure.

They opened the rickety door to find themselves in a long restaurant with a bar that seemed half as long. There was an orange ambience about Pancho's with television screens tuned to sports, the kitchen on the left, a line of two tables each to the right. There wasn't anything fancy about the place. Eight tables were occupied tonight. A Hispanic woman nodded at them, meaning they could find their own table.

They selected a table in the corner with four chairs. Hank faced the TV so he could watch highlights of the game. The woman placed a basket of chips and a bowl of salsa on the table.

The place didn't have menus. Again, that was the beauty of it. A burrito was a burrito, a taco a taco. No nonsense and great food, that's what Pancho's offered.

A guy with long wavy hair and a shirt that said 4:20 on the back approached the table.

"Okay?"

"I'll take a margarita. Want one, Hank?" Dennis asked.

This place didn't fuss with a lot of fancy margaritas. They had one kind, and it wasn't frozen. If you wanted frozen, you could go down the street to 7-Eleven for a Slurpee because Pancho's served margaritas on the rocks. But they were great, with some kind of "special" ingredient added into it that Dennis hadn't identified. Some fruit or spice that made it just a bit different.

"So you really hungry or what?" Hank asked him.

"Sure."

"You haven't even touched the chips."

"So?"

"You showed up at the door with a gun. With a *loaded* gun, to be more precise. Did you bring the gun with you here?"

"It's in the car."

"You paid more attention to the backyard than me. You've been digging in the yard for some reason—"

"What do you mean?"

Hank raised his eyebrows and smiled. "When you went outside I took a look. I mean—what's the deal, man?"

"What if I told you I didn't do that?"

"You keep giving me these 'what if' scenarios. What are you saying?"

Dennis looked around as if they were being watched. He'd picked this place for a reason. Pancho's just felt off the map.

"I'm saying I didn't do that."

"So who did?"

"The ghost is real, Hank. It's real, and it won't go away."

Hank rubbed his temple. "So why'd you want to come to a Mexican restaurant to tell me?"

"I didn't plan on telling you. I was hoping to get you a little more loaded."

"I'm all for that," Hank said, laughing. "But still. For what?"

"I just . . ." Dennis stopped as the waiter brought their drinks.

The 4:20 surfer dude just stood there, as if he had forgotten the question he was supposed to ask. They ordered, and the waiter finally ambled off, looking like he was lost.

"What is it?"

He needed to get it out. He needed to finally tell the truth.

"I did something—something bad."

"What?" Hank asked.

"I stole something."

But just as Dennis was going to continue, he saw the fanatical smile and the wild hair and the narrow shoulders and the lanky figure standing at the door.

Cillian walked over to their table and sat next to Hank.

7.

For a surreal moment, Dennis just sat there wondering if Hank saw the figure sitting next to him. But Hank looked to his right and wrinkled his face.

"Excuse me?"

"Hello, friend of Dennis Shore."

Hank cursed. "Can I help you?"

"Oh, of course you can, Hank," Cillian said, looking at Dennis. "There are many ways you can help me."

Hank glanced at Dennis, then back at the young man.

"Look, whatever you want, it's not the best time, so get up and get out, okay?"

For a moment Cillian waited, then he shook his head. "Such manners, Dennis. Really. After all we've been through."

"You know this guy?" Hank asked.

"Hank, this is, uh . . ."

"I'm the one he's told you about. I'm not wearing my sheet tonight."

For a long minute, Hank stared at Cillian as if sizing him up. Then Hank laughed, nodding, sipping his margarita. "This is who you were talking about? This guy?"

Dennis nodded, and he knew what Hank was thinking.

As Cillian's skinny arm reached out to take a chip, Hank grabbed his wrist. He cursed at Cillian and demanded that he tell them who he was.

"Dennis knows," Cillian said. "He knows well."

Hank dropped the guy's wrist. "That's no ghost, man. This is some kid playing a trick on you, trying to blackmail you, Dennis. Right? What's your name?"

"Cillian."

"Okay then, Cillian. If that's your real name. You're not a ghost. You're some little fan trying to get something out of him. What do you want? Money? Huh?"

"I'd like my life back, if you really want to know, Henry Lee McKinney. Just as much as you'd like Julie back."

Hank's forehead beaded with sweat as he laughed. "That doesn't make you a spirit. Anybody can spy on people. Anybody can look up information. Knowing someone's middle name doesn't mean you're from the afterworld."

"I know about Bailey."

Something changed. Something in Hank. Immediate and deep.

Hank's face reddened. "What'd you say?"

"You heard *exactly* what I said. Your hearing isn't your problem. It's your stupid lack of ambition in this life, Hank."

"What does he mean?" Dennis asked.

"Nothing," Hank told him.

"Bailey was his dog. He accidentally killed it during one of his drunken moments. When you were how old? Seventeen was it? When your parents left you on your own and you decided to have some fun. But it wasn't so fun, was it? You were drunk out of your mind, and the next day you wailed and you buried the dog in a field. And nobody knew. Nobody at all. But the dead talk, my friend. Even dead animals talk."

"There's no way," Hank mumbled under his breath.

"No way what?"

Hank's big hand reached out and grabbed Cillian by the neck. Even unable to breathe and turning blue Cillian spoke. "Your friend tried to do that the other night. It doesn't work."

The server came, apparently oblivious to anything going on.

"Can I get you anything?"

Hank shook his head, looking at Dennis, then at Cillian, then stood up and toppled over his chair as he bolted out of there.

"Oh well, that was short-lived, wasn't it? Guess he finally believes you now, huh? People refuse to see the truth. People don't like to know—they don't like the truth."

Dennis wasn't about to stick around and have a conversation with Cillian. He pushed his chair back.

"Oh, you might not want to do that," Cillian said.

As he stood the lights in the room started to blur together.

"That special little concoction you and your friend had. I put a little something special in it."

A bug crawled over the wall. Then another. Then a dozen. "What?"

"Ah, the memories. Ah, the good ole times of flying high."

"What'd you do?"

"I'm a ghost, so I can do anything, right? That's what you write about? When you get it so utterly *wrong*."

"What'd you do?"

"It's right in front of your eyes, and you don't even know it or see it."

"What?"

"And that's such a shame."

The drink in front of him started to bubble. The television above him started to drip. He felt it on his forehead, sweet warm liquid goop.

"What'd you do?" he shouted.

"Better wait for your burrito," Cillian said, laughing.

"What's right in front of me? Tell me."

Cillian's dark eyes cut into him, not moving. "Evil."

8.

It was the worst trip of his life.

He wasn't sure exactly what Cillian had done and what happened to Hank and what they were drinking, but suddenly the entire world was loopy and messy.

The door to the outside felt like rubber as he pushed against it. Finally it fell off and cracked into a hundred little pieces. Dennis shook his head, opening and closing his eyes. The wall outside was bloodred and dripping, and the sign no longer said Pa cho. It read **Death** and **Pale Rider** and **Ghost** and **Cut** and **Hurt** and **REALREALREAL**.

"Hank?" Dennis called out.

Even his own voice sounded strange and funky. It sounded lower, thicker.

The sidewalk moved beneath his feet, shifting and turning. The walls breathed, expanding in and out. He put his hand against the wall and fell into it, into the marshmallowy texture, his knees in foam, his mouth tasting butter.

I'm losing my mind. I'm utterly losing my mind.

He stood and pushed his way through nothing and then saw someone walk past him.

"Hank? Hank, man, it's me."

But this wasn't Hank. Just some young guy walking the street thinking Dennis was drunk.

For a second or an hour, he didn't know, Dennis walked, calling out for Hank, trying to make sense of this, his eyes and ears not cooperating.

Cars passed as he walked down the sidewalk. One appeared heading right toward him, the lights glowing eyes of fire. But then the car just passed on the other side of the street, far away from him.

Hands that had covered his face now opened in front of him. They were gashed and bleeding. The blood dripped off them.

I've been here before.

He rubbed them together and saw the incisions open, the dark liquid coughing out and leaking between his fingers.

"Hank!"

But Hank was nowhere to be found.

It's another scene from one of my books. Just like the grave digging. How could I forget? How could I not remember?

He needed to get help. He took his cell phone out of his pocket and opened it. A tongue flailed out at him, causing him to drop the phone and stare at it. The phone suddenly looked like a little mouse with a long tail as it scampered away.

If you keep running you'll die. Just like the guy dies in Run Like Hell.

"Hank, man, where are you?" But his body failed him as the words came out: "Tank car all over the wrap dressing!"

Dennis dropped to his knees, biting his lip and forcing himself to try to calm down.

You're going to end up dead, Dennis. And you can't do that, not to Audrey. Not again.

As he opened his eyes to the dark sky, he saw the clouds pulsing, the moon splintering apart, crows flying over him, smiling.

Get up and get help. Get out of here. Get off the street.

So he walked. One foot in front of the other.

Someone passed and screamed out, "You will die before midnight."

But he imagined it just like he imagined the sidewalk being made of chocolate and the bridge he passed over shaking and the railing he gripped becoming a candy cane.

Dennis bumped into something or someone and realized that finally this was not an illusion. It was real. He stared at Hank's red hair and wild face and wide eyes.

"Hank, he put something in our drinks. He spiked them."

Hank just stared at him. Cars passed by as the wind blew, a breeze from the Fox River.

Get off this bridge. Get off now.

"You brought this evil upon us," Hank said.

"Stop it. You're drugged up."

Hank's face turned wrinkly, his eyes blinking, crying blood. A hand came out of nowhere and gripped Dennis's neck.

"You're the evil one. The one they warned about. The one to bring sorrow, to bring pain, to bring evil."

And then Hank grabbed Dennis's belt. With inhuman strength, he lifted Dennis up over the railing and the wall and dropped him.

Dennis fell backward, his face staring up at the heavens, the clouds, the dark night. He seemed to fall forever before he hit cold, deep water. Just as he once described in his novel about demon possession.

When he decided to kill off his main character.

9.

—Hon.

—Yeah.

—It's okay.

—No.

—Yes, it's okay.

—No, it's not. Don't dare say it is. Don't give me your God talk now.

—Hold my hand.

—I just—it's not—

—It's going to be okay. You're going to be okay. You and Audrey are going to be okay.

—No we're not. We can't—you can't leave us, Lucy, not like this, not now. I cannot go on in this world without you.

—Don't crush my hand.

—I wish it was me.

—But it's me. And when I'm gone, you have to do the best you can to stay strong. To be strong. I know you're strong, Den, and you always will be. Even if you don't believe it, you have to know. You have to understand that I believe this. I will be in a better place.

—The best place is right here with us.

—I believe there's an even better place. That's the only hope I have.

—How can you smile?

—Because you can't. But one day, Den. One day I believe you will. You just need to let go of your control. You need to let go . . . and believe.

10.

"One day, Den. One day."

He could hear her whispering in his ears.

"Just not now. Not now, not like this."

"Den."

He opened his eyes and saw darkness and felt himself drifting. His arms and legs floated and for a second he believed he was in heaven. Then he tried to breathe and sucked in water.

"Move, Den. Get out of here."

A flickering streak waved at him far above. He stared at it and suddenly felt his chest burning. The beaming light continued dancing far above, and he did everything he could to move toward it. His arms and legs flailed, and he sucked in water through his nose and mouth as he rushed upward, toward the falling star, toward the laser beam, toward the light of heaven, toward her.

As he finally made it to the glassy surface, he exploded out to the cold air of night and found himself drifting in the middle of the Fox River, the dark night all around him.

There was no light, just flickers of the town in the distance.

He breathed like a newborn and couldn't distinguish the river water from the tears on his face.

He couldn't see Hank on the distant outline of the bridge. He couldn't see Cillian. And he couldn't see any flickers of light urging him onward.

But he had heard and seen something.

Maybe Cillian isn't the only ghost following me around.

All he wants to do is hurt. To reach out and grab something or someone and hurt it.

Bob pulls into the familiar driveway and feels it. It's not anger. It's bloodlust, a tingling in his body, an energy unlike anything else he's ever felt. Nothing can compare to this.

He pulls the truck in and shuts it off.

He knows what he's about to do.

Bob stares at his neighbor's yard. He sees the debris from his parents' house, feels the tormenting wind against his door, begging to come in.

His messy, stupid parents. Always picking at him, always hating him.

He climbs out of the truck. Yet he doesn't go in the front door. Instead he goes around the back and finds exactly what he needs, exactly what he's looking for. Hedge clippers with an *H* branded on their long wooden handles, the black blades as long as his forearm. He crosses the patio to the rusted-out door leading in the back way.

As he steps into the small hallway that goes past an old, broken washer and dryer, he hears their voices in the background.

Their same endless drone about the same endless things.

They're in the living room, just down the narrow hall.

He grips the handles of the hedge clippers. They feel steady in his hands. For a moment he stops and listens to the voices. He closes his eyes, and his body shudders.

Then he moves with a purpose and a mission.

The clippers remain steady, poised to work for him.

Ghosts Can't Hurt

1.

Hell is a place without hope, one day after another after another with absolutely no ounce of hope left.

Dennis thought this as he made coffee. Another October morning, another crack of sunlight in the clouds, another drop in the temperature. No sign of Cillian. Hank was alive and well, sleeping on the couch in the entertainment room. After climbing out of the Fox River and walking off the nightmarish set of events, Dennis found Hank resting in his car. The big guy was passed out and thankfully didn't ask Dennis how he got in the river.

I don't know how I got there myself. If it was Hank or Cillian or if I simply jumped in myself.

One thing Dennis knew for sure: he had ended up in the Fox River. When he woke up this morning after sleeping very little, he checked the clothes on the bathroom tile—still damp.

Like a story with no end. Just repeating over and over again.

And that was why he was thinking about hell as he heard the drips and waited for the hot caffeine to put his thoughts in order. Each day was turning into the same: some unexpected scare, some unseen force, some unknown spirit battling him.

There has to be a point to this.

But does evil have a point? Dennis was beginning to wonder if the point was his death. He assumed ghosts couldn't hurt you, just like Hank said.

Has Cillian hurt you or have you simply hurt yourself?

He didn't know. He certainly didn't know if there was a point, except maybe his growing madness. Was Cillian truly haunting him? Without point or purpose, simply to get back at the living for hurting him in some way?

Hell is Groundhog Day *meets* The Blair Witch Project.

Awaking to see the same things again, not knowing what was out there, and eventually realizing you'd end up in the basement of an abandoned house in the middle of the woods, shrieking and terrified and suddenly blacking out.

Only to have it happen all over again the next day.

Now there was a story idea. He could hear it now, the idiots in Hollywood brainstorming their pitches. *"Yeah, how about this one? This guy is stuck in the same day over and over again, but instead of it being funny it's scary, like* Saw, *except he never dies!"*

Come to think of it, they had probably already made a movie like that.

The coffee was taking forever. Dennis looked across his lawn to the hole, the mock grave. It reminded him that he needed to return Ward's phone calls to make sure his friend was okay and didn't think he was crazy.

Seeing the pile of dirt next to the hole was like looking at a snapshot from his book *Fearless*. He just wondered why it hadn't been apparent to him right away.

The girl on the bridge . . . the zombies in Home De-pot . . . the grave in the backyard . . . the push off the bridge.

These were all scenes from his books.

Hank losing his mind that one night. There's another. It could have come right out of Marooned.

Dennis sipped coffee as he walked over to the door onto the deck.

How could I not have known? Why wasn't it more obvious to me?

An author's books were like his children, as the cliché went, and the memories associated with them grew harder to recall the more of them he had. Sometimes readers would ask about a character he didn't recognize and they'd be shocked. "You don't remember? You're the author!"

You're the author, Dennis. The man in control. The man holding the keys to your fictitious universe. Yet you don't have control of anything anymore, do you?

He recalled a time when he was speaking at a writer's conference and someone asked him bluntly to answer yes or no: was he a controlling person. And without thinking he said yes because he realized he did like to have control, and this showed itself in his writing. He had never been a big fan of Hollywood (even if he had enjoyed a couple of the movies they made out of his books) simply because there were a hundred people to satisfy and work with. When you wrote a book it was just you. Eventually you dealt with an editor and a publisher, but when you were creating the story it was just you and you had all the control in the world.

I can raise the dead and kill my enemies and block out the sun, but in real life I am mortal and flawed and forgetful.

A terrifying thought filled him.

How many of my books' scenes are left to live out? What stories have not yet "happened"?

Dennis was afraid of the answer.

"Anybody home?" a voice called.

Dennis headed inside from the deck to get Hank some coffee.

2.

"What do you remember about last night?"

"A bad burrito."

Dennis wasn't in the mood to laugh and didn't even feign it.

Hank remained stretched out on the couch, sipping coffee and eating a blueberry muffin he'd found in the kitchen.

"Hank, I need to know."

"What? I don't know, to be honest. I don't remember much after the restaurant."

"You remember the guy?"

"What? The creepy guy who looked like a pedophile? Yeah, how can I forget?"

"You remember what he said?"

Hank chewed with his mouth open, the spinning of his brain seeming to make him mute for a moment. Then he shook his head. "Was I that drunk?" he asked.

"No."

"I remember meeting him. But that's it. I guess—maybe I had more yesterday than I thought."

"He put something in our drinks."

"Oh yeah? Probably the date rape drug."

"I'm being serious."

"I feel awful. I haven't felt this awful since I went to New Orleans and woke up several days later wondering where I was."

"You don't remember anything about—anything of what he said?"

As Hank shook his head, Dennis considered reminding his friend.

But was Bailey real? Or was that made up? Was all of it made up? Just like going to the bridge and seeing Hank there and being pushed off by him.

"Do you remember where you went?"

His friend stretched and cursed. "I'm tellin' you, man, it's black. Gone. Bye-bye. I don't remember anything."

"But you saw the guy."

"Yeah. But I'll tell you this, that wasn't any ghost."

"How do you know?"

Hank shook his head. "That guy should be selling Girl

Scout cookies. Well, actually, no, he shouldn't. He's a punk. He's one of your crazy fans who somehow feels warm and fuzzy when he's around you."

"He keeps threatening me."

"Then tell the cops."

"I've told Ryan."

"No, I mean tell someone real. Ryan is a boy with a badge. He's not going to do anything."

Tell him you're scared more than you've ever been before and that you don't know what to do or where to go. Tell him.

But instead Dennis said nothing, sipping coffee and waiting for the next horrific thing to knock at his door.

3.

He'd always said that one day he was going to reread his books. But deep down the task seemed tedious. And even worse, he feared he would get through the books and be bored and unimpressed.

Dennis wasn't bored or unimpressed as he knelt on the carpet in his office and paged through his novels. He needed to know what to expect. To have some idea of what might be coming.

There was his first horror novel, which he remembered quite well, the bold title of *Breathe* calling out to him. He followed in order of publication: *Echoes*, his haunted house story; *Marooned*, his stranded group that meets an alien entity story; *Sorrow*, the serial killer tale; then *Run Like Hell*, about a man demon possessed. He flipped through *Fearless*, which he couldn't remember much of.

And right there in the middle of the book, he found it.

The scene.

A few minutes turned into half an hour as Dennis found himself reading his own prose in a new way.

The scene involved his main character digging a hole in the back of his yard because of feeling "called" to do so. The hole eventually served as a grave for a crazy character killed by the main character.

As he read, picturing Cillian digging the hole, he wondered if Cillian was taunting him with this, mimicking a scene from one of his books.

Dennis came across something that gave him goose bumps. He swallowed and reread it. Thomas, the main character, spoke to the man he was about to kill. *"I'd say it's big enough for a man your size, wouldn't you?"* These were the exact words Cillian had used.

He's mocking you. He's playing with your mind. Don't you get it?

But why?

So what if Cillian picked a scene from one of his books and reenacted it?

During the course of an hour, Dennis compiled his notes:

Girl on the bridge——Breathe
Whatever I saw in Home Depot——Scarecrow
Being haunted in my house——Echoes
Hank flipping out on me——Marooned
Guy digging a grave in backyard——Fearless
Being pushed off bridge——Run Like Hell

Dennis studied the list.

He'd included six books.

Yet he had nine scattered on the floor in front of him.

There was *Sorrow*, his first serial killer novel. Then *Us and Them*, his fantasy thriller that had taken a critical beating. And *The Thin Ice*, another serial killer novel.

Two novels about serial killers and a fantasy left.

Then he thought of the novel he hadn't included.

Empty Spaces.

The book Cillian wrote.

He thought back to that book, to typing it onto his computer. He knew *Empty Spaces* too well, even if it wasn't his own.

Dennis remembered the ending.

And a sickening terror filled him.

He rushed out of the room toward the phone.

Something needed to be done.

He had to protect Audrey.

4.

He called her cell and got nothing.

For the next half hour, he proceeded to call Audrey's roommate, campus security, the local police, and some guy who lived in her dorm. Relief filled him as the phone in his hand rang.

"What are you doing, Dad?" Audrey's breathless voice called out.

It sounded like she was jogging.

"Where are you?" Dennis asked.

"Where are you? The insane asylum?"

"It sounds loud wherever you are."

"I just got three calls—all from people saying my father is freaking out."

"Are you okay?"

"I'm fine. Are you okay?"

"Audrey, there are things—look, even if I tried to tell you everything, I wouldn't be able to. But some things have happened, and I'm really worried."

"I actually had some sheriff call me up. Dad, what's going on?"

How could he tell her? How could he even begin to tell her?

"You just—this guy who's been harassing me. He's dangerous, Audrey. And I'm afraid—I'm not sure what he might do. All I know is that I'm coming out to Biola. I need to make sure—"

"Dad. You can't."

"I can't what?"

"You can't come out here. Not now."

"It doesn't matter if it's not a good time. This is serious, Audrey. I'm not going crazy. I'm scared."

"See—this is why. I'm smart. You know that?"

"What are you talking about?"

"Dad—well, I was going to surprise you, but oh well." Audrey laughed.

How can she be laughing? There's nothing to laugh about. "What?"

"I knew you were—I knew things were not going well. I've been worried about you. And see—you're proving me right. I did the right thing."

"What'd you do?"

"I'm at O'Hare."

For a second he thought he had misheard her.

"What?"

"Yeah."

"Stop laughing. What are you talking about?"

"I was able to get out of a couple of my classes, so I booked an earlier flight. I just got in."

"You're here—now?"

It was both a glorious and terrifying thought.

"Yeah."

"How are you getting home?"

"Mitch is picking me up."

"Oh, he is, huh?"

Mitch was Audrey's quasi-boyfriend during her senior year. They went to different colleges and played things off as being "cool" even though it was obvious they both really liked each other.

"You're not playing a prank on your father?"

"No. But I was going to show up on your doorstep in the middle of the night."

"I wouldn't do that. Not now."

She laughed, but she didn't know he wasn't kidding.

The panic that filled Dennis grew into something more.

A deep, heavy dread.

They talked plans even as Dennis wondered if his phone was bugged or if ghosts could listen in on conversations or if Cillian was in the closet.

"We're going to grab a bite to eat on the way, hope you don't mind."

"Just get here quickly, okay? And next time tell your father."

"I assumed you'd be happy."

"I'm ecstatic. Just . . ." He wanted to tell her to beware of guys with axes and who looked pale as the dead. "Have fun. I'll see you soon." He hung up and sat back in his chair, thinking, wondering, fearing he was being watched.

Everything changed now that Audrey was coming home. He couldn't tell her the full truth. No way. But he needed to protect her. To shield her from whatever might be after her.

Ghosts can't hurt and can't kill. They can only haunt. He kept telling himself this over and over, even as the e-mail popped onto his screen.

Dennis already knew who it was from. He didn't need to check.

Welcome home, Audrey. Just in time for Halloween.
And just like everything plays out in *Empty Spaces*.
Have you read that book, Dennis? The critics say it's pretty good.

October 29, 2009

It's seven thirty on Thursday morning. He's been to Harner's Restaurant before, right next to the Fox River, serving good meals at cheap prices.

But he's not here for the food.

He's here to watch.

Bob followed them this morning, completely unnoticed. He sits at a table where he can see the girl.

She doesn't notice him. Nobody does.

The girl has long arms and long legs and a long neck. He ponders this as he eats his breakfast, as he pours the syrup on his blueberry pancakes, as he sips his coffee, as his large hand surrounds the cup.

She wears slim jeans and high-heeled boots and a fitted shirt.

She smiles at the boy across from her.

They might be late teens, early twenties. She laughs like a little girl. The boy stares like a little boy.

He watches them as he eats.

His fork slices through the soft skin of the pancakes, the blueberries dripping.

And he waits a little longer this morning, getting one more refill than his usual two, having two more creams than his usual one, taking an extra couple seconds stirring the cream with his spoon.

She doesn't know that he watches her.

And she doesn't know that soon he'll kill her father.

And soon after that, despite what the voices told him, he will kill her.

When the young couple leaves, he leaves with them, tossing a distant good-bye to the waitress named Kay. He walks out into the parking lot to see the car driving by. It's a white Ford Mustang. He studies the license plate, remembering the numbers.

The car turns left and he stares after it, studying the car to remember what it looks like.

He thinks of their pretty faces, their smiles, their love of life.

And he knows he will see them again. Sometime very soon.

The Thin Ice

—Den. Wake up. Wake up.

—Huh?

—Something's wrong.

—What?

—It's Audrey. I can't find her.

—Find her where?

—She's missing.

—What?

—I've searched the whole house.

Dennis woke up on the couch downstairs, the Oberweis cups from last night's ice cream shakes still on the table, the television still on, the .38 still under the seat cushion. He was about to run up to see if Audrey was there when he realized Lucy hadn't whispered to him and Audrey wasn't missing. He had just been dreaming of when she had snuck out of her room one morning to go inside the garage to look for hidden birthday presents. She was only five years old, but it had shaken him and Lucy.

It didn't matter if Audrey was five or twenty-five. Nobody was taking her anywhere.

Last night had been fun. A vanilla shake from Oberweis Dairy only made Audrey more animated, and they stayed up late talking about school and Mom and the empty house and books and more school. Dennis didn't say much about writing. There wasn't much to talk about.

He knew Audrey was sleeping in this morning. So he was surprised to find a note in the kitchen. At first he knew who it was from. Cillian. But instead the note was in his daughter's cursive:

Didn't want to wake you. I'm heading to Harner's for breakfast with Mitch. We'll be a while. See you soon.
  A
  PS—You know there are beds in the house? ☺

He loved Audrey's sense of humor. He also loved knowing she was probably worried around the stiffness in his back and neck from sleeping on the couch. He couldn't believe he hadn't heard her this morning.

You sleep better when Audrey's home.

Dennis started the coffee and decided to call Audrey to say good morning. Then he thought twice about it, deciding to give her a little space.

2.

"So how is Mitch?"

Audrey smiled, her wavy hair bouncing as she moved around the kitchen. The girl never stopped. She had a drive just like . . .

Just like you used to have before there was no need to have a drive anymore.

"He's fine."

"Just fine?"

"Don't give me that. There's nothing there."

"Good to hear that."

"But that doesn't mean there can't be."

Dennis asked if she had any plans while she was here.

"I've called several friends. I won't be in your hair."

"I want you to be in my 'hair.'"

"That sounds weird."

"You know what I mean," Dennis said.

"Yeah, but I have a life too, you know."

"Okay. But my time is your time."

"I want to go see her."

Dennis held her eyes for a long moment, then looked away. He knew what she was talking about. It had been a long time since he had gone to Lucy's grave with Audrey. Or even on his own.

"Okay."

"Will you come?"

"Yes."

"Last time you didn't."

"I know. I will. I promise."

"She might be gone, but she's never leaving us, you know. There are reminders of her every day of my life."

"Isn't that something I should say to you?" he asked as he walked over and put his arm around her.

"Probably, but you're not good at the sentimental stuff. Blood and guts. That's your specialty."

"What a legacy," Dennis said, rolling his eyes.

3.

Blood and guts.

He could hear Audrey's words in his head. That was his specialty. At least it used to be.

After spending an hour persuading him to let her go, Audrey had gone out to see one of her friends. He wanted to warn her but didn't know what to say. *"Stay away from any ghosts you see."* She would be more worried about him than ever before. All he was able to do was tell her to come home quickly.

As Dennis sat in his office worrying, staring at the blank screen, the familiar routine mildly comforting even though he had nothing he wanted to write about—his e-mail inbox began to fill, the pings providing yet another distraction. When there were twelve waiting to be read, he decided to check them.

He knew who they were from.

All dozen e-mails were from Demonsaint4424@gmail.com. Some were simple:

Busy Dennis?

Others had profanities, hundreds of times over. One came with an attached snapshot of that afternoon, taken in the kitchen as Dennis spoke with his daughter.

He's just toying with you, that's all. Just ignore it. Ignore the e-mails and Cillian.

Dennis forced himself to start focusing on his novel. He typed something just to prove he could at least do that.

```
Mary had a little lamb, her fleece was white
as snow. Sometimes if you stub your foot,
you'll get a big fat toe.
```

Dennis continued on with this gibberish, reassuring himself that at least he could type, he could spell, he could complete whole sentences.

And then the tapping stopped.

His middle finger pressed *I* and stayed there. He couldn't release it. The computer followed his command.

IIIIIIIIIIIIIIIIIIIIIIIIIIIIIIIIIIIIIIIIIIIIIIIIIIIIIIIIIIIIIIIIIIIIIIIIIIIIIIIIIII

He glanced and saw the caps-lock key lit. He tried desperately to remove his finger from the *I*, but it wouldn't come off. It was stuck, some unseen force holding it there. Slowly, one by one, as he tried to wiggle free of the wireless keyboard pad, his fingers found themselves locked onto letters.

IIIIIIIIIIWWWWWWWWWWWWWWWWWWWWWWWWW
WWWWWWWWAAAAAAAAAAAAAAAAAAAAAAAAAAAA
AAANNNNNNNNNNNNNNNNNNNNNNNNNNNNNNNNN
NNNNNNNNNNNNTTTTTTTTTTTTTTTTTTTTTTTTT
TTTTTTTTTTTTTTTTTTTTUUUUUUUUUUUUUUUUU
UUUUUUUUUUUUUUUUUUUUUUUUUUUUUUUUUUUU
UUUUUUUUUUUUUUUUUUUUUTTTTTTTTTTTTTTT
TTTTTTTTTTTTTTTTTTTTTTTTTTTTTTTTTTTTTT
TTTTOOOOOOOOOOOOOOOOOOOOOOOOOOOOOOOO
OOOOOOOOOOOOOOOOOOOOOOOOOOOOOOOOOOOO
OOOOOOOOODDDDDDDDDDDDDDDDDDDDDDDDDDI
IIIIIIIIIIIIIIIIIIIIIIIIIIIIIIIIIIIIIIIIIIIEEEEEEEEEEEEEEEE

And as the letters continued forming, he stood and tried to jerk the keyboard away. But it was stuck. He shook his arms up and away from his chest and even used his knee to brace against the keyboard.

This is insane.

He tried to break the keyboard in half, but it suddenly became heavier and started to glow.

This is all in your mind, Dennis. Nothing is happening. Your fingers aren't superglued to the keyboard.

But a ripping pain told him otherwise.

His face winced, and he screamed. The wireless pad had turned into a red, glowing blade, a long knife that looked like it had just been taken out of the fire.

He wailed and jerked his arms and heard his skin sizzling and saw pieces of flesh dripping off the knife.

And as he screamed and shut his eyes, he collapsed to the carpeted floor.

4.

This is all in your mind.

But the sickly pink and red hands said otherwise.

He could barely dial 911. Dennis held the phone between

his chin and shoulder, his hands throbbing, shaking, his entire body shuddering.

This is not real. You're going to wake up any moment now.

But he already had woken up. And he had found his keyboard monitor split in half across the carpet. The burns on his hands were real. The tears lining his face were real. The paramedics who arrived were real. The bandages placed over his hands were real. The ride to the hospital was real.

His stomach rolled and ached, his body shaking, and it wasn't because of the pain. It was because of fear. He would have thrown up if he hadn't already done so.

The snarling cry of terror filled his heart and his mind and his soul. And he had no idea what to do about it. Not anymore.

5.

Maybe this is what really happens.

You find yourself staring at the keyboard, your fingers unmoving.

Then you stand up, holding the wireless pad with fingers that have control but a mind that doesn't. You shake and rattle and roll but nothing happens because you don't let it happen. Then you crack the monitor in half and walk out.

You go downstairs and turn on a burner on your stove. Then, as the gas flames warm the black iron grill, you pick it up and sear your hands and scream and wail and imagine that you're holding your keyboard.

This of course is the only logical explanation because fingers don't just get *magically* stuck to keyboards. And keyboards don't suddenly get *magically* turned into hot molten knives. And minds don't suddenly just go loopy.

It takes a long time for a mind to melt away.

Say, nine books or so.

That's when the imagination turns on you like a tidal wave. And when you're forced to lie to the doctors about your third-degree burns, the same way you're going to have to lie to your daughter and everyone else.

The same way you'll lie to yourself that you actually turned on the stove because you know for an absolute positive fact that you didn't.

The only thing you did was write a book about a killer who liked burning things, especially his victims, and he would often work on them slowly and deliberately.

Many times starting with their hands . . .

Rain caresses his forehead, his cheeks, the back of his neck. For a moment Bob stops, looking off across the fields to the highway in the distance. Flickers of light shine from moving cars. He's alone for miles. Nobody will ever see the hole he just dug. Nobody will ever dig up the two bodies he has thrown into it.

There is already a pool of water forming at the base of the hole, where the trash bags lay.

He decided to give them a resting place. They were his parents. Whatever that meant, it meant something different. The regular place he put bodies—the stalls in the barn—just didn't seem to fit. This hole in the middle of nowhere fit. They came from nowhere and ended up nowhere.

Lightning lights up the ground. Behind him are the small house and the big barn.

His back aches, but he piles the mud and dirt back into the hole.

His hands are blistered and raw.

But he knows their work is not done. Not yet.

As he digs he thinks of her, he thinks of them.

He will soon be heading back to town and to the life that awaits him there.

Wife and Mother

1.

Dennis awoke with a deep ache. Even with pain meds he hadn't been able to sleep well. His body burned one minute and shivered the next. He sat up and looked at the bandages on his hands. The thought that ran through his mind had nothing to do with his hands or the fact that he might be losing his mind. It wasn't about the ghosts or the paranormal or the ache or his writer's block.

It was about Lucy.

She passed away a year ago.

That was why Audrey was home.

That was what October 30 would always mean.

And the pain that beat inside him was worse than any third-degree burn could be.

He looked at the photo of her smiling at the age of thirty-five, greeting him in the photo like she did every morning. He delicately grabbed a T-shirt out of the dresser, walked into the bathroom, and examined himself in the mirror. The bags under his eyes said enough, and if they could be unpacked they would say more. His eyes were beginning to look more withdrawn than resilient.

He found some jeans, and his eye caught the plaque Lucy

had put up many years ago, one of the many memories he passed by every day of his life.

EVERY DAY IS A GIFT

He looked at the plaque long and hard, then sat down by the big bathtub that had gone unused for a year. Dennis stared at the plaque as if someone had just hung it there.

I hope you're not up there, looking down at me, not like this, he thought. *Because if you are, you've seen everything that's happened and you probably can't help but be disappointed.*

A deep throb made him wince. He stood up and found some more pills to swallow.

2.

"How are you feeling today?"

"Good," Dennis said, lying to Audrey.

He had called her from the hospital yesterday with assurances that he was okay. Even though he told her not to come, Audrey had come to Delnor Hospital with her friend Natalie to make sure he was okay. The bandages on his hand convinced her it wasn't quite the tiny household mishap he'd said it was. And even after asking half a dozen times if he was telling her the truth, Dennis never wavered.

"I was an idiot for grabbing the grates. I thought the burners were off."

"But how would you think that?" Audrey kept asking.

She didn't understand such a stupid thing because he hadn't done something stupid. But what was he supposed to say?

"I was typing and my computer suddenly became glued to my fingers, then became hot as molten lava."

She would think he was losing his mind, that too many horror stories were turning his brain into Jell-O, the kind they feed you at hospitals.

So he stuck with the explanation and continued even this morning.

"Did you sleep okay?" Audrey asked.

"Well enough."

He hated lying to her, but he didn't want her to worry.

Audrey kicked him out of the kitchen. "I'm making the coffee because I like how I make it better than you. And I'm cooking breakfast. You've lost all your privileges in the kitchen."

He nodded, seeing if he could even lift the remote. The bandages didn't allow him to pick things up. He had to scoop them in his palms.

Audrey watched him as he tried.

"Dad?"

He looked at her, saw the same few freckles Lucy used to have, those dark eyes looking at him with concern.

"What happened to you? What's really going on?"

Tell her. Just tell her.

"Audrey, look—it's complicated."

"Are you okay? I'm worried about you. Not just your hands but *you*."

"Don't be. I'm fine. I am."

"But *what* happened? Did you try to do that to yourself?"

"No. Of course not. Audrey, look at me. I'd never do anything like that."

"I just thought—with Mom's anniversary—that maybe . . ."

He came over and put his arms around her. "No. I didn't do this. I swear. I'd never do anything to hurt myself or hurt you."

Audrey started crying, and Dennis knew it wasn't just for him.

"One year," was all she said.

It was all she had to.

3.

Does it matter what one wears to a gravesite?

Do the dead watch, and if they do, why visit the cold, unmoving stone that rests above their decomposing human remains?

Does a lack of tears mean a lack of feeling?

"Dad?"

"I'm coming."

But what Dennis was doing was sitting in the Volvo SUV they'd picked up earlier that morning. It was as if nothing had touched it, the work on it was that good. He couldn't help hoping his hands would turn out the same way.

Now he couldn't get himself to get out of the car, even as Audrey stood outside the cracked window.

He managed to climb out and follow her.

Lucy had told him that she didn't really care where she was buried. Both of her parents were buried in the hometown they grew up in: Elgin, Illinois. She eventually decided to be buried in the small cemetery where her parents were, in the plot next to theirs.

Burying her anywhere hadn't seemed right, just like the dirt that went over her casket or the cries from people he'd never seen or met. Nothing about the way they said good-bye or the way she died so soon or the way the color of the sun was slightly different after she passed was *right*, nor would it ever be right.

The only reason Dennis was here today was because of Audrey.

But that's not true, is it, Dennis?

He knew he needed to be here, that the teeny, tiny little glimmer of hope that Lucy still lived on mattered and meant something, that it meant enough for him to come back and pay respect and remember the woman he fell in love with and would always love.

Even the words on her tombstone didn't feel right.

Lucy Nessa Shore
March 18, 1957—October 30, 2008
Cherished Wife and Mother

It felt wrong. Four words to describe someone. It was like having to describe a book he'd spent three years working on in just three sentences, yet it was a thousand times worse.

Standing there, his daughter in his arms, sunshine spilling through the trees, the grass still green around the stone, Dennis thought of Lucy.

I could write books the rest of my life and never sum up the joy and goodness of your soul, Lucy.

Audrey wasn't emotional, and neither was he. The cry earlier that morning had gotten it out for his daughter.

Where are your tears, Dennis? They've been strangely missing for a long time, haven't they? Are your tear ducts broken, just like your heart?

A distant memory floated by like a flower petal blowing in the wind.

It was when his first book got published.

The best feeling wasn't holding the book in his hand or flipping through the pages or seeing his name in bold print.

It was seeing Lucy's face when he gave her the first copy, signed.

Her eyes lit up, her face so strong and so proud, her expression saying more than words ever could even though she tried.

"I'm so happy for you. Just remember us little people when you make it big. And you will, Dennis. I know you will."

Even though his first two books tanked, Lucy's faith never wavered, not one bit.

She was so good, in a thousand different ways.

"Dad?"

"Yeah."

"What are you thinking?"

He sighed. "Just thinking about how she never stopped believing in me, even when I did. Even when I almost threw it all in."

"Threw what in?"

"The writing."

"I didn't know that."

"She encouraged me even after my first two books went nowhere. She got me to write *Breathe* when I was contemplating giving up the notion of being a writer."

"She never doubted either of us."

"I know. I think I have enough doubt for all of us."

"Really? You don't ever show it."

Dennis nodded, staring at Audrey. "I mask it. I bury it in words and stories. All the angst in here," he said, tapping his heart, "goes into those stories."

"Does that get rid of it?"

"No. I don't know if anything ever does."

"Mom would disagree."

"Yes, she would. And you know, maybe—maybe she was right."

"Well, if she *was* right, then she still is."

Dennis smiled. Audrey took after him, but she was still both of them, still so much of Lucy that he felt fortunate to be part of her life.

"You think she sees us right now?"

"Yeah," Audrey said. "And she's wondering why your hands look like they're auditioning for a mummy movie."

And then, out of the blue, like when a story took an unexpected turn and his fingers kept going and his mind had to try to keep in stride with them, Dennis spoke out loud:

"I still love you, Lucy."

Audrey smiled and seemed relieved to hear him say that. "Me too, Mom."

The wind picked up as if in answer to their words.

4.

Garbage strewn all over their lawn greeted them back home, ruining the moments shared earlier.

For a second Dennis flashed back to the night he and Maureen found pages of his books scattered everywhere. But this was different. These scraps and pieces were actual garbage—plastic bags, crunched-up boxes, an old glove, paper of all sorts, a soup can.

"I can't believe how much garbage that family has." Dennis would have normally gripped the steering wheel in anger, but his bandaged hands wouldn't allow him to. The anger still burnt inside him. *This is ridiculous.*

As he opened the SUV door, Dennis realized how much the wind had been picking up. Audrey's hair blew around her face.

He had to do something about this.

But as he reached for the cell phone in his pocket, he realized he hadn't carried it with him. He was unable to pick the thing up.

He used the regular phone inside.

Somebody needed to talk to the neighbors, someone who would get their attention.

He called Ryan.

5.

Do you see me, Lucy?

Dennis bolted the front door and proceeded to check the other doors in his house. It had been half an hour since he kissed Audrey on the cheek and said good night. Knowing she was there in the house with him made some of the tension ease.

He couldn't stop thinking about Lucy.

The day had evaporated since they came back from the cemetery. Audrey had spent the afternoon shopping. During that time Ryan had tried to talk to the neighbors about the garbage. The deputy told him nobody was home, but he would check back with them later.

Now, in the silence of the house, life almost seemed normal.

Yet he couldn't shake the feeling that he was being watched.

Is it you?

If ghosts existed, why couldn't angels exist as well?

He wanted to believe. He wanted to tear down the walls and find peace, but he was afraid that after ripping them down he'd find nothing but emptiness.

Can you see these thoughts swirling in my mind, Lucy?

He needed to know. He needed to see, to touch, to really, truly know she was there.

I'd give anything to see you again.

Turning off the light, he walked upstairs, wondering what lurked outside in the darkness.

Wondering if he could keep the ghosts out. For just one more night.

The glass is twisted, deformed, wavering. The rain creates ugly, scowling faces on it. In the dark room, Bob looks through the window across the yard and driveway to the house next door.

He stands and stares, watching the lights from the white sports car shut off as it coasts into the driveway.

He is still dirty, his boots muddy, his jeans stained, his hands crusted over.

The sheet and the bed behind him remain covered in blood. His parents' blood. He tells himself he needs to throw the sheets away just like he threw his parents away.

Lightning exposes everything for a brief second. He sees the girl with long hair and long legs scampering down the driveway and getting into the car. Then the car backs quietly down the driveway, its lights still off.

He eyes the sledgehammer in his hand.

He thinks about walking downstairs and through the door and across the lawn and pounding in the door and then pounding whatever he finds next. The thought of lifting this heavy hammer over his head and wailing away gives him a searing, stretching sensation.

But he wants something else.

He wants her.

And nobody and no voice can stop him. Not now.

Too Late

1.

The bedroom door swung open and pounded against the wall as light blitzed the bedroom. Dennis jerked up and saw the shadowy outline through foggy eyes.

It was Cillian. And he looked angry.

Dennis pointed the .38 at him.

"You fool," Cillian told him.

"What?"

"You stupid, stupid fool."

"Get out of my house."

"Go ahead. Shoot me. Don't you get it, Dennis? I'm dead."

Dennis heard the steady rain outside. It was 2:30 a.m.

"What are you doing here?" Dennis said in a low voice, not wanting to awaken Audrey.

"Don't worry, she's not here."

"What?"

"Yeah, she snuck out. And now. Now it's all over. It's done. Just like in *Sorrow*."

"What's done?" Dennis bolted out of bed and faced Cillian. "Is this another game?"

"It doesn't do me any good if she dies. Because then she'll be in a better place."

Dennis called out Audrey's name, but Cillian remained immobile in front of him, glaring at him. Dennis grabbed him by the throat.

"Don't you get it? It's too late," Cillian choked out. "Too late for her. Even spirits don't have total control. You want to control everything—the whole world—but you can't. You can't control life and death and you can't control the afterlife and even when your own daughter is *right* under your nose, you let her slip away. Into this evil, atrocious world."

Cillian started laughing, even as Dennis dropped him and tore through the open door, running down the hallway to her room.

But just as he feared—just as Cillian had said—she was gone.

No.

He sprinted downstairs, almost falling on the last two steps, calling out her name, wanting this to be a dream, a nightmare he would wake up from.

"Audrey!"

But she wasn't anywhere.

And when Dennis went back upstairs, he couldn't find Cillian anywhere either.

What had he done to her?

Dennis opened the back door and went outside in the rain.

Dear God no.

"Audrey!" he yelled into the darkness.

But she was gone. Just like Cillian.

"Now it's all over. It's done. Just like in Sorrow.*"*

Dennis suddenly understood.

He knew.

Calling the cops wouldn't help. They'd think he was crazy.

This was exactly how things happened in the story.

Dennis raced to find a copy of *Sorrow*. He found a hardcover in his office, shaking uncontrollably as he leafed through the book.

2.

He wasn't sure what page it was. But it was somewhere late in the story. On a night just like this. In a setting very much like this. Rain fell, a cliché in a clichéd story, except this wasn't a cliché. It was real. The rain was real and the killer was real and his daughter was really missing.

The killer was following her.

And the killer was right there.

Right next door.

1:12 a.m. Halloween

The white Mustang is parked in front of a single family house. A light is on in the main room.

He peers into a window and sees the two of them talking in earnest. The boy and the girl. He doesn't see anybody else, nor does he see any other cars.

His hand grips the pipe wrench as he tries the door handle.

They are stupid to leave the door unlocked. Of course he could deal with it if the lock was secure. This just makes it easier.

He opens the door and startles them. The guy stands up and moves toward him.

"I've been looking for you two . . ."

"Look, man, you can't just—"

But that is all the guy can say before the pipe wrench ends the conversation and sends him crashing backward into a table and a lamp.

She screams. He goes over and makes sure the guy won't say anything, won't harm him. And then he glances at the girl, smiling. The screams are louder now, her body running into another room.

He follows.

Part Four

**All You Create
All You Destroy**

Control

1.

Writing *Breathe* brought little Abby back to life, at least temporarily, at least long enough to allow him to say what he needed to say to her, to tell her good-bye.

Writing *Echoes* helped make sense of what they experienced in that haunted house, of the nightmares Lucy and he had, of the loss of faith his wife dealt with afterward.

Writing *Marooned* helped him deal with how isolated and remote he felt after becoming a bestselling author just as his wife was going through her battles with faith issues.

And writing *Sorrow* helped him try to make sense of the evil in this world, of why bad things happen to good people, and finally allowed him to decide once and for all that God did not exist and never had.

He tried to control life as best he could. But he realized that in doing so—in trying to control as much as possible—he'd lost control over everything. Those first books—they had taken so much that ever since then he'd written stories just to scare and entertain. But they weren't written for himself, weren't written out of curiosity and fear and failure. They were written with a formula. And that was all.

What he had never told Audrey was this. That his wife had

left him. For a short time in 2003. And she had given him an ultimatum.

She wanted him back. She wanted his heart and soul. He'd given too much of it to his stories so there was nothing left.

And now, in the empty kitchen with the phone in his hand, Dennis thought of this. As the phone rang and his mind reeled and his body shook, he thought of this.

You've tried to control it all, haven't you, Dennis? And even when she died, you tried to control that. You tried to suppress your grief and be everything to Audrey. And you tried to manage your writing by stealing something that wasn't yours. And even now, even up to this point, you still had to be the man in charge, the guy in control. You needed to keep things from Audrey and CONTROL them. And look what that got you.

He had tried Audrey's cell but had only gotten voice mail. He spoke with someone at the police station, reporting Audrey's disappearance. They told him to give it at least twenty-four hours. They told him more, but he didn't have time to listen. He left a message for Ryan. And now he was leaving a message for Hank.

Where is everybody?

Scattered throughout the kitchen were pages. Torn pages from *Sorrow*. Torn pages that told a story he didn't want to continue living out.

It ended in death.

But even after everything that had happened, Dennis believed he could change the ending.

He could rewrite it.

He knew what had to be done.

You can't control fate and destiny, Dennis. You can't raise the dead. And you can't win.

Dennis gritted his teeth and felt sick, helpless. He couldn't do anything right now.

I don't know where she is. I've tried her cell, and it's not working. She left with her purse but without saying anything else.

He had looked for any contact information for Mitch. But there was nothing.

Go next door. That's where the killer is.

But maybe that was crazy.

What's crazy and what's not?

The story pages he had read—skimmed over in hysteria—had told him enough. He needed to go to the next-door neighbors' house.

He didn't bother trying to find the handgun. He would grab the hatchet on the way over there.

The story he had read had him dying, so what was the point?

If Audrey dies, then I don't care. My life is not worth living. Life is as empty as I've thought it to be.

He opened the door and headed out through the garage.

If he were a praying man, this would be one of those moments.

And if he believed in such things, he would ask God to watch over him.

But Cillian was right on one thing: God had abandoned this family long ago, leaving nothing in his place.

Nothing at all.

2.

Walking through the darkness, under trees that prevented the steady rain from dousing him, Dennis closed his eyes and was transported back in time.

It was one of those Saturday mornings with Dennis at his computer working on a spreadsheet of the family financials, before writing had even entered his life.

But it came, not with a strong breeze but with the gentle laughter of a mother and her child.

It was an April morning, and Dennis was looking outside at the thick pine trees in the backyard of their town house. For a second, he heard cackling. He turned off his stereo to hear

Lucy laughing with Audrey, who was only fourteen months old.

In his home office, a thirty-one-year-old Dennis Shore who nobody had ever heard of or read or interviewed or reviewed sat in his office smiling, with tears coming to his eyes.

And it was there at that moment that an idea hit him, that would be the start of the first novel he would ever write.

It wasn't because he wanted his name in lights or because he wanted to make a lot of money.

It was because he was moved. And because he wanted to document it. He wanted to remember it. He wanted to experience it again.

Sometimes it's that simple. Sometimes you don't need a literary streak of lightning or a voice from the artistic heavens. Sometimes you just need a moment like that, when the world moves you.

Dennis remembered that as he walked over to the neighbors' house this fall day twenty years later. *That* was why he wrote. *That* was what motivated him. Without memories like those, there would be no reason to write. Without emotions like those, there would be no story to tell. Without experiencing love, there would be no way to share it.

Life is a breath, a blink.

He was afraid. Not of what he would find in the house, what monster might await him, but he was afraid that Audrey was gone just like her mother.

And if so, the canvas would remain eternally white, a sea of a thousand questions unanswered.

And it would be my fault. All of this. Every bit of it is my fault.

Dennis took a breath and approached the door.

"Words have power," Lucy once told him. "You have an amazing gift, Dennis. An amazing opportunity to do something with that gift. You can create magic."

All the magic and words in the world couldn't bring her back.

So the magic and the words stopped.

It was that simple.

Are you there? Can you see me down here?

He reached the door.

If you are, help me. Help me, Lucy.

3.

He rang the doorbell a third time, not hearing anything and unsure if it even worked. No light or sound or movement could be noticed.

Dennis held the hatchet in his hand, his shoulders and hair soaked from the rain. He pushed the button again.

Nobody's home.

But of course they weren't. That's what the story said.

Right, Dennis? You read it all, didn't you? Or at least the good parts.

He tried one more time to ring the doorbell, then he knocked on the door.

And as he did, the old wooden door inched open.

Just like the book said it would.

A gust of wind blew it open farther.

Nobody stood at the entrance. A wave of stench hit him.

"Hello?" Dennis called.

But nobody was there.

He glanced behind him, then ahead into the living room area that faced him.

Gripping the hatchet, Dennis stepped into the house.

He wondered if evil would really be there, like it had been on those pages he'd left strewn about his kitchen.

The pages that said he was going to die if he entered this house.

He glances at his hands and sees the chewed-off stubs of his fingertips, the gash on his thumb, the cut on his forearm, the remnants of the scar around his wrist. He grips the steering wheel as he drives through the black hole of night.

The scene he's driving away from is too messy, too revealing. And he knows it's time to leave.

It's time to make one last trip to the coffin of a home in Geneva and then leave for good. Leave and get far away. He's gone unnoticed for this long, but he's been too hungry, too anxious.

His pants are bloody, his cheek gashed from her fingernails. She fought him for a few moments. She had fight in her. But in the end it wasn't enough.

It never is.

The wiper blades hum as the wind blows his white hair.

He pulls into the driveway and passes by the familiar trees, sees the familiar house.

Then he notices the front door slightly open.

And he knows that the killing is not over yet on this night.

Sorrow

1.

Dennis breathed through his mouth.

The smell almost made him throw up. He didn't know if this was another one of Cillian's plans—luring him into this putrid place. All Dennis knew was that something—or someone—had died in this house. And even though everything in him knew he should get out of here, he needed to see if this house had anything to do with her disappearance. He needed to find Audrey.

He turned on a dull light. The hallway from the front door was littered with debris. Old magazines and newspapers. . . . He couldn't tell if the floor was carpeted or wooden. A crumpled shirt lay on the ground. Black stains (coffee, maybe, he hoped) speckled the aged, orange wallpaper. He saw an old dress shoe, dusty and curled. A fire pick. A baseball bat. A set of gloves. More paper. A plastic ball of—something.

Everything about the house seemed dark, the hall light casting a cold glow into the room. There wasn't any noise—nothing seemed alive in here.

You need to get out now.

But Dennis was afraid someone was in here. He thought of the messages he had left for Ryan.

What if he came in here? What would he find? What if . . .

He reached the end of the hallway and stopped at the dark doorway.

"Hello? Anybody there?"

Even with the hatchet in his hand, he didn't feel secure.

Because there are other forces at work, and they've already been killed. You can't kill them again.

"Anybody home?" he called out.

Dennis stepped into a gray, still room and felt for a light switch on the wall. Instead he bumped into something on the ground, some type of furniture. He could see outlines of furniture in this room, faint light spilling from behind him.

His hand eventually found a lamp. He tried it, but it didn't work.

"Hello?" he called, but his voice sounded weak and unsure.

He tried another lamp, and this one worked. The bulb poured flickering light into what appeared to be a living room.

A dusty brown couch faced him, a pillow coated with dark stains.

That's blood, Dennis. Get out of here.

He looked around, making sure no one was going to sneak up on him. The hatchet remained firm in his hand.

There were muddy tracks on the carpet and even on the couch. Another chair contained a torn arm, fabric spewing out and scattered all over the floor.

There were no pictures or decorations on the drab walls.

A television set sat on a small tray table. The TV had wobbly antennas. There was uneaten food still on paper plates, boxes with strange writing on them, old milk cartons, a brown sweater wrapped around something circular.

The filth in here is unimaginable.

His eyes burned. His skin itched. He needed to get out of this cloud of grime.

Another hallway appeared to lead to the back. A door nearby promised more filth.

Dennis knew these people harbored more than simple stench and refuse.

Something evil had happened here. He could feel it. He could see it. And he could smell it.

And without thinking, he called out her name.

"Audrey!"

Saying it weakened him, made this seem more real, more finite.

"Audrey?" The strange echo of his voice made his skin crawl.

As he left the room, he noticed something he could barely make out on the floor in the corner.

That's not—

He squinted his eyes and leaned forward, studying it.

Then he jerked backward and fell on his back, wiping his face and nose with his forearm and coughing.

No, not here. Don't do it. Don't throw up.

He stood and felt like he couldn't move. He wanted to simply vanish, to take a long, hot shower.

Is that really what I think it is?

But Dennis didn't want to find out. He didn't want to see if that belonged to someone. Because if it did, that meant the person was most surely dead.

He didn't bother turning off the lights.

As he hastened down the hallway, his eyes glanced around him uncontrollably. As he moved to swing open the front door, the hatchet still in hand, he glanced back to make sure someone wasn't following him.

His only mistake was not looking ahead to see if somebody was in the doorway.

2.

He saw blank eyes and a terrifying smile.

I've seen you before.

And then something moved and struck him into darkness.

3.

Breathe.

It jerks and moves and shifts and shakes.

Breathe, Den.

He tries. He isn't sure if his eyes are opened or closed. All he sees is blackness. He hears a rumbling.

Breathe.

He swallows and coughs and takes in air.

Then he breathes.

And nauseous pain comes back, and this time the darkness is from blacking out.

He knows someone is in the house.

So he waits outside.

And he watches.

And then he goes and stands by the door. He pulls it shut.

He is patient.

His hands and arms are covered in their blood, his fingernails torn, the skin on his knuckles shredded like beef, the veins in his forearms sticking out.

It was messy with the two of them.

He won't be as messy this time. This time it will be easier.

He waits, the wrench in his hands.

And when the door opens, he strikes methodically, carefully, hitting the side of the man's head and then striking his shoulder.

His neighbor, the author, falls to the ground. The big guy thinks of the kid, the one fascinated by this man, the one who talked about the writer, who dreamed about being one himself, who now comes to him only in whispers and screams.

The writer will be joining the kid very soon.

Empty Spaces

1.

His eyes opened to darkness.

A murky shroud wrapped itself around him. Dennis couldn't see anything more. His forehead beat like a mallet, and he tasted blood in his mouth. His body shook.

A wave of nausea hit him. But then his eyes grew heavy again and closed.

2.

This time he sucked in a breath first, warm and stale. He inhaled and tried to move. But his back ripped in pain, his hands burning, his legs lifeless.

Dennis moved his head, something—a tarp?—pressing against it. He lay on something cold and hard and grooved. He trembled but couldn't move. His hands and feet were tied together. He tried to scream but couldn't muster up enough strength to make much of a sound.

The darkness surrounded him. His eyes grew stronger, but they couldn't discern anything.

"Hello?" he screamed, but his voice grated against his dry throat.

It felt like the word echoed into nothing.

The pain in his back seared. Then came the jutting throb in his head.

He forced himself to breathe slowly, calmly. But he couldn't think. He couldn't figure this out.

Darkness fell over him again.

3.

Something jerked him up. And awake.

It was his hands. He couldn't feel his hands. They were still bound, still immobile.

Another jerk propelled Dennis forward. He couldn't feel anything below his waist, but he struggled until he fell into dirt.

He felt rain against his already wet, sweaty hair.

Wake up, Dennis. Wake up.

A bolt of lightning illuminated everything around him. Then all he could see was darkness. Flat, straight, empty darkness.

Where am I?

A towering figure came out of the darkness, gripping the wire that bound his hands. He crawled forward, his face crashing down into a puddle of mud.

A curse echoed around him.

The blackness swallowed him. For a moment that was all he knew. His hands and wrists burned as something yanked him up. He couldn't feel his legs but tried to shuffle on them anyway.

As Dennis was led somewhere—an empty path, a dirt road, an open, wet field?—he saw it.

At first his mind couldn't comprehend what he was looking at.

But then he did, and it cleared his mind, tore his heart.

The white Mustang.

It was Mitch's car. Audrey's Mitch. The car was latched to the back of a large truck.

And that means . . .

But he couldn't think that.

Just like in Sorrow *. . . after killing them, after killing both of them and disposing of their bodies, he drove the car out here. . . .*

Something pounded the back of his head, sending him to the ground. He lay there for a moment, able to think of only one thing.

Audrey.

She had gone off with Mitch. She had snuck out for the night.

But why?

There could be any number of reasons. Because she was in love. Because she wanted to blow off steam and talk about visiting her mother's grave earlier that day. Who knew?

But now . . .

He tried to say something, but he couldn't. His voice and tongue wouldn't cooperate.

A crack of thunder sounded. And again the world lit up, and he saw the hulking figure with white hair and a long glistening coat standing over him. And he was sure he saw the white Mustang.

No no no no no.

He wanted to cry out, but he couldn't. He wanted to run but couldn't feel his legs. He wanted to reach out and protect himself, but he couldn't move his hands.

No.

His body shook as everything in him started to die.

4.

The storm that smothered the night lit up the stall he'd been thrown into.

He was in a barn in the middle of nowhere. In the middle of flat nothing. And as the cold, pale light slipped in through the cracks, he took in his surroundings.

His heart and soul felt nothing. Slowly ticking away to nothingness.

He lay in a barn stall filled with dead bodies.

Even as he recognized where he was, and what surrounded him, he refused to let his mind go there.

I will get out of here. This is only temporary. This is only made up. This is not real.

But it felt and looked and sounded and smelled and tasted real.

His body shook and shivered. He was cold. But more than that, he was without hope.

She can't be dead. She can't be gone. Not like this. Not like this.

He couldn't think it. It couldn't be.

She left with him and now the car's there and it's all led to this. This is exactly what Cillian wrote about, what he said I could have prevented.

This was it. The end. The last book that would ever have his name on it, *Empty Spaces*, the book he stole from Cillian, the novel that ended with the protagonist dying in a barn . . .

This was Cillian's plan and always had been.

But his own life didn't matter. Not anymore.

"It's not my daughter. It can't be," he said to the darkness.

For the monster to hear. For the bodies around him to hear. For God or Lucy or Audrey or someone, anyone, to hear.

God, get me out of here. Help me, Lucy. Help me, God. Please. I can't, and I won't. I cannot do it alone, not without her.

He opened his eyes and saw the back of a head, dark short hair spilling out of the pile.

That's not her, but maybe just maybe . . .

But he stopped. He had already thrown up and there was nothing left inside him. His hands were bloody and wounded, his legs tied and useless.

I'm useless and have always been useless and I couldn't save her, not even after a dozen warnings. I've never had control, not ever.

He started to cry. Blood filled his mouth and dripped down his cheek as he wailed. Dennis Shore cried out, but his voice was frail. He pressed his arms against his chest to try to keep warm, and he knew that this would be the last night of his life.

I have so much more to do and say and so much more to give. So why was it so hard to find the words? Why? I have so many left.

He tasted salty tears.

This was death and hell and horror.

This is what you wanted, Cillian, and you won. You got it. Are you happy now? Are you happy, you evil waste of a life?

He bit his lip, mouthing the words, his voice gone, his life almost gone.

"Help me. Please help me."

And unseen in a small, square stall in a locked-up barn, surrounded by death and rot, Dennis curled into a ball and closed his eyes and cried.

5.

The last time he'd cried out like this was in an empty field west of his house, off a side road where he had stopped and parked the car and ripped open the door and finally dealt with his pain.

There wasn't any God above to yell at.

There wasn't a heaven above to dream about.

And there was no Lucy around anymore to protect.

Dennis held the picture he had given her.

Some kinda nonsense about this is what heaven should be, what our heaven should be. Nothing but a lie, a terrible awful deluded lie.

He was finally going to do something about it.

Us and Them.

That's what he had called it.

That's our heaven.

That's what he said before she died, but now she was dead and the photo meant nothing.

He cursed out loud and gritted his teeth and took the picture of the old couple and ripped it in half.

This doesn't exist and isn't real, and love is gone. Love is gone. Love is forever and ever gone.

And he took out the matches he had brought and tried to light the picture.

The first one went out. He cursed the wind.

The second one went out. He cursed the skies and the grass and didn't even realize he was barking at nobody and that tears streamed down his face.

The third one went out. This time he threw the matches across the field and took the picture in his hands and crumpled it.

On his knees, he looked at what he had done.

No, no. Don't, Dennis. Don't do this. This is a memory. This is what you gave her. This stands for something more, for something deep.

But he cursed at himself and his weak, sorry, sappy soul.

Dennis stood up and found the matches and this time was very careful and deliberate, guarding the match until it lit and caught the edge of the photograph.

And then it burned, flickering in flames, the color bleeding away, the edges turning to black lifeless ash.

He left it there. Scattered in the wind.

And back in the car he cried and cried and cried.

But nobody saw.

If there was a God above—*if*—then why would he take her? She was the stronger of the two, the cog behind the wheels, the one that gave so much to so many others. She believed in God while he didn't. If her faith was real, then why did that faith end up biting her?

I don't and will never, ever, ever understand.

In the car his body shivered, but he wasn't cold. His hands shook, but he wasn't nervous. He was sad. Bitterly, angrily, spitefully sad.

And the tears were different. They were desperate, vicious. Stored up for too long, tears gushed out.

All alone, he wept, his stomach clenching, his body numb, his eyes blind, his emotions spent.

And if God existed and heaven existed and Lucy floated around with them right now, Dennis hoped she could see him, hoped she could see how much he still loved her and missed her. Not to make her feel sad, but to make her know the sort of life she led, the sort of impact she left behind.

6.

And now, alone again, he dealt with the horrible, horrific truth that Lucy wasn't the only one gone.

That the only reminder of her left on this planet was gone too.

Shivering in the darkness, Dennis cried out for it not to be so.

7.

Lying in the cold black with all hope gone, Dennis heard a whisper. Even with the wind and the storm outside and his shivering breaths, Dennis could hear the voice clearly.

It wasn't Lucy or Audrey.

It was Cillian.

"None of us has control, Dennis. There is only one Creator. And one day, Dennis, one day, you'll find yourself on your knees, not cursing him but asking for forgiveness."

The voice didn't mock him, nor did it sound sympathetic.

It simply stated the words as facts.

There was a pause, then Cillian spoke again.

"But it looks like I'll get there before you do."

He ties the bag at the top, then loops it around to make another knot. The bag is light, about as light as the arm of someone twenty years old.

Bob sits in a chair in the middle of the room. His pants and shirt are soaked through. Even the leather of his boots is damp. All around him on this floor are plastic bags—hundreds of them, tied tightly and piled one on top of the other. On a wall behind him hang dozens of knives. Daggers, swords, carving knives, and cooking knives and stilettos and saws and scalpels.

Some are used. He likes to pick and choose. He keeps them all sharp.

The writer is in the barn, tied in the stall with the rest of them.

Bob will deal with him in a few moments. The sun will be coming up soon.

First he will clean this up. He will take all these bags—every one of them—and drop them off. All in different areas, all around the state. Nobody will know, and even if they're found, nobody will have an idea.

They will find Dennis and his daughter missing, and steps will lead them here. But he will be long gone.

The white bags all look clean, unlike his clothes and his hands.

He will do one more tonight, and then he will be finished.

Us and Them

He opens his eyes and sees the sky moving, the brilliant white plumes of clouds coating the tranquil blue. There is a cobblestone road in front of him, the walls of ancient buildings on each side. And in the distance, some hundred yards or so, an open window.

I know this place. I recognize this place.

Dennis starts to walk, wondering where he is, wondering what's happening.

I'm dreaming, and this is the place I've chosen to rest in.

But that doesn't feel exactly right. This doesn't feel like a dream.

He looks at his hands, and they look slightly different.

They don't look old and torn.

But of course they don't. This is his dream. He doesn't have the bandages on his hands and they look younger and he feels younger. He is desperately trying to cling to something, anything he can.

"Hello, down there," a voice says.

It's the voice of an angel. He looks up toward an open window and sees the unmistakable smile of his wife.

"Lucy?"

"You found me."

"I don't think I was exactly looking."

"Tell me something—what are you feeling? Right now?"

He looks up and sees the colors and the shape of the open window and he seems to remember something but he can't exactly say what.

"Déjà vu."

She nods. Her hair is much longer than he remembers it. "I'll be down in a minute."

And in a minute she is down, opening a door and greeting him with a beautiful smile.

"It's okay."

He can't remember where he was or what he was just doing, but he knows it was bad. He knows it was bad, and he doesn't want to return.

"Where am I?"

"You are safe, that's where you are."

And as hard as he tries, he can't remember. He can't think back.

All he knows is that this place—this is not his place. It's not his dream. It's not his reality.

"Take my hand."

She is the woman he married. She acts like she always did, but she resembles the twenty-something woman he couldn't keep his hands off of. The eyes look vibrant and young but also wise and wonderful.

This is my dream, and I've created her to be something more than she ever was or could be.

"You didn't picture me," she answers his thought.

"Then how come—what—"

"Take my hand," she says again, so he does.

And she leads him down the winding cobblestone street to an opening in the wall. There he sees plush trees and deep blue and sun reflecting off the giant lake. Wind blows flowers. Butterflies bounce around a field of gold.

"I'm imagining this, aren't I?"

"No."

"Then where am I?"

"You are in a barn two hours west of Chicago on an unnamed and unknown farm. You're bound and very close to dying."

"So what is this? A hallucination?"

She still grips his hand, her face so smooth, the smile so perfect.

"No. This, Dennis, is real. It's soft and it's peaceful and it's very much real."

"Is this heaven?"

She nods. "This is a snapshot of it."

"Are you real?"

"Yes. And even though I know you never told Audrey what I asked you to tell her, it still applies. It's still very much true."

He goes to hug her but she stands back. "No."

"Lucy . . ."

"Dennis, your life and your being and everything you've created are but a breath in the rest of time. But there is one thing that endures. One hope."

"Lucy—what—"

"It's love. And love can conquer anything, Dennis."

"Not this," he says. "Not this life and not with the evil that's out there."

"Terror is real, Dennis, but so is love. Love doesn't delight in evil but rejoices with the truth. It always protects, always trusts, always hopes, always perseveres."

"Is this made up?"

"No. The stories you write, they're made up. But they contain pearls of yourself. This place is not a dream or a mirage. It's real. As real as the love you still have inside."

"Then I want to stay here."

"You can't. You have to be invited, Dennis. And you have to

accept the invitation. And all of this—this madness, this darkness—is all part of you being called."

"I don't understand. Called to what?"

"Called to believe. Called to accept that life is not in your
control."

"But what about—what about Audrey—"

"You need to keep that love in your heart. That's what keeps
it beating."

He thinks for a moment but then winces, changing the
thought, unable to consider something so horrible here.

"I'm with you, know that. And know that you're not alone.
You've never been alone. Never."

He knows he could never create something like this, this
pure and this true. He's tried but over and over and over again
he fails because he is flawed.

"I don't want to go back."

"This is but a glimpse, an image you've been allowed to see.
Just like I was allowed to see."

"Why?"

"Because you're loved. And because there are those you love
who believe despite not having seen."

"I don't—"

She nudges his hand. "You're loved. So fight with that love
and don't give up. Don't stop. And always know I'm here."

Lucy, don't.

But he blinks and the lake and the trees and the sky and the
beauty all disappear.

And he finds himself in darkness again.

"Dennis."

Lucy, I don't want to leave you. Don't make me leave you.

"Dennis!"

*I love you and always will love you, and no matter what
happens . . .*

"Dennis, come on, man!"

I will be the man who loves you, the boy who fell in love with a girl.

"Dennis."

He opens his eyes again, and this time he finds himself even more surprised than he was when he saw Lucy.

He sees Hank and knows he's no longer in heaven.

5 a.m. Halloween

Bob sits on the chair, shirtless, his bare feet and bare chest not cold even in the frigid temperature of the house. Sweat runs down his hairy back; his hands grip the knife.

He is debating what to use. On the table in front of him are various tools.

The wind screams, and his house shakes.

There is a rattling, then a whine.

He doesn't notice where it comes from.

The blade he caresses cuts his finger, ever so slightly. But he knows it will do and it will do fine.

A shadow inches out of the back room, the storage room, the room where he keeps waste that he will eventually throw away.

For a long time Bob stares at the foot-long blade with fascination and awe. He doesn't hear the footsteps behind him, nor does he see the face of the man walking toward him.

But he does hear the loud creak in the floor. He turns slowly, not afraid, not surprised.

Bob has never seen the man before in his life. A red-headed man, burly and tough.

And white as a ghost.

As he is about to stand up, the intruder says something.

"What kind of sick perverted freak are you?"

Shaking his head, the redheaded man doesn't hesitate. The gun in his hand doesn't waver. The .38 he's holding doesn't shake. And the first bullet he fires hits Bob right in the chest.

He drops the blade and looks at the man.

"What have you done? Where is he? Tell me where he is right now!"

He starts to laugh, and the redheaded guy walks over to him and presses the gun against his forehead.

He is not afraid.

"Tell me where he is right now. I swear, tell me, you monster! You pig, tell me!"

Bob winces and laughs and then the laughter stops.

It stops when he sees someone behind the redheaded man.

He sees the glaring, leering face of the kid. The boy named Cillian.

And then everything is black, and he begins to hear the screams.

Grim and Unrepentant

1.

"Audrey."

It was the first word he spoke. Ankles and wrists tied with electrical wire, blood dripping, a swollen eye and bloody nose and mouth, Dennis looked like a prisoner of war. And all he could say to Hank was *Audrey*.

"Hey, come on, let's get you up."

But Dennis kept saying it. "Audrey. Audrey. Audrey."

Tears ran down his face.

"Dennis, come on, man."

"No."

"Dennis, she's fine."

"No, no."

"Den—I just came from the house. I just saw her, okay? She's a basket case, but she's okay."

"No."

"I saw her just an hour ago. The police are with her. Ryan just got there, okay? She's in good hands. And she's worried sick about you."

"The car—the boy—the white—Mitch—"

"The cops are coming."

"Give me your phone," Dennis said with a slight slur.

"No, you need to—"

Dennis cursed at him and demanded the phone.

Hank gave it to him and Dennis tried to dial the number but couldn't.

"Here, hold on."

Hank dialed and waited.

"Audrey? Hey—I have your father—"

Dennis took the phone in his right hand. It shook as he held it.

"Audrey?"

"Dad, where are you?"

Never had a voice sounded so refreshingly wonderful.

All he could do was weep.

She's still alive.

A hand went around him, then another took the phone. It spoke, but Dennis couldn't hear what was spoken.

"Thank you, God. Thank you."

Dennis went down to his knees and continued crying, but these tears were tears of joy.

Joy, and humility.

2.

This is what he remembers about the moments that follow.

Hank not saying much, looking pale and horrified, only asking Dennis what he needs.

The flashing lights of a squad car approaching at a maddening pace, followed by more lights and sirens and madness.

One policeman turning into twenty men and women, all around him, their faces changing from tough and curious to faint and appalled.

Several people asking him questions, sensitive, looking for answers.

Paramedics putting him on a stretcher, giving him an IV, checking him over, asking more questions.

Hank staying at his side even when pushed to answer more questions.

Squad cars and ambulances and fire trucks.

Men and women white with disbelief, their faces saying it all.

Such utter and absolute horror.

He's too weak to think anymore, too shocked to put all the pieces together, too relieved, too distraught to ask Hank how come those big hands of his were so bloody.

Dennis doesn't ask because he knows. And he doesn't want to know.

These aren't the pages of a story. They're the life he's living out. Sometimes, on some days, horror and misery and suffering find their place and a life to terrorize. And thus, a tale is told, grim and unrepentant, with no happy ending.

And after what all these people find on this farm, including what surrounded him for a night he'll never forget, there will only be more pain and suffering.

But unlike the character in *Empty Spaces*, Dennis breathes life.

And he knows who allows him to.

3.

At the hospital, finally able to rest, Dennis looks at his friend who had not left his side since finding him in the barn.

"You saved my life." He states the obvious.

"I was lucky."

"How?"

"That guy—your friend, the young guy—that night he saw us at Pancho's. There was no way anybody knew that about me."

"Knew what? What are you talking about?"

"When he referred to Bailey—the dog I drove over one night when I was plastered. The one I buried in my backyard.

Nobody ever knew about that. I never told a soul, Den. In-cluding you."

"You said you didn't remember—"

"He freaked me out. I didn't know what to say. So I did a little research on him."

"What do you mean research?"

"I went to talk to his family. And they told me he got to know a man—this guy named Bob. They said they knew his last name because it was so unique—Holzknecht. They told the authorities that too."

Dennis had heard that name before.

"Why does that . . ."

"Yeah, it sounds familiar, doesn't it? Your neighbors—their last name is Holz."

Dennis nodded, still trying to figure out the connection.

"Your—fan, or whatever you want to call him. He became good buddies with this Bob character. And I believe that's who killed him."

"You believe he's dead."

Hank nodded. "And after what I saw tonight . . ." He let out a sigh. "I think they're going to find that guy's parents. And we're lucky because we could have . . ."

Dennis nodded. He knew.

"But how did you know about—about the barn?"

"I got your message and drove over. You weren't around. You babbled in your voice mail, talking about the neighbors and about Audrey. Your car was there, and it looked like you had just disappeared. I decided to go next door to ask the Holzes some questions, and instead I found—I found a messy place."

"Not as messy as the farm."

"Yeah. The farm is registered under a Bernard and Henri-etta Holzknecht. It took me about an hour to find an address in that outhouse I was in. I just—I'm telling you, man, I just knew. I knew something was up."

"But how?"

"I had a dream. And I saw you—I saw you in mud and darkness and knew you were in trouble. Heck, maybe it was just my imagination after hearing that from that young guy. I don't know. I just know that I needed to find you."

"You did."

"Yeah."

Dennis gave his friend a glance that said more than the words he uttered: "Thanks, Hank."

"If this was one of your books, I'd be dead right now."

Dennis nodded but didn't feel like joking about the dead.

There were plenty of them back there at that farm, plenty of bodies to identify, plenty of families the news would destroy.

"Hank, can you do me one more favor?"

"Yeah."

"Can you go get Audrey?"

Part Five

All That's to Come

Coming Back to Life

1.

"You okay?"

"Dad, I'm fine."

"Just checking."

"It's been six months."

"I can still check."

"You checked on me yesterday."

"I know."

"I'm fine, Dad. Really."

"All right."

"How are you?"

"Hank's still rooming at the house, which has been interesting."

"Getting any writing done?"

Dennis just laughed.

"I gotta go," Audrey said.

"Be careful."

"I have the world watching."

"You have more than that," he said as he told her good-bye.

2.

Sometimes when the phone rang he picked it up expecting to hear Cillian's voice.

Sometimes when an e-mail came in he opened it expecting to see Cillian's address.

But ever since that grisly morning stuck away in some unseen barn, Dennis had not heard from his writer friend.

Cillian had disappeared.

Just like the words he used to use in telling his stories. The words—the magic as Lucy used to call it—were gone.

He believed he'd used up all of that magic.

But that was okay. That's all they were in the end. Just words. Nothing more.

3.

It had been a while since he had gone to his PO box in Geneva. It had been before everything happened, before the media camped out by his property and watched his every move. They had since left, but he knew there was probably a mass of letters and cards awaiting him.

And sure enough, there was.

Three mail bags worth of greetings and get wells and the typical sorry-you-had-a-serial-killer-living-next-to-you cards from Hallmark.

It would take him a week to go through everything.

Back home, he took the bags and dumped them out on his dining room table.

One thing caught his attention right away.

But surely . . .

It made him think of the gift he had given Lucy right after he had discovered she had cancer. He gave it to her as a gesture, a notion, a symbol of the two of them.

I burned that picture in a field a few days after she died.

Of course it wasn't that.

But Dennis looked at the package, the square, flat, cardboard box, and he felt his heart racing.

Is this Cillian again? Has he come back? Is this another game?

Dennis left the package on the table along with all the other contents.

He needed some air.

4.

The package waited on the kitchen table.

He had hoped that maybe it was his imagination, that maybe it wouldn't still be there when he got back.

Dennis was afraid to open it.

He noticed something that he hadn't originally seen: in the corner on the left-hand side was Lucy's name.

Written in her handwriting.

No address, no PO Box 222, North Shores, Heaven insignia.

No, of course not. That would be crazy.

The name in her handwriting wasn't crazy.

It was scary.

So why had she sent something to his PO box and not their home?

It had been marked on the same day he had been knocked out and kidnapped and dragged to a cold barn in the middle of nowhere.

It has to be Cillian. Throw the thing away.

He touched the package. He used to put his hand on her chest, just above her heart. Perhaps this package beat the same way.

I'll never forget. You know? How can I?

He fingered the package to make sure it was real. What was real and what was made up? The line had long since blurred. First in his writing then in Lucy's death and now, after all was said and done, here. With a package she mailed a year after she died.

And I'm thinking I know what's inside.
He took a breath.
Then he took the package in his hands.
They're shaking. God, I'm nervous.
He ripped open the tab in the envelope. He could feel a cardboard backing. Actually, there were two. He carefully slid them out of the yellow package.

It was a sunny April afternoon. The wind was blowing outside, the temperature cold. The sky looked like orange sherbet, the cozy glow filling this room with warmth and life. The day held on, not quite done, the busyness not yet finished.

All of these things mattered because they would be cemented into his mind and his soul until his last breath. He would remember this—standing here, opening this package, peeling the tape from one side of the two cardboard sheets, lifting one of them to see the color photograph, the square shot that wasn't a copy but was the original he had bought years ago and added borders to and named appropriately "Us and Them."

His handwriting was still there, but it was marked over with the same blue pen Lucy had used to sign the outside of the package.

~~Us and Them~~

Next to it Lucy had written something else.
And it made him laugh.
And the orange glow filled his soul.
He knew she wasn't far away, that she was there, watching, waiting.
And he continued to laugh, shaking his head, speechless and utterly moved.

Belief

1.

Sometimes the longer you wait to say the right thing, the necessary thing, the faster time goes by. And sometimes time passes over it altogether, leaving the words and sentiment lost forever.

Memorial Day was drawing to a close. The day had been full of laughter and baseball, both in part due to Hank spending the day with them. He drank remarkably very little and eventually bid Dennis and Audrey good night, and as he did Dennis said words that were obvious but needed to be uttered.

"Thank you, friend."

"For what?" Hank asked, honestly not knowing.

"For allowing this day to happen. And each day to follow."

"I shouldn't get that credit. But I'll take it anyway."

And now, a couple hours later, as Audrey sat with her hands over her knees watching reality TV, Dennis knew it was time. Tomorrow might not come. Tomorrow was not promised to anyone. And this family knew it all too well. There was someone missing tonight, someone who should have been there but wasn't.

"Can I talk to you for a minute?"

She obliged as he sat down on the couch next to her and

turned off the television. Audrey and her curly hair and wide, beautiful eyes faced him on the couch.

He sighed, wondering how to start.

"You doing okay?"

"Dad."

"What?"

"If I hear that question one more time . . ."

"Okay."

"What's wrong?"

"Nothing's wrong. I just—I've wanted to tell you something for a long time now. Something I've needed to tell you."

"I know, I know. You love me," Audrey said, smiling, trying to break the seriousness.

"That's not it, wise guy."

"Wise gal."

Dennis shifted on the edge of the couch, looking at her, feeling strangely nervous about what he needed to say.

"When your mother. . . . Just weeks before she ended up dying, she told me something to tell you after she was gone. I didn't want to hear this, of course. I never truly believed she would die. Never. Part of me always held on to hope that there would be some miracle. But she did die. And, well, I didn't want to tell you this."

"Tell me what?"

"It was just something small that she wanted you to know. And as time passed I knew you already believed this, that you already knew this. It's just—it's just that I never believed it. And I've refused to believe it for a very long time. Until recently."

"Believe what, Dad?"

He smiled at Audrey.

"Your mother had a vision of heaven before she died. It was vivid and real. And she described it to me perfectly. A small town by a lake, with cobblestone streets and a cool breeze that blew between the buildings. She described the place and the scene so perfectly, I told her she should have been a writer. But she said mere words couldn't sum up this place, it was that perfect. It was perfect, and it was full."

"Full?" Audrey asked.

"Full in every way. Full of love. Full of life."

"Why didn't you tell me?"

"Because I thought—I thought she was crazy. I thought it was just a dream. You know? Like the kind we all have."

"So why tell me now?"

"Because I think—because I believe in that place. I think it exists. I don't quite get all of that—that faith thing. But I believe she's there."

"I know she is," Audrey said.

Dennis fought tears.

"It was so simple, you know? So very simple. But I just couldn't get myself to tell you. Because I never believed it. I didn't want to believe she was in a better place. I didn't want to believe she was watching over us. That she would protect us. Because that's my job. That's what *I'm* supposed to do. I was supposed to protect us and watch over us and watch over her, and yet she was ripped away from me and what could I do, you know? What could I do?"

His eyes watered and his jaw felt heavy and he fought but couldn't control his tears.

Audrey held his hand. "Dad, it's okay."

He wiped his eyes. "I know. I just. I'm sorry. Audrey—I'm sorry for not telling you this."

"You didn't need to tell me."

Dennis laughed. "Yeah, that's the thing. My own daughter has more faith than I do."

"Maybe it's easier to have faith," Audrey said. "That's what Mom taught me."

"Yeah."

For a moment they shared the silence, comfortable with it.

Dennis hoped Lucy could see them. That she could feel their love.

He certainly felt hers.

2.

An hour later, in the silence of the dark house, Dennis heard the door to his bedroom open. He jumped up.

"Dad?"

It was Audrey. He let out a deep breath and tried to calm his racing heart.

"Yeah?"

"Can we talk?"

"Sure."

He turned on a light and adjusted his eyes. She came and sat on the edge of the bed in her sweatshirt and flannel pajama pants.

"There's something I need to tell you."

"Uh-oh."

"No. It's nothing bad. It's just—it's something I never told you. I didn't think to tell you, but now—well, this is the night of telling our secrets." She smiled. "I thought you'd like to know."

"To know what?"

"That night with Mitch—when I snuck out of the house to be with him. To go over and hang out with him and Liz. The night both of them were killed. I never went to his house. I told you I had asked him to take me back home. But the truth was—I felt compelled to go to Mom's grave. We had just been there that day, and I was still emotional. But I asked Mitch to take me there because I felt . . ."

"You felt what?"

"I was scared. When I got in that car, something in me told me I needed to get out. And the safest place I thought of going—it wasn't the house. It was her gravesite. And I know—

if I had gone to his place where Liz was waiting—I would have died that night."

"I know."

"It's almost like—I've always believed Mom warned me. And that she wanted me in the safest place. Maybe angels guard her grave. I don't know. But that's where I was. And I walked home from there. Home in the dark."

Dennis took his little girl's hand and held it. "Why didn't you tell me before now?"

"Because I thought—because I knew you wouldn't believe."

"I believe you."

"I know you do, Dad. I know."

3.

The following day arrived with clear skies and bright sun. Dennis awoke before Audrey, just after sunrise. He decided to head to town to get some coffee and pastries. He knew there were a hundred things to do today. And a hundred reasons to be happy.

On the drive toward downtown, he felt light and hopeful.

You can see me now, can't you? Can you read my mind? Can you hear my thoughts? Can you feel my soul?

Dennis drove, music cranked, windows down, Audrey home, the dark madness from last fall finally starting to dissipate.

But Dennis knew that some things would never go away. Joy and pain stayed with you like paintings in a museum, standing in a room of your heart on full display, encased in a protective window that you couldn't break. The joy and pain remained.

But on this bright morning, as he drove toward town, Dennis thought of the joy.

Her laughter and her skin and her touch and her life. A spark a thousand times brighter than the sun, a soul a thousand times richer than anything he could ever conjure up on the page. It kept him going, kept him breathing, kept him feeling.

I still love you, and I always will.

Dennis turned the corner and passed the small church, just like always, waiting to see what the sign said.

Perhaps a love letter from her. Or maybe a few words of encouragement.

But instead the sign surprised him.

The top line read:

YOU'VE COME THIS FAR,
NOW COME A LITTLE FARTHER.

And then on the bottom, it read:

OUR DOORS ARE ALWAYS OPEN.

And he smiled, knowing.

Knowing and believing.

High Hopes

It's the last night in June, the temperature a moderate sixty degrees.

The man wheels the dumpster to the end of the driveway. He places it on the edge of the drive facing Route 31. Just like always. Another weekday night, another routine.

For a moment he looks over to the neighbors' lifeless house with the For Sale sign outside. Then he stares up through the trees toward the moon, barely visible above trees and clouds.

And as always, he wonders.

Does she see me? Does she think of me? Does she remember? Does she still know?

He doesn't know much. But he knows this. If heaven and hell exist, he knows what they are.

Hell is a place without hope.

And heaven is where she lives.

To have lived through hell . . . Dennis knows he's a changed man. But how and in what ways—he still has to figure that out. He's starting to, slowly.

He enters his house and double-bolts the door and double-checks that it's locked. Then he climbs the familiar stairs and enters the familiar office.

He sees the bookcase of all his hardcovers prominently displayed behind his chair.

I'd give them back to have you. I'd erase every single happily ever after to simply have one.

The office is cool and quiet. He sits in his chair and taps his keyboard to awaken his computer.

And for the first time in a long time, he starts typing without thinking, without worrying, without wondering.

It's time again.

He can't remember how long it's been, but it's been at least two years.

He types in the name Lucy gave him, the title Lucy gave with her gift from the grave. The photo that hangs on the wall next to his desk.

He starts to write this story, different from anything he's ever written.

It will be a love story, and it will be about Lucy. And he will try to catch just a tiny fraction of what she was like, what it was like to love her.

And after writing for an hour and feeling like he could go on all night long, he looks at the screen and says the title out loud.

"Wish You Were Here."

A Note from the Author

Authors are a crazy bunch, aren't we? We make these stories out of nothing, spending so much time thinking and plotting and planning and writing. It can't be easy being married to an author or having one as a friend or family member or working with one. So with that said, let me offer some words of thanks to those who put up with me.

Sharon, my wonderful wife—thank you for being down-to-earth when I'm orbiting the planet. Kylie, my feisty little lady—thank you for showing me that passion and zeal can be beautiful things.

Anne—thank you for challenging me and encouraging me and helping me be the best writer I can be. Claudia—thanks for sticking with me on this writing journey.

To my relatives, especially my parents and my in-laws—thank you for loving me and supporting what I do. To my friends, thanks for being there.

I'd like to say a special thanks to all my buddies at Rock Bottom. Especially Kyle—thank you for a conversation that saved my life.

For all my fans and readers, thank you again for coming along for the ride.

About the Author

Travis Thrasher is the author of ten previous novels. A full-time writer and speaker, Travis lives with his wife and daughter in a suburb of Chicago. For more information about Travis, visit www.travisthrasher.com.

A Conversation with Travis Thrasher

Q: Where did the idea for *Ghostwriter* come from?
A: I wanted to do something in the vein of *Isolation*—another "horror" novel. The idea came in the form of a character. I thought, *What if I write about a horror novelist who doesn't believe in the supernatural?* That opened up a lot of possibilities in the story.

Q: Is this a genre you enjoy writing in?
A: I enjoy writing in all types of genre, but it seems like I've found one that I'm really comfortable in. I was encouraged by the overwhelmingly positive response to *Isolation*.

Q: For those readers who have followed your career since your first novel, the self-proclaimed "sweet little love story" *The Promise Remains*, what can you say about the direction your writing is headed?
A: There is a strange link between all my novels. In my mind, they all deal with fears. *The Promise Remains* is ultimately about the fear of not finding that "right" person in life. *The Watermark* is about the fear of not being forgiven by God for something you've done. Each of my books deals with a fear I've had. The only difference is that in the early books,

the tension came out of love stories. Now, I'm taking fears and weaving them into hair-raising tales. But even in *Ghostwriter*, there is the backbone of a love story between Dennis and his wife, Lucy.

Q: Since you have fans in both the general market and the Christian market, are you worried that this kind of story might impact your growing readership and alienate Christian readers by taking on the idea of ghosts?
A: My goal as a writer is to entertain readers while challenging myself. I don't want to preach, nor do I want to teach. But I also don't want to dishonor God in my writing. Look at *A Christmas Carol* by Charles Dickens—look at the message of that story. There were three ghosts in that tale. As I explore the horror/supernatural-thriller genre, I want to take on the staples of that genre and make them my own. *Isolation* dealt with demon-possession (à la *The Exorcist*). *Ghostwriter* is my ghost story. I want to continue to build my readership, but I've never been the type of writer who is driven by other people's expectations.

Q: *Ghostwriter* is your eleventh published novel. How would you describe the Travis Thrasher brand?
A: Like a Happy Meal that contains something different every time you get it. I have an outrageous goal as a writer—not to build a broad readership in one category, but to build a readership that follows me wherever I go. Perhaps that's impossible, but it's what I dreamed of doing when I was growing up, and so far, I've still been able to do it.

Q: What are you working on next?
A: That's one of those questions I can never truly answer, simply because I always have a variety of things in the works. The way I can answer that is this: my next contracted book

will be called *Broken* and is scheduled to come out May 2010. It's another supernatural thriller.

Q: You've been writing full-time for a year now. What's that been like?
A: It's been exciting and scary. God continues to teach me a lot, especially about trusting Him. It's been amazing to see God's hand in my life this past year. The great thing about that is that I'll be able to take some of those experiences and weave them into a story that might get published down the road.

Q: What's something you'd like your readers to know?
A: I'd like them to know my honest appreciation for their taking the time to read my books. I say this a lot. It's not a big deal for someone to pay fourteen bucks for a book. But it's monumental for them to give their time for something I've done. I've put my heart and soul into every single one of my books, and I'm never going to stop doing that. My biggest hope is for a reader to be moved—to be scared silly or moved to tears or inspired. I'm going to keep trying, and hopefully I'll keep getting better.

If you liked *Ghostwriter*,
be sure to pick up

ISOLATION

A masterfully-written story that will grip you from its
mysterious beginning to its chilling end.

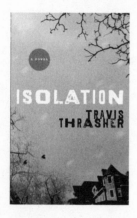

James Miller is a burned-out mission-
ary whose time on the mission field in
Papua New Guinea left him exhausted
and disillusioned. His wife, Stephanie,
feels like she's losing her mind. After
moving to North Carolina, Stephanie
begins seeing strange and frightening things: blood dripping down the
walls, one of her children suffocating. Premonitions, she's sure, of what's
to come. As the visions and haunting images intensify, Stephanie asks her brother to come for a much-needed visit—but
he's hiding secrets of his own that will prove more destructive
than Stephanie can imagine.

Nine-year-old Zachary sees his family's move as an ad-
venture, and as he explores the new house, he discovers every
young boy's dream: secret passageways and hidden rooms. But
what seems exciting at first quickly becomes horrifying.

When a snowstorm traps the Millers, the supernatural dan-
gers of their new home will test everything they thought they
knew about each other, and about their faith.

Available now wherever books are sold!